The God of Love

Justin Huntly McCarthy

Contents

THE GOD OF LOVE

BY

Justin Huntly McCarthy

TO
JUSTIN McCARTHY

I
THE MAY-DAY QUEEN

This is the book of Lappo Lappi, called by his friends the careless, the happy-go-lucky, the devil-may-take-it, the God-knows-what. Called by his enemies drinker, swinker, tumbler, tinker, swiver. Called by many women that liked him pretty fellow, witty fellow, light fellow, bright fellow, bad fellow, mad fellow, and the like. Called by some women who once loved him Lapinello, Lappinaccio, little Lappo. Called now in God as a good religious should be, Lappentarius, from a sweet saint myself discovered--or invented; need we quibble?--in an ancient manuscript. And it is my merry purpose now, in a time when I, that am no longer merry, look back upon days and hours and weeks and months and years that were very merry indeed, propose to set down something of my own jolly doings and lovings, and incidentally to tell some things about a friend of mine that was never so merry as I was, though a thousand times wiser; and never so blithe as I was, though a thousand times the better man. For it seems to me now, in this cool grim grayness of my present way, with the cloisters for my kingdom and the nimbused frescoes on the walls for my old-time ballads and romances, as if my life that was so sunburnt and wine-sweetened and woman-kissed, my life that seemed to me as bright, every second of it, as bright ducats rushing in a pleasant plenteous stream from one hand to another, was after all intended to be no more than a kind of ironic commentary on, and petty contrast to, the life of my friend.

He and I lived our youth out in the greatest and fairest of all cities that the world has ever seen, greater a thousand times than Troy or Nineveh, or Babylon or Rome, and when I say this you will know, of course, that I speak of the city of Florence, and we lived and loved at the same time, lived and loved in so strangely different a fashion that it seems to me that if the two lives were set side by side after the fashion of Messer Plutarch of old days, they would form as diverting a pair of opposites as any student of humanity could desire for his entertainment.

I shall begin, with the favor and permission of Heaven, where I think the business may rightly be said to begin. The time was a May morning, the morning of May-day, warm and bright with sunlight, one of those mornings which makes a clod seem like a poet and a poet seem like a god. The place was the Piazza Santa Felicita, with the Arno flowing pretty full and freely now between its borders of mud. I can see it all as I write, as I saw it yesterday, that yesterday so many years ago when Lappo Lappi was young and Lappentarius never dreamed of.

There is no lovelier day of all the years of days for Florence than May-day. On that day everybody is or seems to be happy; on that day the streets of the city are as musical as the courses of the spheres. Youths and maidens, garlanded and gayly raimented, go about fifing and piping, and trolling the chosen songs of spring. I think if a stranger should chance to visit Florence for the first time on a May-day, with the festival well toward, he might very well think that he had fallen back by fortunate chance into the youth of the world, when there was nothing better nor wiser to do than to dance and sing and make merry and make love. I have heard Messer Brunetto Latini declare, with great eloquence, that of all the cities man has ever upbuilded with his busy fingers, the dear city of Cecrops, which Saint Augustine called the dear City of God--in a word, Athens, was surely the loveliest wherein to live. But with all respect to Messer Brunetto, I would maintain that no city of Heathendom or Christendom could be more beautiful than Florence at any season of the year. What if it be now and then windy; now and then chilly; now and then dusty? I have talked with a traveller that told me he had found the winters mighty bitter in Greece. But I think that in all the history of Florence there never was a May-day like that May-day. It was gloriously green and gold, gloriously blue and white, gloriously hot, and yet with a little cool, kissing breeze that made the flaming hours delectable. And, as I remember so well, I sat on the parapet of the bridge of the Holy Felicity.

Where the parapet of the embankment joined the beginning of the bridge of the Santa Felicita there stood, in those days, a large, square, ornamental fountain. May be it stands there now. I was banished from Florence at the same time as my friend, and we left our Mother of the Lilies to seek and find very dissimilar fortunes.

This fountain had a niche above it, in which niche he that built the fountain designed, no doubt, to set some image of his own design. But he never carried out his purpose, why or wherefore I neither knew nor cared, and in that niche some Magnifico that was kindly minded to the people had set up a stone image, a relic of the old beautiful pagan days, that had been unearthed in some garden of his elsewhere. It was the figure of a very comely youth that was clothed in a Grecian tunic, and because, when it was first dug up, it showed some traces of color on the tunic and the naked legs and arms and the face and the hair, therefore one of the artificers of the said Magnifico took it upon himself to paint all as, so he said, it had once been painted. And he made the limbs a flesh color, and gave the face its pinks, and the lips their carnation, and the eyes their blackness, very lively to see; and he adorned the hair very craftily with gold-leaf, and he painted the shirt of the adorable boy a very living crimson. It was a very beautiful piece of work with all these embellishments, and though there were some that said it was an idol and should not be tolerated, yet, for the most part, the Florentines liked it well enough, and it saved the cost of a new statue for the vacant space.

So it stood there this day that I think of and write of, a very brave and radiant piece of color, too, for the eye to rest on that had wearied of looking at the gray stone palace hard by, the palace of Messer Folco Portinari, that showed so gray and grim in all weathers, save where the brown rust on its great iron lamps and on the great rings in the wall lent its dulness some hint of pigment. Over the wall that hid the garden of the palace I saw and see crimson roses hang and scarlet pomegranate blossoms. Opposite this gloomy house of the great man that was so well liked of the Florentines, against the pillars of the arcade, there stood, as I recall it, a bookseller's booth, where manuscripts were offered for sale on a board. Here he that had the means and the inclination could treat himself at a price to the wisdom of the ancient world. I fear I was never one of those so minded. The wisdom of my own world contented me to the full, and ever it seemed to me that it mattered less what Messer Plato or Messer Cicero said on this matter and on that matter than what Messer Lappo Lappi said and did in those affairs that intimately concerned him.

Now, on this day, which I see again so clearly, I was seated, as I say, on the parapet of the bridge, propped against the fountain. If I turned my head to the left, I could please myself with a sight of the briskly painted statue of the young Greek youth. If I turned my head to the right, I could look on the river and the smiling country beyond. But, as it happened, I turned my head neither to the left nor to the right, but straight before me and a little below me. For I was singing a song to a lute for an audience of pretty girls who looked up at me, some admiringly and some mockingly, but all very approvingly. One of the girls was named Jacintha, and one was named Barbara, and another, that had hair of a reddish-yellow and pale, strange eyes, was called Brigitta. There were also many others to whom, at this time, I cannot give a name, though I seem to see their faces very clearly and hear the sound of their voices, as well I might, for I was very good friends with most of them then or thereafter. And this is the song that I was singing:

"Flower of the lily or flower of the rose,   My heart is a leaf on each love-wind that blows.   A face at the window, a form at the door,   Can capture my fancy as never before.   My fancy was captured, since-well, let us say   Since last night, or the night before last, when I lay   In the arms of--but, hush, I must needs be discreet;   So farewell, with a kiss for your hands and your feet.   I worship your fingers, I worship your toes,   Flower of the lily or flower of the rose."

Then the girl Brigitta, she that had the red-gold hair and the eyes like pale glass, thrust her face very near to me and said, laughing, "Messer Lappo, Messer Lappo, who is your sweetheart?"

And I, who was ever ready with a brisk compliment to pretty maid or pretty woman, or pretty matron, answered her as swiftly as you please, "She shall be named by your name, dainty, if you will lend me a kiss of the lips."

And, indeed, I wished she would give me my will, for at that time I had a great desire for Brigitta; but she only pinched up her face to a grin, and answered me, teasingly, "Nay, I cannot kiss you; I think you have a Ghibelline mouth."

Now this seemed to me a foolish answer as well as a pert one, for, besides that I was ever a Guelph and a Red, I think that politics have no business to interfere with the pleasant commerce and suave affairs of love, so I answered her reprovingly. "Kisses have no causes," said I; "I will kiss Guelph-wise; I will kiss Ghibelline-wise; I will kiss Red; I will kiss Yellow; it's all one to me, so long as the mouth be like yours, as pink as a cleft pomegranate, and the teeth as white as its seeds."

Now at this Jacintha, who had eyes the color of amethysts, and dark hair with a purplish stain in it, wagged a finger at me reprovingly, saying, "I fear you are a wanton wooer." And at this all the other girls laughed like the jolly wantons they were.

But I pretended to take it all mighty seriously, and answered as solemnly as any philosopher, "Never say it, never think it. I am the golden rose of constancy; I have loved a lass for three days on end, and never yawned once."

Now, while I was talking thus, and pulling my face to keep it from laughing, the girl that was named Barbara had come up very close to me, and I was minded to slip my arm about her waist and draw her closer with a view to the kissing of lips. But she had only neighbored me to mock me, for she cried aloud, "Mirror of chivalry, I will give you a Guelph cuff on your Ghibelline cheek." And as she spoke, being a girl of spirit, she kept her word very roundly, and fetched me a box on the ear with her brown hand that made my wits sing.

Now this was more than my philosophy could stomach, so I made a grab at her, but she dipped from my outstretched fingers and slipped into the midst of the crowd of other girls, and straightway I dropped from my parapet and ran after her, vowing the merriest, pleasantest skelping. However, she was too swift for me, and too nimble, capering behind this girl and that girl, and ever eluding me when I seemed to be on the point of seizing the minx, till at last, what with laughing and running and calling, my breath failed me, and I stood in the midst of the pretty jades, panting.

"Nay, I am fairly winded," I protested. "If some sweet she do not give me a kiss, I shall die of despair."

Then Brigitta, who was nearest to me, came nearer with a kind look in her strange eyes. "Nay then," she said, "for your song's sake, and to save your life." So she said and so she did, for she kissed me full on the mouth before all of them, and, indeed, this was the first time I had kissed her, though I thank Heaven it was not the last.

And because there is nothing so contagious as kindness and so stimulating as a good example, the other girls were now ripe and ready to do as she did, and Jacintha cried, "I will be generous, too!" and set her red lips where Brigitta's kiss had rested, and then one kissed me and another, and at the end of it all, Barbara herself, that had been so ready with her fingers, surrendered and kissed me too. And it was while she was kissing me, and I was making rather a long business of it, seeing how

she was the last to be kissed, and how she had provoked me, that there came unob-
served into our group another youth whose coming I had not noticed, being so busy
on pleasant business.

But I heard a very sweet and tunable voice speak, and the voice asked, "When
the air is so brisk with kisses, is there never a kiss for me?" And I looked up from
the lips of Barbara and saw that my very dear friend, Messer Guido Cavalcanti, was
newly of our company.

It is many a long year since my dear friend Messer Guido dei Cavalcanti died
of that disastrous exile to which, by the cynical irony of fate, my other dear friend,
Messer Dante dei Alighieri, was foredestined to doom him. That sadness has nothing
to do with this sadness, and I here give it the go-by. But at nights when I lie awake
in my cell--a thing which, I thank my stars happens but rarely--or in the silence
of some more than usually quiet dawn, I seem to see him again as I saw him that
morning, so blithe, so bright, so delightful. Never was so fine a gentleman. It is to
be regretted, perhaps, that his was not a spirit that believes. I that am a sinner have
no qualms and uncertainties, but credit what I am told to credit, and no more said.
After all, why say more? But Messer Guido was of a restless, discontented, fretting
spirit, that chafed at command and convention, and would yield nothing of doubt
for the sake of an easy life. Well, he was the handsomest man I have ever known,
and he never seemed fairer than on that May morning--Lord, Lord, how many cen-
turies ago it seems!--when he came upon me in the sunlit Place of the Holy Felicity,
and thereafter, for the first time, made the acquaintance of Messer Dante.

When the girls heard that complaint of Messer Guido's, they gathered about
him noisily, crying, "Surely, Messer Guido, surely!" and pushing their impudent
faces close to his, and catching him with their hands, for indeed Messer Guido was
a very comely personage, and one that was always well-eyed by women.

But it seems that for all his asking he had little mind for the amorous traffic,
for he laughingly disengaged himself from the girls, and I said to him, pretending
to be jealous, "If you taste of their bounty, I shall tell Monna Giovanna"--for so was
named the lady he loved--"and then you will weep red tears."

Messer Guido pointed to me with a mock air of indignation. "See what it is," he
said, "to take a traitor to one's heart." He ran his laughing eyes over the little knot
of us, and went on, "Sweet ladies, and you, sour gentleman, I have news for you."

But I protested, drolling him, for it was always our custom when we met to toss jests and mockery to and fro, as children toss a ball. "Do not heed him," I said, "Guido's news is always eight days old."

Then the girls laughed at him, for I think in their hearts they were vexed because he had not taken their kisses--at least, most of them; for I have it in mind that Brigitta was content with my kissing and none other. But Guido was not to be downed by their laughter.

"This is not an hour old," he said. "You should all be at the Signory. The fair ladies of Florence have chosen Monna Beatrice, of the Portinari, for the queen of their May festival, and will bear her about the city presently in triumph."

Now this was no piece of news for me, but I was where I was for a reason, which was to meet Messer Dante. It was news to the girls, though, for Brigitta cried, "Monna Beatrice, she who has been away from Florence these nine years?" and Jacintha questioned, "Monna Beatrice! Is she daughter of Folco Portinari that builds hospitals?" and Barbara sighed, "Monna Beatrice, whom some call the loveliest girl in the city?"

And Guido gave to their several questions a single answer: "Even she. For her beauty's sake and in compliment to Messer Folco, because he builds hospitals."

Now, though I had little interest in this news of Guido's, I was so glad of his coming that I was as ready to be rid of the girls by this time as I had been eager before to keep them about me. So I waved my hand at them as housewives wave their hands to scare the chickens, and I called to them: "So! Away with you girls to join the merry-making. I will kiss you all another day."

Then the girls began to mock at me again, and Jacintha hailed me as prince of poets, and Brigitta, half laughing and half earnest, called me prince of lovers, and Barbara shot out her pink tongue at me, saying, "Prince of liars!"

Straightway I made as if I would catch them and slap them, and they all ran away laughing, and Messer Guido and I were left alone, at the corner of the bridge of the Holy Felicity, with the image of the God of Love hard by.

"Good-bye, lilies of life!" I called after the flying fugitives, kissing my hand at them; and then I turned to my friend. "This lady Beatrice," I questioned, "is she very fair?" For though I had heard not a little of her return to our city from Fiesole, I had not yet seen her, and I am always curious--I mean I was then always curious--about fair women.

"Angel fair," Guido answered, briskly. "Our Florence is ever a nest of loveliness, but no one of her women is fairer than Folco's daughter."

"May be she seems fairer, being strange," I hinted, quizzically. "Are we not Athenian in our love of new things?"

Guido answered me very gravely. "I think we should have held her as precious if she had never left us."

Now, I had never given the affairs of the Portinari many thoughts, and though I had heard how Messer Folco had brought his daughter home of late from Fiesole, I knew nothing more than so much, wherefore I questioned, less because I cared, than because Messer Guido seemed to care, "Why did she leave us?"

Guido seated himself by my side on the parapet, swinging his slim legs, and told the tale he wanted to tell.

"It is nine years ago. She was one of those fairy children--I remember her very well--too divine, too bright, it might seem, to hold in the four walls of any mortal mansion. That as it may, the physicians found her a delicate piece of flesh, and so banished her out of our hot Florence into the green coolness of the hills."

I do not think that I cared very much about what Messer Guido was telling me, but because I loved him I feigned to care.

"And has she lived there ever since?" I asked, with such show of interest as I could muster.

And he answered me, very lively. "There she has lived ever since. But now Messer Folco, being reassured of her health, brings her to Florence, where her beauty will break hearts, I promise."

I think he sighed a little, and I know that I laughed as I spoke. "Well, I that have broken my heart a hundred times will break it again for her, if she pleases."

Messer Guido grinned at me a little maliciously. "Better not let Messer Simone dei Bardi hear you," he said, and his words suddenly brought before me the image of a very notable figure in the Florence of my youth, a very forward man in the squabbles of the Yellows and the Reds.

It would, I think, be very hard to make any stranger acquainted with the state of our city at this time, for it was more split and fissured with feuds and dissensions than a dried melon rind. It had pleased Heaven in its wisdom to decide that it was not enough for us to be distraught with the great flagrant brawls between the Guelphs and the Ghibellines, between those that stood for Roman Emperor and those that stood for Roman Pope. No, we must needs be divided again into yet further factions and call ourselves Reds and Yellows, and cut one another's throats in the name of these two colors with more heat and zeal in the cutting than had ever stirred the blood of the partisans of the two great camps.

This Red and Yellow business began simply enough and grimly enough in a quarrel between two girls, distant kinswomen, of the House of the Casa Bella. One of these girls maintained, at some merry-making, that she was comelier than the other, which that other very stoutly denied, and from the bandying of words they came to the bandying of blows, and because it is never a pretty sight to see two women at clapper-claws together, those about bestirred themselves to sunder the sweet amazons, and in the process of pulling them apart more blows were given and exchanged between those that sought at first to be peacemakers, and there were many hot words and threats of vengeance.

From this petty beginning, like your monumental oak from your pigmy acorn, there grew up a great feud between the families of the two girls, and like a poison the plague of the quarrel spread to Florence, and in a twinkling men were divided against each other in a deathly hatred that in their hearts knew little of the original quarrel, and cared nothing at all for it. But as all parties must needs have a nickname, whether chosen or conferred, the first of these parties was called Yellow, because the girl that began the quarrel had yellow eyes; and the other party in mockery called itself Red, because the girl that was, as it were, the patron saint of their side of the squabble had red hair. These Reds and Yellows fought as fiercely in Florence as ever the Blues and the Greens in Constantinople of old time. And in our city the Donati sided with the Reds, and the Cerchi with the Yellows, and all that loved either of these great houses chose their color and conducted themselves accordingly. But you must not suppose that the heads of the great houses of the Donati and the Cerchi publicly avowed themselves as the leaders of these whimsical factions, however much they might, for their own purposes, foster and encourage their existence. At the time of which I write Messer Guido Cavalcanti was ostensibly the chief man among the Reds, and the chief man among the Yellows was Messer Simone dei Bardi.

Here, in consequence of this business of Reds and Yellows, was a thickening of the imbroglio of Florentine life. For now it was not enough to be told whether a man was Guelph or Ghibelline in order to know how to deal with him. It was not merely prudent but even imperative to inquire further, for a rooted Guelph might be Red or Yellow in this other scuffle, and so might a rooted Ghibelline. Thus our poor City of the Lilies was become a very Temple of Discord, and at any moment a chance encounter in the street, a light word let fly--nay, even no more than a slight glance--might be the signal for drawn swords and runnels of blood among the cobbles. Truly, therefore, it is not to be denied that for such poor gentlemen as, like myself, desired their ease, together with much singing and kissing and sipping, Florence was by no means an Arcadia. And yet there was no one of us that would willingly have lived elsewhere, for all the quarrelling and all the feuds.

Now I do not say it because I was a Red myself, but I do think that the Reds were of a better temper than the Yellows. Very certainly no one was less eager to fan the flames of these quarrellings and feuds than the man that was by my side, Messer Guido Cavalcanti. And no less certainly of those that were hottest for quarrellings and keenest to keep old feuds alive, and to enforce distinctions of faction, and make much of party cries, there was no one hotter and keener than Messer Simone dei Bardi, whose name had just come to Messer Guido's lips.

Messer Simone came of a house that was of excellent good repute in our city. Bankers his folk were, very busy and prosperous, and bankers they had been for many a long day before Messer Simone was begotten. Messer Simone was not the greatest heir, but I think in his way he was the most notable, though his way was not quite the way of the family, no less steady-going than honorable, from which he came. For, indeed, it was his chief delight to lavish the money which his forebears had amassed, and there was no one in all Florence more prompt than he to fling hoarded florins out of the window. By rights he should have been a free-companion, and received on the highroad at the heads of a levy of lesser devils, for of a truth he was too turbulent and quarrelsome for Florence, which is saying much. The men of my spring days, as I have written, were ranged in many ways of opposition, Guelph against Ghibelline, Red against Yellow, Donati against Cerchi, and Messer Simone should have been content to be Guelph and Yellow and Cerchi, but at times he carried himself as if he were ranged against every one, or perhaps I should rather say that he carried himself as if his single will was above all the wranglers of others, and that it was given to him to do as he pleased, heedless of the feelings of any faction. Had he had but the wit to balance his arrogance, Messer Simone might have been a great man in Florence. As it proved, he was only a great plague.

Now I laughed at Guido's words, for it seemed strange to me to think of Messer Simone dei Bardi as a wooer of countrified damsels. "What has that Bull-face to do with it?" I asked, and whistled mockingly after the asking.

Guido still looked grave. "Why, I think his fist gapes, finger and thumb, to seize Monna Beatrice," he said, and he said no more, but looked as if he could say much.

Here was an oracle anxious to be interrogated, so I questioned him further. I knew by report that the girl was fair, but I could not think of her in any fashion as a maid for Messer Simone, and I conveyed my doubts to Guido. "Is the girl to be snared so?" I asked.

Guido looked cryptic. "That is for father Folco to settle," he said. "And father Folco is a man that loves his fellow-men, but would have his children obey him even to the death, like a Roman father of old."

I began to take the matter hotly, thinking it over and looking at it this way and that way. "Well, if I were a woman," I protested, "which I thank Heaven I am not," I interpolated, fervently, "I would drown in Arno sooner than be bride to Simone of the Bardi."

Guido shrugged his shoulders. He was a man that believed anything of women. "Yet I think Vittoria loves him," he said, softly, more as if to himself than to me.

But, bless you, I caught him up nimbly, seeing the weakness of his argument. "Vittoria, the courtesan! She loves any man, every man."

Guido looked at me very thoughtfully. Then he said, slowly: "I will tell you a tale I heard yesterday. Some while ago our bull-headed Simone, being with Vittoria at supper at her house, and as drunk as is his custom at the tail of the day, dozed on a sofa while the company began to talk of fair women."

I was horrified at the ill-manners of the hog, though it all seemed of a piece with his habitual hoggishness. "One should never be too drunk," I averred, "to talk on that illuminating theme."

Now Guido was fretted at my interruption, and he showed it with a frown and a silencing gesture of his hand. "Peace, Lappo, peace!" he cried; "this is my story.

Some praised this lady, some praised that, all, as was due to their guesthood, giving the palm to Vittoria, till some one said there lived a lady at Fiesole that was lovelier than a dream."

"Who was this nonesuch?" I asked, all agog over any word of loveliness.

Guido chastened my impatience with a grave glance. "I come to that," he continued. "She was named Beatrice, daughter of Folco Portinari, and he that praised her averred that whoso might wed her would be the happiest of mortals."

Now, though the air was warm, I shivered at his words, as if it had suddenly turned cold, for, indeed, I was never a marrying man, and my pleasantest memories of women are not memories of any wife of mine. "Marriage--and happiness?" I said, questioning and grinning. "I am not of his mind."

Guido looked at me with a good-humored smile, as one that was prepared to bear with my interruptions. "Nor he of yours," he answered. "Now, as they talked thus, our Simone stirred in his stupor, and swore that if this were true he would marry the maiden. Vittoria laughed, and her laughter so teased the ruffian that he swore a great oath he would take any wager he would wed this exquisite maiden."

"Who took him?" I asked. The tale promised to be interesting, and spurred my curiosity.

Guido went on with his narrative. "No man. Simone's luck is proverbial as his enmity deadly. But Vittoria grinned at him, swearing no such maid would marry him, and at last so goaded him that he defied her to a wager. Then she dared him to this--staking her great emerald, in a ring that the French prince gave her, on the terms that if he failed to gain the daughter of Folco Portinari he was in all honor and solemnity to marry her, Vittoria."

I remember as well as if it were yesterday my amazement when I heard this story, and am inclined now to uplift my hands as I then uplifted them in wonder, and am inclined to say again, as I said then, "Gods, what a wager!"

Guido seemed amused at my astonishment, for he laughed a little while softly to himself, and then went on with his tale-telling. "Simone's red gills winced, like a dying fish, but he was too drunk to qualify. He swore a foul oath, 'I will marry this lily,' says he, 'within a year, and if I do not, why I will wed you, you--' And he called Vittoria by such lewd names as your wit can picture. But she, turning no hair, called for pen and parchment, and had it fairly engrossed and Simone's sprawling signature duly witnessed before even the company departed. So it stands--Simone must win the maid or wed the light o' love."

Then I said, "I take it he will win the maid."

Guido nodded his head gravely. He did not like Simone any better than I did, but he had a way of accepting facts more readily. "Simone mostly wins his wish. See how far he has gone already. He has so worked it that her father has brought his lovely daughter from the hills to the city. Old Folco favors him, and small wonder, Messer Simone being the power he is in Florence. As for this triumph of Folco's daughter through our streets, I take it to be rather Simone's displaying of his prize, that all men may envy him his marvel."

For my part, I protested very honestly and from the core of my heart. "If I were old Portinari, I would rather rot in exile than have Simone dei Bardi for my son-in-law."

Guido tapped me on the shoulder. "That is," he said, "because you have the heart of an amorist that would let none be lover save himself."

I laughed in his face, and gave him the lie courteously. "No, because I have the heart of a poet, and the full-favored brute vexes my gorge."

Guido still seemed to mock me. "As you will," he said. "Shall we go to the Signory and stare at the pageant?"

I shook my head. I was sorry to deny Messer Guido in anything or to deprive myself of the comfort of his company. But I had come to that place to keep a tryst. "I cannot," I said. "I wait here for young Dante of the Alighieri."

Now Messer Dante and I had been friends for some years past, friends not indeed because we were both Florentines, but perhaps I should say in spite of the fact that we were both Florentines. For in those days, as in the days before them, and in the days that since have come to pass, while every Florentine loved Florence with all the passion of an old Roman for the city of Romulus, Florentine very often loved Florentine as day loves night, eld youth, health sickness, poverty riches, or any other pair of opposites you please. But I was never much of a politician, I thank my stars, and though a good enough Guelph to pass muster in a crowd, and a good enough Red to cry "Haro!" upon the Yellows if need were, I bothered my head very little about such brawls so long as there were songs to sing, vintages to sip, and pretty girls to kiss.

In Messer Dante I found one of my own age, or, perhaps, a little less that was in those days scarcely more pricked by the itch political than I myself was, and for a while he and I had been jolly companions in the merry pleasant ways of youth. But of late days this Dante, that was ever a wayward fellow, had suddenly turned away from sports and joys, and devoted himself with an unwholesome fervor to study, and seemed, as it were, lost to me in the Humanities. Which is why I had made a tryst with him that day to upbraid him and bring him to a better sense, and so I could not go with Messer Guido as he was good enough to wish.

Guido looked at me with a sudden interest. "You are much his friend, are you not?" he questioned.

Now I had for long been mightily taken with Messer Dante, and, indeed, for a while I seemed to see the world as he saw it, and to speak as he would have spoken. I am of that mood now, after all these years--at least, in a measure. But just then I was in a reaction and vexed, and I voiced my vexation swiftly. "Why, I thought so once. But I wash my hands of him. We were as one in the playthings of youth. Now he dances no more to my piping. He will not laugh when my wit tickles him. He is no longer for drinking or kissing, for dicing or fighting. He has a cold fit of wisdom come upon him, and rests ever with Messer Brunetto, the high dry-as-dust, reading of Virgilius, Tullius, and other ancients, as if learning were better than living. I have made a tryst with him here to upbraid him; but I doubt he will keep it."

"I know little of him," Guido said, thoughtfully. "I should like to know more, to know much."

Now, it was a great compliment to any youth in our city that Messer Guido should desire his acquaintance, yet I feared in this case he had made a rash choice.

"Lord," I said, "he is hard to know. Yet, laugh if you will, but I think there are great things in him."

Messer Guido did not laugh. Rather he looked grave. "Pray God there be," he said. "For indeed the age lacks greatness."

"So every man has said in every age," I protested. "But our Dante baffles me. He changes his moods as a chameleon changes his coat, and feeds each mood so full. Yesteryear he was mad for the open air, and the games, and the joy of life. To-day he is mewed in the cloisters of knowledge. He is damned in his Latin. I will wait no more for him."

So I spoke in my impatience, and made as if to go; but Guido caught me by the sleeve and restrained me, saying, "Why, here, as I think, he comes, by way of the bridge."

Now, even as he spoke, I looked where he looked, and whom should I see coming toward us on the shady side of the bridge than this very lad we were talking of, and with him Messer Brunetto, the great scholar. So I went on with a new anger in my voice, "It is he, indeed, in Messer Brunetto's escort," and then I plucked Guido by the arm and pulled him round about, so that we were out of ken of the coming pair. "Let us stand off one side till he be alone."

So I urged and so I persuaded, and Messer Guido and I, that were curious to have speech with Dante, but had no desire to have speech with the elder, slipped apart and hid ourselves in the shadow of the pillars of the Arcade that faced the Portinari palace.

II
A CHILD AND A CHILD

Guido and I had scarcely taken cover when Messer Brunetto came into view on the lip of the bridge. He was talking as he walked, but he walked and talked alone, for unperceived by him Dante had lagged behind and stood with his elbows rested on the parapet looking down at Arno below him. Messer Brunetto was discoursing very learnedly about Messer Virgilius, and how he did, in a measure, form and model himself upon Messer Homerus, when he suddenly became aware that he was wasting his periods upon empty air--for of us where we lurked he knew nothing. Turning round, he saw where Dante stood pensive, and called to him sharply, asking him why he dawdled.

Dante, thus addressed, raised his head from the cup of his palms and his elbows from the parapet, and, with a pleasant smile on his face, came down to where Messer Brunetto had halted. I have never known a man's face that could be blither than Dante's when he smiled, and in those days, when he and I were young together, before that happened which was so soon to happen, I had seen him smile many a time, though for the most part his countenance had a great air of gravity. Now he and Messer Brunetto stood in talk, and from where I lay hid I could catch most of the words these two spoke, and my wit was nimble enough to piece out the rest at my convenience; and you must take it with a good will that what I set down was spoken or might be spoken by my friend. And the first I heard him say was this, in a grave voice, "Forgive me for lingering, Master; I was listening to the Song of the River."

And Messer Brunetto echoed, in surprise: "The Song of the River! What in the name of all the ancients is the Song of the River?"

Messer Dante seemed to muse for a while, and then I heard him answer his master in that strong voice of his, that even then was deep and full, and always brought to my mind the sound of a bell.

"The Song of the River, the Song of Life. I cannot sing you the Song of the River. If I could tell you its meaning, I should be a greater poet than Virgilius."

Messer Brunetto held up his hands in a horror that was only part pretended. "Do not blaspheme!" he cried. Dante smiled for a moment at his whimsical vehemence, and then went on with his own thoughts, talking as one that mused aloud.

"It must be glorious to be a great poet, to weave one's dreams into wonderful words that live in men's hearts forever. Master, I would rather be a great poet than be the Emperor of Rome."

Then the elder looked at the younger with a smile and shook his head at his ambition. "It is given to few to be great poets; there have been fewer great poets than emperors since the world began."

But my friend was not to be so put off. I knew him ever to be persistent when once his mind was made up, and it may be that he knew well enough that such warnings had been addressed idly to all the great poets in their youth. He answered Messer Brunetto slowly.

"My mother, who died young--I cannot remember her--dreamed a strange dream of me. She dreamed that I stood a shepherd beneath a laurel-tree, and strove to gather the leaves thereof, and failed in my strivings and fell, and rose again, and lo! no longer a man, but a peacock, a glory of gold and purple."

The youth paused for a moment as if he lingered lovingly over the bequeathed vision, then he questioned Messer Brunetto. "What could this dream mean, Master?"

Messer Brunetto looked sour. "Who shall say? Who shall guess?" he answered, fretfully. "Your peacock is a vain bird with a harsh voice."

Dante seemed to pay no heed to the impatience or the disdain of his master. He went on talking as if he were talking to himself, or to some congenial companion such as I would be.

"Sometimes I dream of that laurel-tree, and then I wake with joy in my heart and verses humming in my brain. They vanish when I try to set them down, but they sweeten the leave of the day."

I think Messer Brunetto did not like the turn which his pupil's thoughts had taken. "Dreams are but dreams," he answered, impatiently. "Wisdom, philosophy, these are the true treasures. There is no harm in a Latin ode after the manner of Messer Ovidius, but for the most part poets or those that call themselves such are foolish fellows enough, and keep very bad company. Ply your book, my son, and avoid them."

"Messer Guido Cavalcanti is a poet," Dante objected, firmly, yet gently, for he was speaking to his elder, and to a very great and famous man, and he always carried himself with a becoming reverence to those that should be revered.

The scholar smiled a little acidly. "He is of a noble house, and he may divert himself with such trifles and no harm done."

Then I saw Dante raise his head, and his eyes flashed and his cheeks flushed. "I, too, am of a noble house," he asserted, proudly; and indeed this was true, for he could claim descent from people of very pretty genealogy. "I, too, am of a noble house," he insisted. "I derive from the Alighieri of Ferrara, the Frangipani of Rome. Heaven my witness, that matters little, but to be a great poet would matter much."

Messer Brunetto patted my Dante very kindly on the shoulder, and looked at him with the look that old men wear when they are advising young men.

"I have better hopes for you," he declared, "for I swear you have in you the makings of a pretty scholar."

He smiled as he spoke, paternally, as one that feels he has spoken the last word that has any need to be spoken on any matter of dispute.

But Dante seemed to be little impressed by his advice, and he showed his own thoughts in his words, for when he spoke it was rather as if he were speaking to himself than to his companion. "Am I a fool to feel these stirrings of the spirit? God knows. But my dreams are full of stars and angels, and the sound of sweet words like many winds and many waters. And then I wake in an exultation and the words die on my lips."

Messer Brunette lifted his hands in protest. "Thank Heaven they do die. It must needs be so. Purge yourself of such folly. Poetry died with the ancients. Virtue, my young friend, not verses. Will you dine with me? We will eat beans and defy Pythagoras."

Dante shook his head.

"I thank you," he answered, slowly, and I supposed it grieved him a little to deny so wise a man, "but I may not. I keep a tryst here."

Messer Brunetto instantly assumed an air of alarm, and he allowed his voice to tremble as he said, "With no woman, I hope."

Dante looked at him squarely. "With no woman, I swear. I have no more to do with women. What woman is as fair as philosophy, as winsome as wisdom?"

Messer Brunetto beamed on him with an admiring smile.

"Right, my son, right!" he cried, delighted. "Better Seneca for you than sensuality; Virgilius than venery. When you are as ripe as I, you may trifle awhile if you like with lightness." Here I, listening, sniggered, for it was blown about the city that Messer Brunetto had his passions or fancies or vagaries, call them what you will, and humored them out of school hours. "For the present," he went on, "read deep and lie chaste, and so farewell."

He patted Dante again paternally on the shoulder and wished him good-day, and went off down the street, muttering to himself, as I make very little doubt, his wonder that any could be found so foolish as to wish to string rhymes together when they might be studying the divine philosophies of the ancients. As for Messer Dante, he stood for a while where his master had left him, as one that was deep in thought, and we, though we had a mind to spring out and accost him, yet refrained, for I knew of old that when my friend was deep in his reflections he was sometimes inclined to be vexed with those that disturbed him. So we still lingered and peeped, and presently Dante sighed and went over to where the bookstall stood and began turning over some of the parchments that lay on the board. As he did so the bookseller popped his head out at him from the booth, as a tortoise from his shell, and I never beheld tortoise yet so crisp and withered as this human. Messer Cecco Bartolo was his name. And Dante addressed him. "Gaffer Bookman, Gaffer Bookman, have you any new wares?"

The bookseller dived into the darkness of his shop again and came out in a twinkling with an armful of papers, which he flung down on the board before Dante. "There," he said. "There lie some manuscripts that came in a chest I bought last week. Is there one of them to your taste?"

We watched Dante examining the manuscripts eagerly, and putting the most part of them impatiently aside. One seemed to attract his attention, for he gave it a second and more careful glance, and then addressed the bookseller. "This seems to be a knightly tale," he said, extending the volume. "What do you ask for it?"

The bookseller took the manuscript from him, glanced at it, and then handed it back to him. "Take it or leave it, three florins is its price."

We heard Dante sigh a little, and we saw Dante smile a little, and he answered the bookseller, humorously: "My purse is as lean as Pharaoh's kine, but the story opens bravely, and a good tale is better than shekels or bezants. What do you buy with your money that is worth what you sell for it?"

The bookseller shrugged his stooped shoulders. "Food and drink and the poor rags that Adam's transgression enforces on us."

Dante laughed at his conceit. "You are a merry peddler," he said, and took out of his pouch a few coins, from which he counted scrupulously the sum that the bookseller had asked, and gave it to him. Then he moved slowly away from the stall, reading in his new purchase until he came to the fountain that had the painted statue over it. There he sat himself down on a stone bench in the angle of the wall and buried himself in his book.

And by now we were resolved to address him, but again we were diverted from our purpose, for there came by a little company of merrymakers, youths and maidens, that were making sport as is fit for such juvenals in that season of felicity which is named May-day. Some had pipes and some had lutes and some had tambourines, and all were singing as loud as they could and making as much noise as they might, and when they came into the open space hard by the fountain they paused for a while in their progress, and broke into as lively a morris-dance as ever I had seen skipped. How they twisted and turned and tripped; how bravely they made music; how lustily they sang. I recall them now, those bright little human butterflies. I can see the pretty faces and slim figures of the girls, the blithe carriage of the lads. The musical tumult that they make seems to be ringing in my ears as I write, and my narrow room widens to its harmony.

But would you believe it, no sound of all that singing and dancing served to rouse Messer Dante for one moment from his book. Though the air was full of shrill voices and sweet notes and the clapping of hands and the flapping fall of dancing feet, he remained motionless, and never once lifted up his eyes to look at the merry crowd. As for the dancers, I do not think that they saw him, certainly they paid him no heed. Why should such merry fellows as they take note of a book-worm while there were songs to sing and tunes to turn and dances to dance? And by-and-by, when they had made an end of their measure, they fell into procession again and went away as quickly as they had come, leaving me mightily delighted with their entertainment. As they trooped off over the bridge, Guido and I made up our minds that now we would have speech with Dante; so we came out from where we had lain hid and walked softly across the space that divided us from him, and stood by his side and called his name loudly into his ears. Then, after a while, but not at all at first calling, Dante slowly lifted his eyes from his book and looked at us, and the look on his face was the look of a man that is newly wakened from a pleasurable dream. Then he smiled salutation on me, for, indeed, I believe he always liked me, and recognizing Messer Guido, he rose and saluted him courteously.

"Now, Heaven bless you, brother," I cried, "that you seem to sleep in the midst of all these rumors."

Dante gazed at me with untroubled curiosity. "What rumors?" he asked, indifferently.

"Why," replied Guido, staring at him, "here was the daintiest dancing."

Now by this I remembered that of us three present two were not known one to the other, and I hastened to amend the matter.

"Nay," said I, "here is another that can tell you better than I. Here is Messer Guido of the Cavalcanti that has kicked heels with me on this ground for the wish to make your acquaintance."

Now, Messer Guido, that had stood quietly by, made speed to speak to Dante. "It is very true," he declared. "I have heard your praises." And as he spoke the face of Dante flushed with pleasure, for it was no small honor to be sought in friendship by Messer Guido. So he answered him very gladly, yet with a certain calmness that was his character in all things.

"Messer Guido," he said, "I am honored to the top of my longing, though, indeed, I have no greater claim to your favor than this: that I know by root of heart every rhyme that you have written and given."

At this Messer Guido laughed joyously. "Heaven, friend," he cried, "what better recommendation could a man have to one that writes verses?"

"Is there one in Florence," Dante asked, "that could not say as much?" Then, as if to break away from bandying of compliments, he asked: "But what were the rumors you spoke of?"

"Why," replied Guido, looking at him in some wonder, "here was the daintiest festal ever devised: delicate youths and exquisite maidens footing it to pipe and cymbal as blithely as if they would never grow old."

Dante shook his head a little. "I did not mark them."

As for me, I marvelled, and I cried, "A beatific disposition that can sleep in such a din."

But Dante reproved me with that gravity he always showed when there was any matter of truth to be considered. "I did not sleep," he asserted. "I read."

"What, in Heaven's name," asked Guido, "did you read, that could shut your ears to such a din?"

Dante lifted up toward him the manuscript he had newly bought. "The love-tale of Knight Lancelot and Queen Guinevere. The fellow that wrote it discourses nothing but marvels."

Now I was curious, for I love all strange tales, and I questioned him: "What marvels?"

Dante answered me smiling, and his face was always very sweet when he smiled. "Why, the rogue will have it that when such a cavalier as Lancelot tumbles into love he becomes a very ecstatic, and sees the world as it never is, was, or shall be. The sun is no more than his lady's looking-glass, and the moon and stars her candles to light her to bed. You are a lover, Messer Guido. Do you think thus of your lady?"

Messer Guido answered emphatically, for he was indeed deep in love with a lady well worth the loving. "Very surely and so will you when the fever wrings you."

Dante turned to me, still with that same luminous smile on his face. "And you, Lappo?"

Now, it was then and ever my creed that it is a man's best business to be in love as much and as often as he can, and I answered him according to my fancy. "I should scorn myself if I did not overtop every conceited fancy that lover has ever sighed or sung for his lady."

Dante still smiled, but there was now a little scorn in his smile that nettled me. "It is strange," he said. And then made a feint of returning to his book, saying,

"Well, I will read in my book again if you are no wiser."

But Guido laid his hand upon the pages and protested. "Plague on your reading, brother; you read too much. You are young to be so studious of pothooks and hangers. The Book of Life is a brave book for a youth to read in."

And here I put in my word. "And the two best chapters, by your leave, are those that treat of Squire Bacchus and Dame Venus."

"You are a pretty ribald," Dante said to me, mockingly. "Leave me to my ease. Let our star wheel where it pleases; I cannot guide the chariot of the sun. Let me bask in its bounty, warm my hands at it, eat the fruit it ripens, and drink the wine it kindles. I am content. Florence is the fairest city in the world. I shall be happy to grow old in Florence, studiously, peacefully, pleasantly, dreaming my dreams."

Guido protested against his placidity. "What a slugabed spirit! Rings there no alarum in your blood?"

Dante said nothing, but looked at me, and I supported Guido's theme. "There are ladies in Florence as lovely as the city's lilies. I would rather lie in white arms than dream dreams."

Dante shook his head, and he fluttered the pages of his book as he answered us slowly: "Restless, feverish Titans, forever challenging the great gods of Love and War. Give me the dappled shade of a green garden, the sable shadows quivering on a ground of gold, a book of verse by me to play with when I would be busy, and a swarm of sweet rhythms like colored butterflies floating about my drowsy senses. What to me are wars and rumors of wars in that delicious ease? What to me are the white breasts of the fair Florentines?"

Guido and I looked at each other in wonder, and then Guido asked again, "Tell me, comrade, have you ever been in love?"

Now, when Guido asked him that question, I expected to hear from Dante a mocking answer, but instead, to my surprise, he sat quite still for a little while, almost like a man in a trance, with his hands clasped about his knees, and it seemed to me as if he were seeing, as indeed he was seeing, things that we who were with him did not see and could not see. After a while he spoke in a soft voice, and for the most part his words came sharp and clear, like the words of a man that speaks in a dream.

"Once, when I was still a child, I saw a child's face, a girl's face; it lives in my memory as the face of an angel. It was a sunny morning, a May morning, such a morning as this, one of those days that always make one think of roses. I had a rose in my hand, and I was smelling at it--and then I saw the child. She was younger than I--and I was very young."

Now, although I am a liberal lover of women, I have, I thank Heaven, such a nature that any talk of love pleases me and interests me, and I can listen to any lover with content. But this talk of children only tickled me, and I turned to my comrade Guido, that was known to be a very devoted swain to his lady, and that served her in song and honor with all fidelity, and pointed Dante out to him now, as if laughing at the radiant gaze on his face. "Look at the early lover, Guido," I said, and laughed; but Messer Guido would not humor me by laughing too, and he told me later that he never found a love-tale a thing to laugh at.

Dante seemed neither to heed nor to be vexed at my mirth. "Laugh if you like," he said, good-humoredly, "but I learned what love might mean then, as I peeped over the red breast of the rose at the little maiden. She was younger than I was; she had hair like woven sunlight, and her wide eyes seemed to me bright with a better blue than heaven's. Oh, if I had all the words in the world at my order, I could not truly tell you all I thought then of that little child."

Guido said very gravely, "A boy may have great thoughts." And he said no more, but looked steadfastly upon the rapt countenance of Dante.

Now by this time I was all afire with curiosity, for this strange talk stirred me to wonder, and I entreated Messer Dante very zealously to tell me who this child was. Dante went on as if he had not heard my question, telling his tale in a measured voice. "She looked at me and she looked at my red rose, and I felt suddenly as if that rose were the most precious gift in the world, a gift for a god, and that I should give it to her. I held out my hand to her with the rose in it, and she took the flower, and her fingers touched my fingers as she took it. They still thrill with the memory."

As I have but just recorded, to my shame, I took all this story of our friend's in a spirit of mockery. "O father Socrates," I cried, "listen to the philosopher!" And then, because I was still burning with desire for more knowledge in this strange business, I repeated my question. "Who was she?"

And this time Dante heeded me and answered me. "I do not know. I never saw her again."

Guido's amazement at this answer found speech. "You never saw her again?" he questioned. "A girl in Florence?"

And indeed it was a strange thing for our city, where one sees every one every day.

But Dante nodded. "It is strange, but so it is. I never saw her again. That is nine years ago now."

Guido's eyes were filled with a tender pity. Never before saw I true lover so moved by a profession of true love. "Are you sure you ever really saw her?" he questioned, somewhat sadly. "Are you sure that you did not dream this wonder?"

Dante showed no anger at this doubt, though indeed at other times he was quick enough to take offence if he found just cause. But I guessed then what I know since, that he found this matter at once so simple and so sacred that nothing any man could say concerning it could in any way vex him. So he answered very mildly, "Sometimes I almost doubt, but the scent of a red rose on a May morning always brings her back to me."

Now I grieve to record it, but the silly spirit of mockery within me had so far infected my wits that I cried out in pretended astonishment, "O marvellous fancy that can so ennoble a neighbor's brat!" The which was very false and foolish of me, for I know well enough now, and knew very well then, that love, while it lasts, can ennoble any child, maid, or matron. Lord, the numbers of girls I have likened to Diana that were no such matter, and the plump maids I have appraised as Venus, though, indeed, they would have shown something clumsy if one had caught them rising from the sea! But, as I say, Dante never heeded my jeers, and sat there very quiet and silent, very much as if he had forgotten our existence, and was thinking only of that gracious child he spoke of. And I, my laughter being somewhat abashed by his gravity, and the edge of my jest being blunted by his indifference, as well as by the reproof on Guido's face, stood there awkwardly, not knowing whether to abide with him or leave him, when there came, to break my embarrassment, the presence of a mighty fair lady.

III
VITTORIA

The lady that now came toward us over the little bridge was one whose acquaintance I could claim, and whose beauty I admired very greatly. Madonna Vittoria Crescimbeni was a very fair lady that was generous of her favors to those that were wealthy, and even to those that were not, if they happened to take her fancy, as indeed I am pleased to recall. She lived on the other side of Arno, in a gracious dwelling that had been built for her by a great lord that had given her everything, except his name, while he lived, and had died and left her a fortune. For all that, she was a light child; she carried herself with much show of discretion, and was only to be come at warily, as it were, and with circumspection; and because of her abundance she was at no man's beck and call, and could choose and refuse as it liked her. She was made something full of figure, with a face like an ancient statue, which was the less to be wondered at because her mother was a Greek; but her hair, of which she had a mighty quantity, was of that tawny red tincture that is familiar to those that woo Venetian women. As for her mouth, it was like flame, and her eyes were flames too, though of another hue, having a greenish light in them that could delight or frighten as she pleased. She went her ways in great state, having two small knavish blackamoor pages in gold tissue at her heels, and a little ways off she was followed by a brace of well-armed serving-rascals.

For my own part, I was mightily pleased to see her, for though she was, in the native ways of affairs, somewhat out of my star, still, as I said, she was to show later that she had an eye for a pretty fellow and owned a spirit above mere dross. I say no more. She seemed content enough to see me, but still more content to see Messer Guido. This was an experience in the ways of ladies with which those that walked with Messer Guido were familiar. Every woman that saw him admired him highly. So Vittoria smiled a little on me and a great deal on Messer Guido; and as for Dante, she glanced at him slightly and gave him little heed, for his habit was modest and his looks were not of a kind at once to tickle the fancy of such as she. Yet Dante looked at her curiously, though without ostentation, as one whose way it is instinctively to observe all men and all women with an exceeding keenness and clearness of vision.

Messer Guido greeted Madonna Vittoria very courteously, as was ever his way with women. Were they fair or plain-favored, chaste or gay, he was ever their very gentle servant. And by this time Vittoria, being very close to us, paused and gave us the greeting of the day; and her pages came to a halt behind her, and her men-at-arms stood at ease a little space away.

The beautiful lady looked at us with a kind of wonder and a kind of mockery in her dark eyes. And when she spoke to us her voice was marvellously soft with a rich softness that made me, being then of a very sensual disposition, think instantly of old wine and ripe fruit, and darkened alcoves, and the wayward complaining of lutes. Indeed, wherever Monna Vittoria went she seemed to carry with her an atmosphere of subtle seclusion, of a cloistered lusciousness, of dim, green, guarded gardens, where the sighs of love's novices are stifled by the drip of stealthy fountains and the babble of fantastic birds. I suppose it was no more than my fancy, or a trick of my memory confusing later things with earlier, that makes me now, as I write, seem to recall what seemed like a smile on the face of the pagan effigy of Love as Madonna Vittoria swam into her company, as if the Greekish image recognized in the woman a creature of the early days when cunning fingers fashioned him. For, indeed, Vittoria was not modern in the sense that we Florentines are modern. She derived from a world long dead and buried. Heavens, how Messer Alcibiades would have admired her!

"Good-morrow, gentle gentles," she began, in that caressing voice, "why are you absent from the sacrifice?"

Guido looked for the instant perplexed by the woman's words, and he moved a little nearer to her. As for Dante, he seemed to have forgotten us all, even to have forgotten his book, and though he had risen when Monna Vittoria approached, he had by this time sunk onto the stone seat again, and seemed drowned in a brown study.

"What sacrifice, lady?" Guido asked of Vittoria; and whenever Guido spoke to a woman, he spoke as if all the pleasures and destinies of the world depended upon that one woman's interest and caprice.

Madonna Vittoria smiled, self-satisfied, as all women smiled when Guido so addressed them. "Why, the sacrifice of the pearl to the pig," she answered; and she still smiled as she spoke, but there was a kind of anger in her eyes. "The sacrifice of a clean child to a coarse churl, the sacrifice of Folco Portinari's little Beatrice to my big Simone, that I do not choose to lose."

Here I broke in, laughing, for I took the drift of her meaning, and was wishful to prove myself alert. "Most allegorical lady," I protested, "I take you very clearly when you explain your own fable." And I rubbed my hands, instantly pleased with myself and my nimbleness.

But Messer Guido still looked thoughtful. "If the ladies of Florence," he said, slowly, "make Madonna Beatrice their May-queen, that dainty deed does not deliver her to Simone of the Bardi."

Madonna Vittoria turned upon him with a sharpness seldom seen on a woman's face when it bent toward Messer Guido of the Cavalcanti. Her smooth forehead wrinkled with an unfamiliar frown; her full lips seemed to tighten and narrow to a red thread; her eyes were as a cat's eyes are when the cat is very, very angry.

"Who goes by her side," she asked, sourly, "as she goes through the city?" And she answered her own question with a name. "Simone dei Bardi." She went on: "Who is her father's faithful friend? Simone dei Bardi." She glanced from one to the other of us--Messer Guido and I, I mean, for Dante took no heed of her and she seemed to take no heed of him. "I will tell you," she said, fiercely, "the trap is baited for the prey, and, as things go, it seems as if I were like to lose my emerald, that I can spare ill, as well as a husband, that I could spare very readily were it not that I had a mind to marry him."

Now at this there was a pause, and in a little while I turned to Dante, thinking that it was high time he took a share in our parley.

"Is not," I said, "Monna Vittoria much to be pitied?"

Being thus questioned, Dante seemed to shake himself free from his lethargy, or his disdain, or whatever you may call it, and he answered very indifferently, as one that speaks of another that is not present, "I do not know the cause of her sorrow."

Monna Vittoria turned to him now very directly and faced him, and there was a kind of challenge in her carriage.

"Messer Dante," she said, "if you know nothing of me, I know something of you, for Messer Brunetto, your philosopher, is one of my very good friends. I had this trinket of him a week ago." And as she spoke she fingered an enamelled and jewelled pendant against her neck that must have cost the scholar a merry penny. "Well, Messer Dante, you who are young and of high spirit, would you have a queen of beauty married to a king of beasts?"

Dante shrugged his shoulders a little, feigning no interest in the handsome creature that addressed him. "The alliance sounds unnatural," he answered, carelessly, and looked as if he would be glad that the matter should end.

But Vittoria would not have it so. "Well, now," she said, "when all Florence is luting and fluting for the queen of beauty, the king of beasts walks warden by her side."

Still Dante showed no interest. "Who is this queen of beauty?" he asked, listlessly. And when Guido made answer that she was Folco Portinari's daughter Beatrice, he only shook his head a little and declared that he did not know her.

"She is new to Florence," I explained.

And Vittoria went on. "I will give her this credit, that she is a comely piece. Let us go and see the girl in her triumph." She addressed herself directly to Guido, but she had an after-glance for me as well.

Guido turned toward his new-made friend. "Will you come with us, Messer Dante?" he asked.

But Dante denied him. "Not I, by your leave," he replied. "I find folly enough here in my book without tramping the highways to face it in its pageant."

Now I felt a little vexed at his churlishness, for Madonna Vittoria was a lovely lady, and very pleasant company, and one worth obliging. So I spoke to the others, saying, "Well, well, let us not starve because Dante has no appetite." And therewith I caught a hand of Guido and a hand of Vittoria, and made to lead them from the place. And they both responded well enough to my summons.

But Monna Vittoria checked me a little and paused, and spoke again to Dante. "Farewell, Messer Dante," she said, sweetly. "Will you come visit me one of these days?"

But Dante, who had poked that hooked nose of his now in his book again, shook his head and made her no very civil answer. "Madonna," he said, "I have little money and less lust. God be with you."

So, lapped in that mood, we left him, and went our ways toward the Signory, and our Dante was soon out of sight, and, if truth be told, out of mind.

IV
THE WORDS OF THE IMAGE

Now I proceed to tell under all caution what happened to our Dante, sitting there alone in the shady angle of that sunny place, after we had left him to go to the Signory. For, indeed, I did not see it, although I heard it from his lips, that had the gift, even then, to make the strangest things seem as real as, say, the door of a house. The tale was so told, in such twists of thought and turns of phrase, that it might, if you chose, be taken as an allegory or the vision of a dream; but, for my own part, I prefer to believe that it came about just as I shall set it down, for the world is merrier for a spice of the marvellous in its composition, and, for myself, I could believe anything of that same painted image.

It seems, then, that when Dante was left alone he turned to his book again, and set himself very resolutely to reading of the loves of Lancelot and Guinevere, in the hope, most like, to still that stirring of the spirit occasioned by our talk. And when the fall of our footsteps and the babble of our voices could be heard no more, he confessed that at first he felt grateful for the silence and the peace. But of a sudden it appeared to him that the silence was greater than there was any need or reason for it to be, that it seemed to him as if all Florence held its breath in the suspense of a great hush which lapped the world in its embrace--such a hush as might perchance occur before the coming of Doom. Then, after an interval that seemed too age-long to be endured, out of the very core of the silence Dante heard a voice calling to him that he had never heard before, and that spoke to him with such a sweet imperiousness that he was as physically and spiritually bound to obey and attend as ever Moses was on the holy hill. And the commanding voice cried to him, "Dante, behold a deity stronger than thou, who comes to govern thee."

Then it seemed to Dante that at the sound of that voice his consciousness returned to him, and, looking up from his book, he called aloud, "Who speaks to me?" And as he spoke he saw, or thought he saw--but I give it to you as he gave it to me--to his amazement, how the painted image of the beautiful youth that stood above the fountain seemed slowly to quicken into being, and how all the gaudy colors and gilding of the figure seemed to soften to the exquisite and tender hues of a life that was more marvellous than life. The hair of the youth was radiantly sunny, his cheeks flamed and paled with a divine white and red, his perfect limbs and perfect body seemed moulded with such exquisite rounded flesh as the immortal gods assumed long ago when they deigned to descend from Olympus or appear in Cytherea, and speak to men and love them. And the pagan boy that stood above the plashing fountain lifted a hand toward Dante and parted his lips and spoke, and this was what he said: "The God Love speaks to you, Dante, and to none but you. Lift up your heart, for soon your happiness shall be made manifest unto you."

At this Dante, though, as he told me thereafter, he felt no fear, was full of a great astonishment, and he strove to speak and could not for an instant, and at last he cried out, "Must I believe you?" For it seemed to him as if the image uttered the very voice of truth, but that he, listening, rebelled against it.

Then the beautiful, breathing boy, that had been the beautiful, silent image, stretched out a hand to him in command, and said, "You that denied me must now believe me, for henceforth I shall govern your soul."

At these words Dante crossed himself, for all this seemed strange work for commonplace Florence in full day, and he tried to repeat a prayer, but wonderfully could remember none, and only his ears buzzed with the words of all the love-songs he had ever heard, and he entreated, "Leave me in peace." And as he spoke he stretched out his hands in supplication to the quickened image.

Now it is to be said that it seemed to Dante as if a kind of pale flame appeared to blaze all about the living image, and to spread from him in fine and delicate rays till it seemed to play on Dante's body and burn through the armor of the flesh and lurk about his naked heart. And the agony of that burning was beyond words, yet there was a kind of joy in it that was beyond thought.

And the God that was Love cried out again: "You pray in vain for peace who shall ever be peaceless from this time forth. For the unavoidable hour is at hand when you shall know my power. Farewell awhile." As the figure spoke those last words it seemed slowly to stiffen into stone again, and the beautiful, vital coloring faded away, and the pale, leaping flames vanished, and Dante found himself sitting and staring at the painted image above the lisping water that he had looked at unmoved a thousand times, as he passed it going to and fro on his way through the city.

Dante rubbed his forehead and wondered. "I have been dreaming," he murmured, "and the love-tale in the book colored my thoughts."

Now, though all this vision, or whatever you may please to call it, seemed brief enough, it took longer than the telling, for Messer Dante told me that the next thing he knew was that he heard my voice calling to him. Wherefore, the most will probably say that Messer Dante had fallen asleep in the heat of the day and dreamed a dream, but I do not think so. Now, Guido and I and Monna Vittoria had gone on our ways to the Signory, thinking to witness the crowning of the lady Beatrice of the Portinari, but we had not travelled very far when we heard the noise of many people mixed with the sound of music, and we knew that the procession was coming our way and that the ceremony at the Signory was over and done with. Then it seemed a shame to me that my friend should lose all the pleasure, and I said I would go back for him, and Messer Guido came with me because Monna Vittoria had found other friends and stayed in speech with them. And when Guido and I came back to the place where we had left Dante, I found him, as I say, seated upon the stone seat. His closed book lay by his side, and he was staring straight before him, as a man that is newly awakened from a trance. But I, taking little notice of his state at the moment, ran toward him and clapped him on the shoulder, calling to him: "They are moving this way!" I cried. "Come and see!"

But Dante did not seem to hear me, and sat gazing at that painted image that was such an old friend of mine and his, as if he had never seen it before. But presently, partly by persuasion, and partly by pushing and urging, we got him to turn from the statue and accompany us a little ways till we came to a stand in the neighborhood of the Palace of the Portinari, toward which the procession of the May-day was making its way.

The open space of the Piazza of the Santa Felicita was now pretty well filled with the curious and the seekers for amusement, and all the air was full of sweet noises, and all the smiling faces shone in the warm sunlight. And Guido and I, piloting our Dante, pushed our way to the inner circle of the loiterers, and paused there, waiting for the coming of the merrymakers. And even as we paused the folk that we expected came upon us. They were a gallant company of youths and maidens, dressed all in their best and brightest, and there were excellent musicians with them that made the most noble of cheerful music, and the comely girls scattered flowers on the cobbles, and the comely youths laughed and shouted, and in the midst of the throng a dozen of the strongest lads were tugging at a chariot that carried a gilded throne, and on that throne was seated Madonna Beatrice of the Portinari. She was dressed in a robe of crimson silk, and she carried red roses in her hand, and I think that all who looked upon her held her as the loveliest maid in all Florence. I know that, for my part, I frankly admitted to myself that none of the girls that I was in love with at that time could hold a candle to her. Yet I knew for my sins that I could never be in love with Madonna Beatrice of the Portinari. Standing by her side was a big, thick-set, fierce-looking man, with a shag of black hair and a black beard like a spade, whom I knew well enough and whom all there knew well enough to be Messer Simone dei Bardi, the man of whom Guido and I had talked that morning. There was a great crowd behind the chariot, Reds and many Yellows, seemingly at peace that day, friends of Guido, and followers of Simone, and revellers of many kinds and townsfolk of many classes. I could see that Monna Vittoria was in the thick of the crowd that followed the Car of Triumph, and presently she made her way beneath the shelter of the arcade, and stood there hard by one of the pillars, watching the lady Beatrice on her throne and Simone dei Bardi keeping so close beside her. And Simone, as I believe, had no knowledge of Vittoria's presence.

Now, when that brave company came into the place where we stood, Dante, that had stood by our sides listlessly enough, turned away from us as suddenly and sharply as if he had received an order. So he turned, and, turning, he saw in full view the face of the lady Beatrice as she sat on her car of triumph; and, at the sight of her, he gave a great cry, and then stood silent and stiff as if spellbound.

Guido, delighted by the girl's beauty, cried to him, not looking at him, "Is she not fair?"

But I saw what strange case our Dante was in, and pulled at Guide's sleeve and jerked his attention to my friend, saying, "Our Dante stands at gaze as if he were sun-dazzled."

Guido turned to Messer Dante and saw the rapture in his face, and, seeing, questioned him. "Is she not fair?" he asked, and his glance travelled again to where the May-queen sat.

And Dante answered him, speaking very slowly, as a man might speak in some sweet sleep when he dreamed a dear dream, "She is the loveliest woman in the world." He paused for a moment, and then added, in a lower tone, "She is the child I worshipped."

Now, I could plainly read amazement and doubt on Messer Guido's face when he heard Dante speak thus strangely, and he caught at his arm and shook it a little gently, as one would do that wishes to wake a sleeping man. "You are dreaming, for sure," he said.

But Dante only answered him very quietly, still keeping his rapturous face fixed on the girl as she and her company came nearer. "She is the lady of my dreams."

Now I, that was glancing in much bewilderment from Dante, where he stood at gaze so radiant, to the fair girl on her gilded car, saw, or thought I saw, all of a sudden, a look in the girl's eyes that betokened more knowledge of Dante than merely the knowledge that a man stood in the roadway and stared at her beauty. So I whispered to Guido in his ear, "See, she seems to note him, and, as I think, with recognition."

Now, even as I said this, the little company that carried the Queen of Beauty came to a halt some yards from the gate of the gray palace, and Messer Simone dei Bardi, quitting the side of her chariot, advanced toward the Palace of the Portinari to give the formal summons that the Queen of May demanded admittance, all of which was part and parcel of the ceremonial of the pretty sport. At the same instant Dante, quitting Guido's side, advanced a little nearer to the girl, who did not descend from her chair, but sat still in her chariot as if waiting for his coming, and the little crowd of juvenals about her fluttered aside before his resolute advance, and I thought even then how strong his young face looked, and how purposeful, for all his youth, that grim nose of his and the steady eyes above it, in contrast with the pink-and-white prettiness of the many slim lads that were the Queen of Beauty's satellites.

And Dante raised his voice and called to the girl as a friend calls to a friend: "Give me a rose for my rose, madonna! Give me a rose for my rose!"

Now the girl, as she sat, had in her lap a great quantity of roses exceedingly red and large, and she took up one of these in answer to the call and cast it through the air to Dante, who caught it as it fell, and, catching it, lifted it to his lips with his eyes fixed on the girl. Then, whether because of his action or the eagerness of his gaze above the crimson petals I know not, but Madonna Beatrice flushed a little, and she gathered the rest of her roses into her arms and rose from her chair, and descended from her chariot and mounted the steps of the great house, whose doors had now opened to Simone's summons. Messer Folco of the Portinari stood smiling on his threshold, but Messer Simone, by his side, was not smiling, for he had seen that pretty business of the given rose, and I could note that its prettiness pleased him little. I think he would have stepped down then and there and eased his spleen, but Messer Folco, as his way was ever, wished to improve the occasion by making a speech.

"Friends and neighbors," he began, in his ample, affable voice, "Florentines all, in my daughter's name, and for my own sake, I thank you." Thereat there came a little cheer from the crowd, and then Folco turned toward his daughter, plainly very proud of her, but still flagrantly paternal and pompous.

"Come, child," he said, solemnly. "Come, you have been queen for a day, but your reign is over, and you are no more now than honest goodman Folco's daughter. Get you within." Then Madonna Beatrice she paused for a moment with two of her girl friends by her side and looked down upon her company very graciously and sweetly, and wished them farewell. Then the door of the palace opened and swallowed her up with her two companions, and when she had gone it seemed to us watching as if the sunshine had gone with her, though the street was still flooded with its light.

Then Messer Folco spoke again to the multitude, saying that there would be simple cheer and sport provided in his gardens that lay in the meadow-land on the other side of Arno for such as chose to go so far, at which his hearers cheered again, and made all speed to take him at his word and hurry away over the bridge. Thereafter Messer Folco turned to Messer Simone, as if inviting him to enter.

But Messer Simone shook his head. "Later, Messer Folco," I heard him say, "later; I have some busy hours before me." Then Messer Folco, acquiescing, entered his great house, and its great doors closed behind him, and those that were conveying the car wheeled it about and pulled it away, returning on the road by which they had come, and by this time most of the revellers had departed over bridge.

Guido and I, that were not tempted to travel so far as Messer Folco's river gardens, turning to our companion, noted that Dante was standing entranced with his eyes fixed upon his rose, and I heard him murmur to himself, "O wonderful world, that can boast of so wonderful a woman!"

Now, when I say that all of Madonna Beatrice's escort had gone from there, I mean that the gay youths and maidens had departed, but Messer Simone dei Bardi had remained behind, leaning against the wall of the house with his arms folded and an evil smile on his face.

Messer Simone's own followers, seeing him, lingered, waiting upon his pleasure, and though most of the May-day merrymakers had disappeared, there were not a few idlers and passers-by.

There were a certain number of Messer Guido's friends there, too, that had joined him in the procession, and that now lingered in the hope to bear him with them to some merriment more to their liking than Messer Folco's transpontine hospitality. So that the open place was far from empty for all its bigness.

V
ONE WAY WITH A QUARREL

Now when the door had shut upon Beatrice, Messer Simone shook himself from the wall and advanced with a steady, heavy stride to where Dante stood lost in contemplation of his rose, and I thought he looked like some ugly giant out of a fairy-tale, and his sullen eyes were full of mischief. He came hard by Messer Dante, and spoke to him roughly. "I do not care to see you and that flower in fellowship."

Now both Guido and I feared that this might breed a quarrel, so we lingered, and Messer Simone's people drew together, watching their lord, and some that were passing paused to note what was toward. But Messer Dante lifted his head very quietly, and looked calmly into Simone's angry face and spoke him seemingly fair. "The world is wide, friend," he said, very smoothly; "you have but to turn the corner, and I and my flower will no longer vex your vision."

But Simone was not to be so put off. "I have a mind to wear that rose myself," he said, savagely, and he came a little nearer to Dante as he spoke, and his followers dogged his advance, ready to obey his orders.

He looked so big and so strong and so brutal by the side of our friend that I was ill at ease, for I knew well what a truculent ruffian this Simone was.

But Dante seemed to be no more troubled than he would have been by the buzzing of a wasp. "Then you had better change your mind speedily," he answered, in an even voice, "lest being crossed in a peevish whim sour your blood."

Now, the being spoken to so sweetly, and yet with words that had so little of sweetness in them and no fear at all, teased Messer Simone's black blood till it bubbled like boiling pitch, and his voice had got a kind of silly scream in it, as he cried: "Why, you damnable reader of books, you pitiful clerk, do you think I will bandy words with you? Give me that rose instantly, or I will cut out your heart and eat it!"

Dante was still unruffled, and answered him very suavely, "If you cut out my heart you would still find the rose in it and the name of earth's loveliest lady."

Now at this Messer Simone's face showed as red as an old roof-tile, and his voice was hoarse with anger as he called, furiously, "Give me the flower!"

For a breathing while Dante made him no answer, while he gathered the rose carefully together in the cup of his hand and then slipped it into his bosom. Then he spoke to Simone with a grave impatience. "You are a boisterous braggart, and you scream like the east wind. I am very weary of you."

Simone slapped his big hand to the hilt of his sword. "Patter an Ave quickly," he growled, "ere I slay you with the sight of a drawn sword."

It was such a menace as might have fretted many a man that was brave enough, for Simone was out of the common tall and strong, but it fretted our Dante no whit, and he only smiled derisively at the giant.

By this time the brawl--for such it was proving to be--had begun to attract public notice, and those that walked halted to watch the altercation between the big man and the slim youth. I caught a glimpse of Monna Vittoria beneath the arcade, and saw amusement on her face and wonder, and some scorn of Simone and much admiration of Dante. But I had no time to concern myself with Vittoria, for now Messer Simone's fingers were gripping at the hilt of his weapon, but he did no more than grip the hilt of it. Indeed, I do not think that he would have drawn on an unarmed man, and very likely he meant no more than to frighten the scholar. If this were Messer Simone's purpose, it was frankly baffled by the fact that Dante did not seem to be frightened at all, but just stood his ground and watched his adversary with a light of quiet amusement in his eyes that was very exasperating to Simone. The whole quarrel had kindled and thriven so quickly that Messer Guido, who was standing apart and talking with certain of his friends, had as yet no knowledge of it, but now I moved to him and plucked him by the sleeve and told him what was toward. In truth, I felt no small alarm for my friend, for I knew him to have no more than that passable facility with the sword which is essential to gentility. Then Messer Guido turned and came with me, and his friends followed him, and our numbers added to the circle that was forming about the disputants. So now, while Messer Simone was still angrily handling his sword-hilt, and while the smile still lingered on Dante's lips, Messer Guido stepped nimbly between the two, being eager to keep the peace for the sake of his new-made friend that seemed so slight a thing by the side of Simone.

"How now!" Guido cried, aloud. "I hear shrill words that seem to squeak of weapons. What is your quarrel, gentles?"

If every man there present knew who Messer Simone of the Bardi was and what he stood for in Florence, so also every man there present knew who Messer Guido of the Cavalcanti was and what he stood for, and there were few that would have denied him the right to speak his mind or to question the cause of the quarrel. So Messer Guido stood between Dante and Simone, looking from one to the other of the pair and waiting for his answer.

Dante answered in a kind of ironic simplicity, and he seemed to me as I looked upon him like a man exalted out of all reason by some great joy. "It is but a gardener's wrangle--how best to guard roses from slugs."

Simone began to frown upon the brawl that himself had caused, and he looked toward Messer Guido, whom he knew, with a forced show of friendliness, and spoke with a gruff assumption of good-humor. "Messer Guido, will you tell this blockhead who I am?"

Now, Guido was as good a swordsman as the best man in Florence, and far better than the most that handled steel, and he thought and spoke in the wish to protect his new-made friend, whom he took to have no such skill as his own.

"Gently, gently," he said to Simone, and his tone was by no means gentle. "My friend's name is my name, and I take terms from no man. You will answer me now." And as he spoke he placed his hand upon his hilt, and made ready to draw.

Now at this Simone frowned again, for he had no personal quarrel with Messer Guido Cavalcanti, yet from the very bullness of his nature he would take a dare from no man. So he showed his teeth and eased his blade to make ready.

But Dante moved swiftly forward and pulled Messer Guido from between him and Messer Simone, doing this with a courtesy due to one of Messer Guido's standing, yet with a very plain decision. "Messer Guido," he said, "I entreat you to refrain. I guess your purpose, but I will not have it so. This is my quarrel, and, believe me, I can handle it."

Guido plucked him a little apart, and whispered him hurriedly. "This is Simone of the Bardi, a very notable soldier," he said.

I heard Dante answer him very calmly. "Were he a very notable devil, I would stand to him enough."

By this time Messer Simone was in such a black rage at being thwarted that he cared not what might come of it, and he called out to Dante, in a bellowing voice, "Come, sir, come! Will you fight or yield?"

Messer Dante's carriage showed very plainly that he would not yield; of a contrary, he moved composedly a little nearer to Simone, still smiling and stretching out his hands as he went, as if to show that he held no weapon. "Surely I will not yield," he said; and then questioned, "But how shall I fight, being swordless?"

Simone grinned hideously at him. "You should have remembered that," he said, "before you chose to play hufty-dufty." Then he scowled and pointed to the armed men about them. "Some one will lend you a sword if you have the courage to hold it," he said, scornfully.

Once again Messer Guido intervened, eagerly, passionately. "For God's sake, forbear," he entreated Dante, and thrusting himself against the other. "Messer Simone," he said, "you cannot deny me if I take up this quarrel."

My Dante laid an arresting hand upon Messer Guido's arm. "Gently, Messer Guido," he said, "you are too good, and if I were a woman I could not choose a nobler champion. But being no better than a man, I must even champion myself to the best of my wit." He paused, and his eyes followed the course of Simone's gaze and then came back to Simone. "You are a soldier," he said; "it is your business to kill. You prize the life of other men lightly; 'tis but a puff of your heavy breath and out goes his candle. I am no such butcher, and though I am not unskilled in arms, we should be ill-matched, you and I." And as he spoke he laughed softly, as at some jest known only to himself.

Now Messer Guido, that was growing very angry, as I could see from the way in which the color quitted his cheeks, thrust himself in front of Dante, and he spoke to Simone boldly. "He says rightly," he cried. "A stripling against your bulk. It were murder."

Simone always addressed Messer Guido with as much courtesy as he could compass, for the sake of his great house and his great friends, and his standing with the Reds, that was as high as his own with the Yellows. "Then he should not steal roses," he answered, quietly enough. But immediately thereafter, as if the mention of roses had stirred him to fury, his wrath foamed over again, and, turning to Dante, he shouted, "Give me the rose, you cowardly clerk, or I will pinch out your life between finger and thumb!" He held out his huge hand as he spoke, and to those who looked at it, or to me, at least, among the multitude, it seemed easy enough for him to carry out his threat, for Messer Dante looked so slight and spare in the front of such a ruffian.

But Messer Dante was in no ways discomposed, and he still kept smiling while he shook his head, and he answered very quietly: "Idle giant, you will do no such thing. For if you prize my life very little, you prize your own life very well. Now, while I think nothing of your life, I also think nothing of my own, and would rather end it here in this instant than surrender this flower. Why, I would see a hundred fellows like you dead and damned to save a single petal of it from the pollution of such filthy fingers." He paused for a moment and paid Messer Simone the tribute of a mocking inclination of the head. Then he spoke very clearly and sweetly. "I hope I make myself clear to your thick head."

Simone's red face grew redder. "By Paul's jaws, I will wring your squeaking neck!" he said, savagely, and made a move nearer to Dante.

But here Guido's paling face grew paler, and again he thrust himself between Dante and Simone, and his sword flashed into the air. "By Paul's jaws, you will not!" he cried; and then looking about him, he shouted, "A Cavalcanti! a Cavalcanti!"

At that cry all those that inclined to Messer Guido, and there were many in the place, bared their swords likewise and rallied about him in an eager press of angry men.

When Simone saw that the swords were out, he drew his own sword and raised it aloft and cried his cry, "A Bardi! a Bardi!"

Then the people of his following bared their weapons and gathered to his side, and such of the spectators as took no part in the quarrel drew a little apart, for fear they might come to harm in the brawl, but still went not very far, so eager is the curiosity of all Florentines to see sights. So the folk stood, two little armies of fighting men facing each other, as Greek and Trojan faced each other long ago, and ready for fighting, as Greek and Trojan fought, and as men always will fight with men, for the sake of a woman. And I, with my sword drawn, being never so intent upon battle that I have not an eye to all things about me, could see, looking aloft, that a curtain was drawn from a window in the great house of the Portinari, and that a woman stood by the window, and I made sure that the woman's name was Beatrice.

But this Dante saw not and knew not, for he stood between the two opposing forces very composedly, with the same quiet smile upon his face, and he held up his hands toward either party as a man might do that wished to sunder and pacify quarrelling children. "Gently, friends, gently," he said; "there is a pleasant way to end this dilemma." Then he turned to me, and I never saw his face serener. "Friend Lappo," he said, "will you lend me your dice-bones a minute?"

It was characteristic of his readiness in the pinch of emergency that he knew where to apply for what he needed, for I was at that time a most inveterate game-ster, and loved to stake my all, which for the most part was truly little enough, upon the toss of a die; and for my greater ease in this exercise, I ever carried the bones with me in a little inner pocket at my breast. Now, then, for Dante's pleasure, though indeed I did not know what he would be at, I lugged them out of their con-cealment, and dropped the three, one after the other, into his open palm, which he held to me extended there as steady as the palm of a stone image.

Dante laughed a little softly to himself as he looked at my dice where they lay, and indeed it was curious to see him and them in such close companionship, for Dante had no taste for those gamblers' games that I delighted in. Then he turned and showed the dice to Simone, who stared at him in amazed rage, and he spoke very pleasantly and evenly as he dandled the tools of chance. "Messer Simone," he said, "here be three cubes of bone that shall settle our quarrel better than shearing steel. We will throw on this ground here, you and I in turn, and he that has the ill-fortune to make the lowest cast shall, on his honor, very presently kill himself."

At this drolling challenge most of the spectators began to laugh, and the laugh-ter ran through the ranks of Cavalcanti's adherents, and even found some echo, albeit soon stifled, among Bardi's men.

But Simone saw no laughter in the matter. "You are a fool!" he fumed. It was plain that he felt himself to be at a disadvantage before the gravity of Dante's dis-dainful courage, and that he was better with blows than with words. "You are a fool!" he repeated.

But Dante denied him. "I am wise." Then he moved his head a little this way and that, as if to show that he was addressing all his audience, and, indeed, there was not a man in all that assemblage that did not listen to him intently, Simone's own following not excepted. "Fellow Florentines," he said, "here is a straight challenge. It equals the big man with the little; it fills me to the giant's girth and inches. It saves him from shame if he wins, for it were little to his credit to kill a civilian. It denies me if I win the vainglory of overcoming a Titan. Is not this an honest dare?"

As he finished speaking he looked about him, and saw sympathy and approval on the faces of most. As for me, I was so taken with his ingenuity and his insolence in thus braving the big fellow that I cried aloud, "Well dared; well done." And Guido called out sharply, addressing the Bardi, "Do you take him, Messer Simone? I will be surety for his pledge."

As Messer Guido dei Cavalcanti ended there went up a great shout of applause from the spectators, who were tickled with the thought of witnessing so new a way of ending a quarrel. While they were clapping their hands and laughing, a cunning, sharp-faced fellow named Maleotti, that was one of Bardi's men, came close to his master, and spoke to him in none so low a whisper that I could not hear his words. "Consider, signor," he said; "this were a mad wager to accept, for the State cannot spare you, and who can say how scraps of bone may fall? Yet, if you refuse and force a quarrel, the Cavalcanti outnumber us." As he spoke he indicated with quick glances of his evil eyes that there were indeed many more in the place that seemed to side with Guido than friends to the Bardi.

While Messer Simone, seeing this, sucked his lips like one puzzled, Dante again addressed him in the same bantering manner. "Come," he cried, "'tis but a toss of three ivories and the world is lighter by one of us, and purgatory the more populous. You shall toss first or last, as you please." As he spoke he shook the dice invitingly on his extended palm, and laughed as he did so.

Simone answered him with a great frown and a great voice. "You should have been a mountebank and cried cures on a booth, for your wit is as nimble as an apothecary's flea. But if you have any man's blood in you, you will make such friends with master sword that hereafter we may talk to better purpose. Come, friends." So, with a scowling face, Messer Simone jammed his sword back again into its scabbard, and he and his fellows went away roughly, and the crowd parted very respectfully before them.

At the wish of Messer Guido, his friends and sympathizers went their ways; and as for the crowd of unconcerned spectators, they, understanding that there was nothing more to stare at, went their ways too, and in a little while the place that had been so full and busy was empty and idle, and Guido and I were left alone with Dante.

As we stood there in silence, Madonna Vittoria came forward from her shelter under the arcade and advanced to Dante, and addressed him. "Give me leave," she said, "to tell you that you are a man whose love any woman might be proud to wear. Beware of Simone dei Bardi. I know something of him. He is neither clever enough to forget nor generous enough to forgive. Remember, if you care to remember, that I am always your friend."

Dante saluted her. "I thank you," he said, in a dull, tired voice.

Then Madonna Vittoria went her way over the bridge with her people after her, and when she was gone I made bold to go up to where Dante stood thoughtful, and clapped him on the back in very hearty commendation of his courage and daring. "You have bubbled Simone well," I said, joyously.

But, to my surprise, Dante turned to me with a face that was not at all joyous. "I think he had the best of me in the end," he said, sadly. And as he spoke he hung his head for all the world like a schoolboy that had been reproved before his class.

Messer Guido, that was as tender to melancholy as a gentlewoman, caught him by the hand. "Are you teased by that fellow's taunt?" he asked.

Dante sighed, as he answered: "To the quick of my heart. Will you leave me, friends, to my thoughts?"

VI
LOVER AND LASS

I sighed in my turn to see him so perverse who had been so triumphant. "He is as humorous as a chameleon," I protested. Then Guido and I took Dante by the arms to lead him away, I applauding him for his cunning, and Guido gently reproving him for his foolhardiness in getting into a quarrel with such a man of might as Messer Simone--had got him and us some few yards from the scene of the scuffle when Dante suddenly came to a halt and would budge no farther. When we asked him what ailed him, he told us that he had left his book behind him, the book that he had been so deep in a little while ago; and for all we could say to him, he would not be prevailed upon, but must needs return for his precious love-tale. So he quitted us and returned on his steps, and Guido and I looked at each other in some amusement, thinking what a strange fellow our Dante was, that could play scholar and lover and soldier in so many breaths, and could show so much care for some pages of written parchment. Then Guido would have me go with him, but I was of a mind to see what Dante would do next, and was fain to watch him. Guido disapproved of this, and he would not share in it, saying that it was not for us to dog the heels of a friend.

Guido went his way without me, for it seemed to me less scrupulous and seeking only to be amused that one who had done so much in a short time might well be counted upon to do more. I hid in the arcade, and I saw how Dante went straight to the seat where he had left his book, and found it still lying there, and took it up and thrust it into his bosom. And when he had done this he turned and went like one that walked in a dream--and I spying on him from my hiding-place--till he came to the front of the Palace of the Portinari, and there he paused and gazed wistfully at the gray walls. And I, concealing myself behind a convenient pillar of the colonnade, observed him unseen, and presently saw how the small door in the great door of the gray palace opened, and how Madonna Beatrice came out of it, followed by two girls, her companions. They both were pretty girls, I remember, that would have suited my taste very pleasantly. All three maidens stood on top of the steps looking at Dante where he stood, and Dante remained in his place and looked up at them silently and eagerly.

Madonna Beatrice seemed to hesitate for a moment, and then, quitting her companions, descended the steps and advanced toward Dante, who, seeing her purpose, advanced in his turn toward her, and they met in the middle of the now deserted square. I was very honestly--or dishonestly, which you may please--anxious to hear what these two might say to each other, so I lingered in my lurking-place, and there I lay at watch and strove to listen. And because the time was very peaceful, and I very quiet and the air very still and their young voices very clear, I could hear much and guess more, and piecing out the certain with the probable, record in my memory this delicate dialogue.

Madonna Beatrice spoke first, for Dante said nothing, and only gazed at her as the devout gaze at the picture of a saint, and there was some note of reproof in her voice as she spoke. "Messer," she said, "they tell me that you have fought for a rose."

Then Dante shook his head, and he smiled as he answered, blithely, "Madonna, I fought for my flag, for my honor, for the glory of the sempiternal rose."

Beatrice looked at him with a little wonder on her sweet face. "Was it very wise to risk a man's life for a trifle?" she asked.

Dante was silent for a short time, then he said: "There are trifles that outweigh the world in a true balance. I would die a death for every petal of that rose."

Beatrice began to laugh very daintily, and spread out her pretty palms. "This Florence is a very nest of nightingales," she said, softly; and then she added, quaintly, "You talk like a poet."

I heard Dante sigh heavily as he answered her fancy. "I would I were a poet, for then my worship would have words which now shines dumbly in my eyes."

Beatrice gave him a little mocking salutation. "You are very gallant," she said. "Farewell." There was a hint of reproof in her voice, and she made as if to go.

But Dante stopped her. "Stay, lady, stay," he protested. "I speak with a simple heart. I have been your servant ever since you took a rose from my hands. I am your servant forever, now that you have given me a rose. We are old friends, sweet lady, though we wear young faces, and friends may speak their minds to friends."

Then Beatrice asked him, "Who are you who risked your life for my rose?"

Dante answered her: "I am named Dante Alighieri. Yesterday I was nobody. To-day I would not change places with the Emperor, since I declare myself your servant."

Beatrice smiled a smile of sweet content, and I could see that she was both amused and pleased. "I am glad we are old friends," she said, "for so it was not un-maidenly of me to speak to you, but indeed I was grieved to think I had put you in peril. I did not think what I did when I threw you that flower. I only felt that we were children again, you and I. Forgive me."

"It was a happy peril," Dante declared, gladly.

Again Beatrice said him farewell and turned to go, and again Dante stayed her, and when she had paused he looked as if he knew not what to say; but at last he questioned, "When may we meet again?"

Beatrice answered him gravely. "Florence is not so wide a world that you should fear to lose sight of a friend."

Once more she made as if she would join her companion maidens, but as she did so Dante looked all about him with an air of great surprise, and I heard him say: "How dark the air grows. I fear an eclipse."

Beatrice, pausing in her path, cried to him, marvelling, "Why, the sun is at its brightest."

Dante shook his head. "I do not find it so when you are leaving me."

Then I think that Beatrice looked half alarmed and half diverted at the way of Dante's speech, and I heard her say, "Is not the spring of our friendship something too raw for such ripeness of compliment?"

Dante persisted. "I would speak simpler and straighter if I dared."

Then Beatrice shook her head and tried to wear an air of severity, but failed because she could not help smiling. "The arrows of your wit must not take me for their target," she said, and made a pretence to frown.

Then Dante, at a loss what to say, made the best plea he could when he pleaded, "Pity me."

At that cry the growing gravity on the girl's face softened to her familiar gentleness, for she was touched, as all women who are worthy of womanhood must be
touched by that divine appeal. "Are you in need of pity?" she said, softly.

And Dante answered, instantly, "Neck-deep in need."

Then he sighed and Beatrice sighed, and she said, very kindly, "In that case,
I pity you," and made again to leave him, and again the appeal in his eyes stayed
her.

"Can you do no more than pity me?" he asked.

Beatrice was smiling now, for all she strove to be serious. "Why, you are for a
greedy garner; you want flower, fruit, and all, in a breath."

I could see Messer Dante's face suddenly stiffen into solemnity; I could hear
Messer Dante's voice, for all its youthful freshness, take upon it the gravity of age.
"For nine years, day in and day out, I have thought of you," he sighed. "Have you
ever thought of me?"

He looked steadfastly at the girl as he spoke, and if there was much of entreaty
in his question there was something of command also, as if he chose to compel her
to tell him the very truth. And the girl answered, indeed, as if she were compelled
to speak and could not deny him, and her cheeks were as pink as the earliest roses
as she answered him: "Sometimes."

Again Dante spoke and questioned her, and again in his carriage and in his
voice there was that same note of command. "With what thoughts?"

But I could plainly see that if our Dante would seek to give orders to the girl
with an authority that was beyond his years, the girl could meet his assumption
of domination with a composure that was partly grave and partly humorous and
wholly adorable.

She nodded very pleasantly at him as she answered, "Kind thoughts for the
gentle child who gave his rose to a little girl."

I knew very well, as I leaned and listened, that the mind of Dante leaped back
on that instant to the day he had told us of so little a while before, the day nine
years ago when, as the sweet lady said, he gave his rose to a little girl. I knew, too,
that the chance meeting with Madonna Beatrice on this fair morning must in some
mighty fashion alter the life of my friend. The fantastic love which he, a child of
nine, felt or professed to feel for the little girl of a like age was now, through this

accident, setting his soul and body on fire and forcing him to say wild words, as a little while back it had forced him to do wild deeds, out of the very exhilaration of madness. And Dante spoke as all lovers speak when they wish to touch the hearts of their ladies, only making me who was listening not a little jealous, seeing that he spoke better than most that I knew of.

"Madonna," he said, "Madonna, the lover-poets of our city are very prodigal of protestations--what will they not do for their lady? They offer her the sun, moon, and stars for her playthings--and in the end she is fortunate if she gets so much as a farthing rushlight to burn at her shrine."

Beatrice was listening to him with the bright smile upon her face which for me was the best part of a beauty that, if I had been in Dante's place, I should have found a thought too seraphic and unearthly for my fancy.

"My heart," she assured him, "would never be touched by such sounding phrases."

Now Dante's face glowed with the fire that was in him, and his words seemed to glow as he spoke like gold coins dropping new-moulded from the mint. "I am no god to give you a god's gifts," he protested. "But of what a plain man may proffer from the heart of his heart and the soul of his soul, say, is there any gift I can give you in sign of my service?"

The bright smile on the face of Beatrice changed to a gracious air of thoughtfulness, and I think I should have been glad had I been wooing a woman in such fashion to have seen such a look on the face of my fair. "Messer Dante," she said, "you have some right to be familiar with me, for you risked your life for my rose. So I will answer your frankness frankly. Men have tried to please me and failed, for I think I am not easy to please greatly."

Dante stretched out both his hands to her. "Let me try to please you!" he cried.

The girl answered him, speaking very slowly, as if she were carefully turning her thoughts into words and weighing her words while she uttered them. "That is in your own hands. I do not cry for the sun and stars and the shining impossibilities. But I am a woman, and if a man did brave deeds (and by brave deeds I do not mean risking two souls for the sake of a rose) or good deeds (and by good deeds I do not mean the rhyming of pretty rhymes in my honor), and did them for love of me, why, I have so much of my grandmother Eve in me that I believe I should be pleased."

I saw Dante draw himself up as a soldier might in the ranks when he saw his general riding by and thought that the rider's eye was upon him. "With God's help," he vowed, "you shall hear better things of me."

There was a look of such fine kindness on Beatrice's face while he spoke thus as made even me, that am a man of common clay, and like love as I like wine and victuals, thrill in my hiding-place. "I hope as much," she said, softly--"almost believe as much. But I linger too long, and my comrades wonder. Farewell."

She gave him an enchanting salutation, and Dante bowed his head. "Farewell, most fair lady," he murmured.

Then Beatrice moved away from him, and ascended the steps where the two girls stood and waited for her, and she laid her white finger on the ring of brass that governed the lock of the little door, and the little door opened and she passed into the gray palace, she and her maids, and to me too, as I am very sure to Dante, the world seemed in a twinkling robbed of its sweetness. For though, as I have said, Madonna Beatrice was never a woman for me to love, I could well believe that to the man who loved her there could be no woman else on the whole wide earth, which, as I think, is an uncomfortable form of loving.

When she had gone Dante stood there very silent for a while, and it may be that I, tired of watching him, drifted into a doze, and leaned there for a while against my sheltering pillar with closed lids, as sometimes happens to men that are weary of waiting. If this were so, it would explain why I did not see what seems to have happened then--or perhaps it was because I was of a temper and composition less fine than my friend's that I was not permitted to see such sights. But it appears, as I learned from his lips later, that as he stood there in all the ecstacy of his sweet intercourse with the well-beloved, the painted image of the God of Love that stood beside the bridge, above the fountain, came to life again, and moved and came in front of Dante and looked upon him very searchingly. The God of Love lifted the hand that carried his fateful arrow and pointed with the dart toward the gray palace, and it spoke to Dante in a voice of command, and said, "Behold thy heart." Then Dante felt no fear such as he had felt at the first appearance of the God of Love, but only an almost intolerable sense of joy at the glory and the beauty and the divinity of true and noble love. And he said to himself, as if he whispered a prayer, "O Blessed Beatrice," and therewith the figure of the God of Love departed back to its familiar place.

If I had, indeed, been dozing, my sleep lasted no longer than this, and I was conscious again, and saw Dante, and I leaped from my hiding-place and ran to where Dante stood alone in the square, with his hands against his face. I called to him, as I came up, "Dante, are you drowned in a wonder?" and at the sound of my voice Dante plucked the fingers from his face and stared at me vacantly, as if he did not know me. This gaze of ignorance lasted, it may be, for the better part of a minute.

Then Dante, seeming to recognize me, all of a sudden drew me toward him and spoke as a man speaks that tells strange truths truly. "Friend," he said, "you are well met, for you see me now as I am who will never see me again as I was. I am become a man, for I love God's loveliest woman. Enough of nobility in name; I mean to prove nobility in deed. Say to my friends that Dante of the Alighieri, a Florentine, and a lover, devotes himself for love's sake to the service of his city."

And when he had spoken he stood very still with his hands clasped before him, and I, because it is my way to laugh at all things, laughed at him, and cried out: "Holy Saint Plato, what a hot change of a cold heart! Bring bell, book, and candle, for Jack Idle is dead and Adam Active is his heir."

But Dante turned his face to me, and his eyes were shining very bright, and he looked younger than his youth, and he spoke to me not as if he were chiding my mirth, but as if he were telling me a piece of welcome news, and he said, very gently, "Here beginneth the New Life."

VII
CONCERNING POETRY

Now you must know that after that whimsical encounter of wit between Dante and Simone, which I have already narrated, Messer Dante seemed to change his mood again, as he had changed his mood oft-time before. Messer Brunetto Latini saw much less of his promising pupil, and a certain old soldier that was great at sword-play much more, and there was less in Dante's life of the ancient philosophies and more of the modern chivalries. I presently found out that Messer Dante, having taken much to heart that gibing defiance of Simone of the Bardi, had set himself, with that stubborn resolution which characterized all his purposes, to making himself a master of the sword. Of this, indeed, he said nothing to me or other man, but Florence, for all that it is so great and famous a city, is none so large that a man can easily hide his business there from the eyes of those that have a mind to find out that business. So I learned that Dante, who had been, as I told you before, no more than a passable master of the weapon, now set himself to gain supremacy over it. Day after day, through long hours, Dante labored at his appointed task, bracing his sinews, strengthening his muscles, steadying his eye, doing, in a word, all that a spare and studious youth must do who would turn himself into a strong and skilful soldier. And because whatever Dante set head and heart and hand to he was like to accomplish, I learned later what I guessed from the beginning--that his patience had its reward.

By reason of his white-hot zeal and tireless determination, Dante gained his desired end sooner than many a one whom nature had better moulded for the purpose. And being of a generous eagerness to learn, he did not content himself with mastering alone the more skilled usage of the sword, but made his earnest study of the carriage and command of other weapons, and he applied himself, besides, to the investigation of the theory and practice of war as it is waged between great cities and great states, and to the history of military affairs as they are set forth and expounded in the lives of famous captains, such as Alexander, and Caesar, and their like. Had he been in expectation of sudden elevation to the headship of the Republic, he could not have toiled more furiously, nor more wisely devoured a week's lesson in a day, a month's lesson in a week, a year's lesson in a month, with all the splendid madness of desireful youth.

But the marvel of it all was that he did not suffer these studies, arduous as they were, to eat up his time and his mind, but he kept store of both to spare for yet another kind of enterprise no less exacting and momentous, albeit to my mind infinitely more interesting. I will freely admit that I was never other than an indifferent soldier. I did my part when the time came, as I am glad to remember, not without sufficient courage if wholly without distinction, but there was ever more pleasure for me in the balancing of a rhyme than in the handling of a pike, and I would liefer have been Catullus than Caesar any day of the week. So the work that Dante did in his little leisure from application to arms is the work that wonders me and delights me, and that fills my memory, as I think of it, with exquisite melodies.

It was about this time that sundry poets of the city, of whom let us say that Messer Guido Cavalcanti was the greatest and your poor servant the least, began to receive certain gifts of verses very clearly writ on fair skins of parchment, which gave them a great pleasure and threw them into a great amazement. For it was very plain that the writer of these verses was one in whose ear the god Apollo whispered, was one that knew, as it seemed, better than the best of us, how to wed the warmest thoughts of the heart to the most exquisite music of flowing words. These verses, that were for the most part sonnets and longer songs, were all dedicated to the service of love and the praise of a nameless lady, and they were all written in that common speech which such as I talked to the men and women about me, so that there was no man nor woman in the streets but could understand their meaning if once they heard them spoken--a fact which I understand gave great grief to Messer Brunetto Latini when some of these honey-sweet verses of the unknown were laid before him.

To Messer Brunetto's eyes and to Messer Brunetto's ears and to Messer Brunetto's understanding there was but one language in the world that was fit for the utterances and the delectation of scholars, and that language, of course, was the language which he wrote so well--the Latin of old-time Rome. If a man must take the love-sickness, so Messer Brunetto argued, and must needs express the perfidious folly in words, what better vehicle could he have for his salacious fancy than the forms and modes and moods which contented the amorous Ovidius, and the sprightly Tibullus, and the hot-headed, hot-hearted Catullus, and the tuneful Petronius, and so on, to much the same purpose, through a string of ancient amorists? But we that were younger than Messer Brunetto, and simpler, and certainly more ignorant, we found a great pleasure in these verses that were so easy to understand as to their language, if their meaning was sometimes a thought mystical and cryptic.

The fame of these verses spread widely, because no man of us that received a copy kept the donation to himself, but made haste to place abroad the message that had been sent to him. So that in a little while all Florence that had any care for the Graces was murmuring these verses, and wondering who it was that wrote them, and why it was that he wrote. It seems to me strange now, looking back on all these matters through the lapse of years, and through a mist of sad and happy memories, that I was not wise enough to guess at once who the man must be that made these miraculous stanzas. I can only plead in my own excuse that I did not live a generation later than my day, and that I had no means of divining that a work-a-day friend possessed immortal qualities. Everybody now in this late evening knows who that poet was, and loves him. I knew and loved him then, when I had no thought that he was a poet. Even if it had been given me to make a wild guess at the authorship of these poems, and my guess had chanced all unwitting to be right, as would have been thereafter proved, I should have dismissed it from my fancy. For I conceived that my friend was so busy upon that new red-hot business of his of fitting himself to be a soldier and use arms, and answer the taunt of Simone dei Bardi, that he could have no time, even if he had the desire, of which, as far as I was aware till then, he had shown no sign, to try his skill on the strings of the muses. You may be pleased here to remind me of the discourse between Messer Brunetto Latini and Dante, which I strove to overhear on that May morning in the Piazza Santa Felicita, to which I will make bold to answer that I did not truly overhear much at the time, and that the substance of what I set down was garnered later, both from Dante and from Messer Brunetto. But even if I had caught sound of those poetical aspirations of Dante's, I doubt if they would have stuck in my memory.

I suppose it was not for such an idle fellow as I, to whom to do nothing was ever better than to do--I speak, of course, of any measure of painful labor, and not of such pleasing pastime as eating or drinking or loving--to guess how much a great brain and a great heart and a great purpose could crowd into the narrow compass of a little life. In the mean time, as I say, these songs and sonnets were blown abroad all over Florence, and men whispered them to maids, and the men wondered who wrote the rhymes and the maids wondered for whom they were written.

They would come to us, these rhymes, curiously enough. One or other of us would find some evening, on his return to his lodging, a scroll of parchment lying on his table, and on this scroll of parchment some new verses, and in the corner of the parchment the words in the Latin tongue, "Take up, read, bear on." And he of us that found himself so favored, having eagerly taken up and no less eagerly read, would hurry to the nearest of his comrades and read the new gift to him, delighted, who would busy himself at once to make a fair copy before speeding the verses to another. So their fame spread, and so the copies multiplied, till there was never a musical youth in Florence that did not know the better part of them by heart; and still, for all this publicity, there was no man could say who wrote the rhymes, nor who was the lady they honored. I think and believe, indeed, there were many in Florence who would gladly have declared themselves the author, but dared not for fear of detection, and who contented themselves by slight hints and suggestions and innuendoes, which earned them, for a time, a brief measure of interest, soon to be dissipated by the manifest certainty of their incapacity.

And the first of all these sonnets was that which is now as familiar as honey on the lips of every lover of suave songs--I mean that sonnet which begins with the words:

"To every prisoned soul and gentle heart--"

To this sonnet it pleased many of our poets of the city to write their replies, though they knew not then to whom they were replying, and Messer Guido Cavalcanti wrote his famous sonnet, the one that begins:

"Unto my thinking thou beheldst all worth--"

Now I, being fired by the same spirit of rhyming that was abroad, but being of a different temper from the most of my fellows, took it upon me to pretend a resentment of all this beautiful talk of Love and My Lady. So I wrote a sonnet, and here it is, urging the advantages of a plurality in love-affairs:

"Give me a jolly girl, or two, or three--
The more the merrier for my weathercock whim;
And one shall be like Juno, large of limb
And large of heart; and Venus one shall be,
Golden, with eyes like the capricious sea;
And my third sweetheart, Dian, shall be slim
With a boy's slimness, flanks and bosom trim,
The green, sharp apple of the ancient tree.
With such a trinity to please each mood
I should not find a summer day too long,
With blood of purple grapes to fire my blood,
And for my soul some thicket-haunting song
Of Pan and naughty nymphs, and all the throng
Of light o' loves and wantons since the Flood."

I showed this sonnet to Messer Guido, who laughed a little, and said that I might be the laureate of the tavern and the brothel, but that this new and nameless singer was a man of another metal, whom I could never understand. Whereat I laughed, too; but being none the less a little piqued, as I think, I made it a point thereafter, whenever Guido had one of these new poems come to him, to answer it with some poem of my own, cast in a similar form to that chosen by the unknown. But my verses were always written in praise of the simple and straightforward pleasures of sensible men, to whom all this talk about the God of Love and about some single exalted lady seems strangely away from the mark of wise living. For assuredly if it be a pleasant thing to love one woman, it is twenty times as pleasant to love twenty. But I will not give you all of these poems, nor perhaps any more, for you can read them for yourselves, if you wish to, in my writings.

Now in a little while this same unknown poet was pleased to put abroad a certain ballad of his that was ostensibly given over to the praise of certain lovely ladies of our city. Florence was always a very paradise of fair women. An inflammable fellow like myself could not walk the length of a single street without running the risk of half a dozen heartaches, and never was traveller that came and went but was loud in his laudations of the loveliness of Florence feminine. A poet, therefore, could scarcely have a more alluring theme or a livelier or more likable, and the fact that the mysterious singer had taken such a subject for his inspiration was rightly regarded as another instance of his exceeding good sense. It was a very beautiful ballad, fully worthy of its honorable subject, and it paid many compliments of an exquisite felicity to many ladies that were indicated plainly enough by some play upon a name or some praise of an attribute. But it was, or might have been, plain enough to all that read it that this poem was written for no other purpose than to bring in by a side wind, as it were, the praise of a lady that was left nameless, but that he who wrote declared to be the loveliest lady in that noble city of lovely ladies. This ballad seemed to be unfinished, for in its last stanza the writer promised to utter yet more words on this so favorable theme. Now when I had heard of this poem and before I had read it--for Guido, to whom the first copy was given, loved it so much and lingered so long upon its lines that he kept it an unconscionable time from his fellows--I bethought me that I, too, would write me a set of verses on the brave and fair ladies of Florence, and that in doing so I could bring in the name of the girl of my heart.

It was easy enough for me to write a passable ring of rhymes that should introduce with all due form and honor the names of those ladies that all in that time agreed to be most eminent for their beauty and gentleness in the beautiful and gentle city. And so I got a good way upon my work with very little trouble indeed, for, as I have said, rhymes always came easy to me and I loved to juggle with colored words. My difficulty came with the moment when I had to decide upon the introduction of my own heart's desire.

Now about this time of the year when I began my ballad, I was myself very plenteously and merrily in love with a certain lady whose name I will here set down as Ippolita, for that was what I called her, seeing in her a kind of amazonian carriage, though that was not the name she was known by among the men and the women, her neighbors. She had dark eyes whose brightness seemed to widen and deepen as you kissed her lips--and, indeed, the child loved to be kissed exceedingly, for all her quaint air of woman-warrior--and she had dark hair that when you, being permitted to play her lover, uncoiled it, rolled down like a great mane to her haunches, and her face, both by its paleness and by the perfection of its featuring, seemed to vie with those images of Greece by which the wise set such store. To judge by the serenity of her expression, the suavity of her glances, you would have sworn by all the saints that here if ever was an angel, one that would carry the calm of Diana into every action of life, and challenge passion with a chastity that was never to be gainsaid. But he that ever held her in his arms found that the so-seeming ice was fire, under those snows lava bubbled, and she that might have passed for a priestess of Astarte quivered with frenzy under the dominion of Eros. To speak only for myself, I found her a very phoenix of sweethearts.

She was married to a tedious old Mumpsiman that kept himself and her in little ease by plying the trade of a horse-leech, which trade, for the girl's felicity, held him much abroad, and gave her occasion, seldom by her neglected, to prove to her intimate of the hour that there can be fire without smoke. Now I, being somewhat top-heavy at this season with the wine of so fair a lady's favors, thought that I might, with no small advantage to myself and no small satisfaction to my mistress, set me to doing her honor with some such tuneful words as the unknown singer was blowing with such sweet breath about Florence in praise of his lady. For it is cheaper to please a woman with a sonnet than with a jewel, and as my Ippolita was not avaricious, I was blithe to oblige her in golden numbers in lieu of golden pieces.

Wherefore I set my wits to work one morning after an evening of delight, and found the muse complaisant. My fancy spouted like a fountain, the rhymes swam in the water like gilded or silver fishes, so tame you had but to dip in your fingers and take your pick, while allusion and simile crowded so thickly about me that I should have needed an epic rather than my legal fourteen lines to make use of the half of them. I tell you I was in the very ecstasy of composition that lasted me for the better part of a fortnight. But by the time that I had come to this point the pretty Ippolita, whose name I had intended to place there, was no longer the moment's idol of my soul, and between the two dainty girls that had succeeded her I sat for a long while embarrassed, like the schoolman's ass between the two bundles of hay, not know-ing, as it were, at which to bite.

At last I bethought me that the best way out of my trouble was to set down the names of all the sweet women whom I loved or had loved, and to let those oth-ers and more famous, of whom I knew nothing save by sight or renown, stand to one side. So it came to pass that this poem of mine proved, at the last, more like an amorous calendar of my own life than a hymn in praise of the famous beauties of Florence. For with famous beauties I have never at any time had much to do. It has always been my desire to find my beauties for myself, and I have ever found that there is a greater reward in the discovery of some pretty maid and assuring her that she is lovelier than Helen of Troy or Semiramis or Cleopatra, than in the paying of one's addresses to some publicly acclaimed loveliness.

By the time my tale of verses was complete, it was as different as it might be from that which it set itself, I will not say to rival, but to parody, for it contained few names of great ladies that were upon the lips of every Florentine, but sang the praises of unknown witches and minxes that were at the time of writing, or had been, very dear to me. If my song was not so fine a piece of work as that of Messer Dante, though Messer Dante was at that time only in the earlier flights of his efforts, and his pinions were, as yet, unfamiliar to the poet's ether, it was perhaps as true a picture, after its fashion, of a lover's heart. After all, it must be remembered that there are many kinds of lovers' hearts, and that those who can understand the "New Life" of Messer Dante's are very few, and fewer still those that can live that life. But I here protest very solemnly that it was with no thought of scoff or mockery that I made my ballad, but just for the sake of saying, in my way, the things I thought about the pretty women that pleased me and teased me, and made life so gay and fragrant and variegated in those far-away, dearly remembered, and no doubt much-to-be-deplored days.

It was the dreaming of this ballad of mine that led me to think of Monna Vit-toria, whom you will remember if you bear in mind the beginning of this, my his-tory, the lady that Messer Simone of the Bardi was whimsically pledged to wed if he failed to win a certain wager that I trust you have not forgotten. And thinking of Monna Vittoria led, in due time, to a meeting with Monna Vittoria that was not without consequences.

It is not incurious, when you come to reflect upon it, how potent the influence of such a woman as Vittoria may be upon the lives of those that would seem never destined by Heaven to come in her way. My Dante was never in those days a wooer of such ladies. As to certain things that are said of him later, in the hours of his despair, when the world seemed no better than an empty shell, I shall have somewhat to say, perhaps, by-and-by, for there is a matter that has led to not a little misunderstanding of the character of my friend. As for Madonna Beatrice, she that was such a flower in a guarded garden, why, you would have said it was little less than incredible that the clear course of her simple life could be crossed by the summer lightning of Madonna Vittoria's brilliant, fitful existence. Yet, nevertheless, from first to last, Madonna Vittoria was of the utmost moment in the lives of this golden lass and lad, and this much must be admitted in all honesty: that she never did, or at least never sought to do, other than good to either of them. I should not like to say that she would have troubled at all about them or their welfare if it had not served her turn to do so. But whatever the reasons for her deeds, let us be grateful that their results were not malefic to those whose interests concern us most. If Messer Simone had never made his brutal boast, Madonna Vittoria would never have made her wild wager. But having made it, she was eager to win it at all costs, and it was her determination that Simone of the Bardi should never wed with Beatrice of the Portinari, that led, logically enough if you do but consider it aright, to the many strange events which it is my business to narrate.

VIII
MONNA VITTORIA SENDS ME A MESSAGE

Monna Vittoria dwelt in the pleasantest part of the country outside the city, in a quarter where there were many gardens and much thickness of trees and greenness of grass and coloring of bright flowers-- all pleasing things, that made an agreeable background to her beauty when she went abroad in her litter. For, indeed, she was a comely creature, and one that painters would pause to look at and to praise, as well as others that eyed her more carnally minded. Now I myself had but a slight acquaintance, albeit a pleasant one, with Vittoria. This was partly because my purse was but leanly provided, and partly because I had ever in mind with regard to such creatures the wise saying of the Athenian concerning the girl Lais, that it was not worth while to spend a fortune to gain a regret. Moreover, I was too much occupied with my own very agreeable love-affairs, that were blended with poetry and dreams and such like sweetnesses, as well as with reality, to make me feel any wish for more extravagant alliances. But I had it in my mind now that it might be a good thing for me, in the interests of my poem in praise of fair Florentines, to pay this lady a visit, and I hoped, being a poet, though I trust not over puffed up with my own pride of importance, and knowing that she was always fain to be regarded as a patroness of the arts, that I might, without much difficulty, gain access to her.

So I spent a careless morning on a hillside beyond the city in the excellent company of a flask of wine and a handful of bread and cheese, and there I sprawled upon my back among the daisies and munched and sipped, and listened to the bees, and looked upon the brown roofs of beautiful Florence, and was very well content. And when I had stayed my stomach and flung the crumbs to the birds, and had emptied the better part of my flagon, I stretched myself under a tree like a man in a doze. I was not dozing, however, for the flowers and the verdure about me, and the birds that piped overhead, and the booming bees, and the strong sunlight on the grass, and the glimpses of blue sky through the branches, were all busying themselves for me in weaving the web of the poem I wanted to carry home with me.

As I shot the bright verses this way and that way, and caught with a childish pleasure at the shining rhymes as a child will catch at some glittering toy, I had perforce to smile as I reflected on what a different business mine was to that of the unknown singer of those days. For those poems of his that he had sent to Guido and to others were exceeding beautiful, and full of a very noble and golden exaltation. I think if the angels in heaven were ever to make love to one another they would choose for their purpose some such perfection of speech as Dante--for I knew the singer to be Dante a little later--found for his sonnets and canzone. For myself, I frankly admit, being an honest man, that I could not write such sonnets even if I had my Dante's command of speech, to which Heaven forbid that I should ever pretend. Those rhymes of his, for all their loveliness--and when I say that they were lovely enough to be worthy of the lady to whom they were addressed, I give them the highest praise and the praise that Dante would most have cared to accept--were too ethereal for my work-a-day humors. I liked better to write verses to the laughing, facile lasses with whom my way of life was cast--jolly girls who would kiss to-day and sigh to-morrow, and forget all about you the third day if needs were, and whom it was as easy for their lover to forget, so far as any sense of pain lay in the recollection of their graces. And I would even rather have the jolly job I was engaged on at that moment of some ripe, rich-colored verses for Vittoria, for I could, in writing them, be as human as I pleased and frankly of the earth earthly, and I needed to approach my quarry with no tributes pilfered from the armory of heaven. I could praise her beauty with the tongue of men, and leave the tongue of angels out of the question; and if my muse were pleased here and there to take a wanton flutter, I knew I could give decorum the go-by with a light heart.

So I wallowed at my ease in the grasses and tossed verses as a juggler tosses his balls, and watched them glitter and wink as they rose and fell, and at last I shaped to my own satisfaction what I believed to be an exceedingly pleasant set of verses that needed no more than to be engrossed on a fair piece of sheepskin and tied with a bright ribbon and sent to the exquisite frailty. And all these things I did in due course, after the proper period of polishing and amending and straightening out, until, as I think, there never was a set of rhymes more carefully fathered and mothered into the world. And here is the sonnet:

> "There is a lady living in this place
> That wears the radiant name of Victory;
> And we that love would bid her wingless be,
> Like the Athenian image, lest her grace,
> Lifting a siren's-tinted pinions, trace
> Its glittering course across the Tyrrhene sea
> To some more favored Cyprian sanctuary,
> Leaving us lonely, longing for her face.
> O daughter of the gods, though lovelier lands,
> If such there be, entreat you, do not hear
> Their whispering voices, heed their beckoning hands;
> Have only eye for Florence, only ear
> For Florentine adorers, while their cheer
> Between your fingers spills its golden sands."

Now this sonnet may be divided into four parts. In the first part, I make my statement that there is a lady dwelling in Florence whose name is Vittoria. In the second part, I allow my fancy to play lightly with the suggestions this name arouses in me, and I make allusion very felicitously to the famous statue of the Wingless Victory, which the Athenians honored in Athens so very specially in that, being wingless, it could not fly away from the city. In the third part, I express my alarm lest her loveliness should spread its vans in flight and leave us lonely. In the fourth, I entreat her to pay no heed to the solicitations of others, but to remain always loyal to her Florentine lovers so long as they can give her gifts. The second part begins here: "And we that love." The third begins, "Lest her grace." The fourth part begins, "O daughter of the gods."

That simile of the Wingless Victory tickled me so mightily that I was in a very good conceit with myself, and if I read over my precious sonnet once, I suppose I read it over a score of times; and even now, at this distance of days, I am inclined to pat myself upon the back and to call myself ear-pleasing names for the sake of my handiwork. Of course I am ready to admit quite frankly that most, if not all, of Dante's sonnets are better, taking them all round, than my modest enterprises. But there is room, as I hope, for many kinds of music-makers in the fields about Parnassus. I know Messer Guido spoke very pleasantly of my sonnets, and so I make no doubt would Dante have, but somehow or other I never showed them to him.

Now, when I had scrolled my rhymes precisely, I had them dispatched to Monna Vittoria by a sure hand, and, as is my way, having done what I had to do, thought no more about the matter for the time being. It was ever a habit of mine not merely to let the dead day bury its dead, but to let the dead hour, and, if possible, the dead minute and dead second bury their dead, and to think no more upon any matter than is essential. I think the sum of all wise living is to be merry as often as one can, and sad as seldom as one can, and never to fret over what is unavoidable, or to be pensive over what is past, but to be wise for the time. So I remember that days not a few drifted by after I had sent my rhymes and my request to Monna Vittoria, and I was very busy just then paying my court to three of the prettiest girls I had ever known, and I almost forgot my poem and Monna Vittoria altogether.

But I recall a grayish morning along Arno and a meeting with Messer Guido, and his taking me on one side and standing under an archway while he read me a sonnet that the unknown poet had composed in illustration of his passion for his nameless lady, and had sent to Messer Guido. It was a very beautiful sonnet, as I remember, and I recall very keenly wishing for an instant that I could write such words and, above all, that I could think such thoughts. I think I have already set it down that love has always been a very practical business with me. If one girl is not at hand, another will serve, and the moon-flower, sunflower manner of worship was never my way. But if one must love like that, making love rather a candle on God's altar than a torch in Venus her temple, there is no man ever since the world began, nor will, I think, ever be till the world shall end, to do so better than Messer Dante. When I had done reading the sonnet, and had parted from friend Guido, I found myself in the mood that this then unknown poet's verses always swung me into, of wonder and trouble, as of one who, having drunk over-much of a heady and insidious wine, finds himself thinking unfamiliar thoughts and seeing familiar things unfamiliarly. While I was thus mazed and arguing with myself as to whether

I were right and this poet wrong or this poet right and I wrong in our view of love and women. I was accosted in the plain highway by a dapper little brat of a page that wore a very flamboyant livery, and that carried a letter in his hand. And the page questioned me with a grin and asked me if I were Messer Lappo Lappi, and I, being so bewildered with the burden of my warring thoughts, was half of a mind to answer that I was no such man, but luckily recalled myself and walked the sober earth again soberly. I assured him that I was none other than poor Lappo Lappi, and I pinched a silver coin from my pocket and gave it to him, and he handed me the missive and grinned again, and whistled and slipped away from me along the street, a diminished imp of twinkling gilt. And I opened the letter then and there, and read in it that Monna Vittoria very gracefully gave me her duty, and in all humility thanked me for my verses--Lord, as if that ample baggage could ever be humble!-- and would be flattered beyond praise if my dignity would honor her with my presence on such a day at such an hour. And I was very well pleased with this missive, and was very careful to obey its commands.

The house where Monna Vittoria dwelt was a marvel of beauty, like its mistress--a fair frame for a fair portrait. It seemed to have laid all the kingdoms of earth under tribute, for, indeed, the lady's friends were mainly men of wealth, cardinals and princes and great captains, that were ever ready to give her the best they had to give for the honor of her acquaintance. Her rooms were rich with statues of marble and statues of bronze, and figures in ivory and figures in silver, and with gold vessels, and cabinets of ebony and other costly woods; and pictures by Byzantine painters hung upon her walls, and her rooms were rich with all manner of costly stuffs and furs. He that was favored to have audience with Monna Vittoria went to her as through a dream of loveliness, marvelling at the many splendid things that surrounded her: at the fountain in her court-yard, where the goldfish gambolled, and where a Triton that came from an old Roman villa spouted; at her corridors, lined with delicately tinted majolica that seemed cool and clean as ice in those summer heats; at her antechambers, that glowed with color and swooned with sweet odors; and, finally, at her own apartments, where she that was lady of all this beauty seemed so much more beautiful than it all.

Madonna Vittoria would have looked queenly in a cottage; in the midst of her gorgeous surroundings she showed more than imperial, and she knew the value of such trappings and made the most of them to dazzle her admirers, for her admirers, as I have said, were all great lords that were used to handsome dwellings and sumptuous appointments and costly adornings, but there was never one of them that seemed to dwell so splendidly as Monna Vittoria.

Now I, that came to her with nothing save such credit as I might hope to have for the sake of my verses, could look at all this magnificence with an indifferent eye. Yet I will confess that as I moved through so much sumptuousness, and breathed such strangely scented air, I was stirred all of a sudden with strange and base envy of those great personages for whom this brave show was spread, and found myself wishing unwittingly that I were some great prince of the Church or adventurous free-companion who might not, indeed, command--for there were none who could do that--but hope for the lady's kindness. Although I assured myself lustily that a poet was as good as a prince, in my heart, and in the presence of all this luxury, I knew very dismally that it was not so, and that Monna Vittoria would never be persuaded to think so. As I have already said, I had no great yearning for these magnificent mercenaries of the hosts of Love, for these bejewelled amazons that seemed made merely to prove to man that he is no better than an unutterable ass. My pulses never thrilled tumultuously after her kind, and in the free air of the fields I would not have changed one of my pretty sweethearts against Monna Vittoria. But somehow in that fantastic palace of hers, with its enchanted atmosphere and its opulent surroundings, my cool reason of the meadows and the open air seemed at a loss, and I found myself ready, as it were, to surrender to Circe like any hog pig of them all.

If this were the time and the place, I should like to try to find out, by the light of a dry logic, and with the aid of a cold process of analysis, why these Timandras and Phrynes have so much power over men. Perhaps, as I am speaking of Monna Vittoria, I should add the Aspasias to my short catalogue of she-gallants, for Vittoria was a woman well accomplished in the arts, well-lettered, speaking several tongues with ease, well-read, too, and one that could talk to her lovers, when they had the time or the inclination for talking, of the ancient authors of Rome, and of Greece, too, for that matter--did I not say her mother was a Greek?--and could say you or sing you the stanzas of mellifluous poets, most ravishingly to the ear. She knew all the verses of Guido Guinicelli by root of heart, and to hear her repeat that poem of his beginning,

"Love ever dwells within the gentle heart,"

what time she touched a lute to soft notes of complaining and praise and patience and desire, was to make, for the moment, even the most obdurate understand her charm. But if I at all seem to disfavor her, it may be because she was too costly a toy for such as I, save, indeed, when she condescended to do a grace, for kindness' sake, to one whose revenues were of small estate. It is plain that such ladies have their fascination, and in a measure I admit it, but, day in and day out, I prefer my jolly dollimops. This has ever been my opinion and always will be, and I think those are the likelier to go happy that think like me.

IX
MADONNA VITTORIA SOUNDS A WARNING

Madonna Vittoria received me so very graciously that for a while I began to think no little good of myself, and to reconsider my latest opinion as to the value of poets and poetry in the eyes of such ladies. But this mood of self-esteem was not fated to be of long duration. After some gracious words of praise for my verses, which made me pleased to find her so wise in judgment, she came very swiftly to the purpose for which she had summoned me, and that purpose was not at all to share in the delight of my society.

"Are you not a friend," she said, very gravely, "of young Dante of the Alighieri?"

I made answer that for my own poor part I counted myself his very dear and devoted friend, and that I had reason to believe that he held me in some affection. I was not a little surprised at this sudden introduction of Messer Dante into our conversation, and began to wonder if by any chance Monna Vittoria had taken a fancy to him. Such women have such whims at times. However, I was not long left in doubt as to her meaning.

"If you are a true friend to him," she said, "you would do well to counsel him to go warily and to have a care of Messer Simone of the Bardi, for I am very sure that he means to do him a mischief when time shall serve."

Now I had seen nothing of Dante since that day of the little bicker with Simone, long weeks earlier, but as I had heard by chance that he was busy with the practice of sword-craft, I took it for granted that he was thus keeping his promise to a certain lady, and was by no means distressed at his absence. As for Messer Simone, he went his ways in Florence as truculently as ever, and I hoped he would be willing to let bygones be bygones.

"Does he still bear such a grudge for a single rose-blossom?" I asked. And it seemed to me that it was scarcely in reason to be so pettily revengeful toward a youth that had carried himself so valiantly and so cunningly in the countenance of a great danger.

Monna Vittoria answered me very swiftly and decidedly. "Messer Simone has a little mind in his big body, and little minds cling to trifles. But it is not the matter of the rose alone that chokes him, but chiefly the matter of the poems."

I stared at Monna Vittoria with round eyes of wonder. "What poems?" I asked; for, indeed, I did not understand her drift.

She frowned a little in impatience at my slowness. "Why, surely," she said, "those poems that Messer Dante has written in praise of Beatrice of the Portinari, and in declaration of his service to her. Have you not seen them? Have you not heard of them? Do you not, who are his friend, know that they were written by young Dante?"

Now, indeed, I knew nothing of the kind, and I could not, in reviewing the matter, blame myself very greatly for my lack of knowledge. Who could guess that a scholarly youth who was now very suddenly and wholly, as I had heard, addicted to martial exercises, should, in a twinkling and without the least warning, prove the peer of the practised poets of Florence? Nor was there in the poems that I had seen any plain hint given that the lady they praised was Madonna Beatrice.

"Are you very sure?" I asked. And yet even as I asked I felt that it must be so, and that I ought, by rights, to have known it before, for all that it was so very surprising. For when a man is in love and has anything of the poet in him, that poet is like to leap into life fully armed with equipment of songs and sonnets, as Minerva, on a memorable occasion, made her all-armored ascent from the riven brows of Jove.

The lady was very scornful of my thick-headedness, and was at no pains to conceal her scorn, for all that I had written her so honorable a copy of verses.

"Am I sure? How could I be other than sure? Why, on that day when Madonna Beatrice flung your Dante the rose from her nosegay, I knew by the look in the lad's face that he no less than worshipped her. Was I not standing in the press? Did I not see all, even to the humiliation of Simone? It needed no very keen vision to divine the beginning of many things, love and hate and grave adventures. So when a new and nameless poet filled the air of Florence with his sweetness it did not take me long to spell the letters of his name."

I felt, as I listened, very sure that it ought not to have taken me long either, and the thought made me penitent, and I was about to attempt apologies for my folly when Madonna Vittoria cut me short with new words.

"It mattered little," she went on, "for me to guess the secret of the new poet's mystery, but it mattered much that Simone should guess it. Yet he did guess it. For my Simone, that should be and shall be mine, though he knows nothing and cares nothing for poetry, guessed with the crude instinct of brutish jealousy the authorship that has puzzled Florence."

I felt and looked disturbed at these tidings, and I besought Monna Vittoria to give me the aid of her counsel in this business, as to what were best to do and what not to do. And Madonna Vittoria very earnestly warned me not to make light of Messer Simone's anger, nor to doubt that my Dante was in danger.

"It were very well," she said, after a few moments of silent thoughtfulness, "if Messer Dante could be persuaded to pay some kind of public addresses to some other lady, so as to divert the suspicions of Messer Simone. Let him show me some attention; let him haunt my house awhile. Messer Simone will not be jealous of me, now that he is in this marry mood of his."

I have sometimes wondered since if Madonna Vittoria, in her willingness to help Dante, was not also more than a little willing to please herself with the society of one that could write such incomparable love-verses. Whatever the reason for it might be, I found her idea ingenious and commended it heartily, but Madonna Vittoria, that seemed indifferent to my approval, interrupted the full flood of my eloquence with a lifted hand and lifted eyebrows.

"I know your Dante too well," she said, "though I know him but little, to think that he will be persuaded to any course in order to avoid the anger of Messer Simone."

I knew that this was true as soon as Madonna Vittoria had said it, and I admired the insight of women by which they are so skilled to distinguish one man from another, even when they have seen very little of the man that happens to interest them. I may honestly confess that if the case had been my case, I would cheerfully have availed myself of Monna Vittoria's suggestion and seemed to woo

her--though, indeed, I could have done it very readily with no seeming in the mat-
ter--that I might avoid the inimical suspicions of Messer Simone or his like. Not,
you must understand, that in the heart of my heart I was so sore afraid of Messer
Simone or of another man as to descend to any baseness to avoid his rage, but just
that there was in me the mischievous spirit of intrigue which ever takes delight in
disguisings and concealments and mysteries of all kinds. But I knew when Madonna
Vittoria had said it, and might have known before Madonna Vittoria had said it, if
I had reflected for an instant, that my Dante was not of this inclination and must
walk his straight path steadfastly. Wherefore, I felt at a loss and looked it, staring at
Monna Vittoria.

"Messer Dante," she went on, "must do this thing that I would have him do,
not for any care or safety of his own, but for the sake and for the safety and the
ease and peace of mind of Madonna Beatrice. If it gets to be blown about the city
that the lad Dante of the Alighieri is madly in love with her, and can find no other
occupation for his leisure than the writing in her praise of amorous canzonets, not
only will Messer Simone, her suitor, be fretted, but also Messer Folco, her father,
be vexed, neither of which things can in any way conduce to her happiness. Let
Messer Dante, therefore, for his love's sake, be persuaded to wear the show of affection for some other lady, and as there is already nothing in the wording of his
verses to betray the name of the lady he serves, let him by his public carriage and
demeanor make it seem as if his heart and brain were bestowed on some other, such
another even as myself."

Here, for an instant, Madonna Vittoria paused to take breath, and I nodded approval, and would have spoken, but she was too quick for me.

"Get him to do this," she said, earnestly. "Let him be made very sure that I thoroughly know that he does not care and never could care two fig-pips for me, and tell
him, if you like, that I could never waste a smile or sigh on the effort to make his
sour face look sweet. Besides, I am not urging this to serve him, but to help myself,
for I do not wish Messer Simone to marry Madonna Beatrice, the which thing is the
more likely to happen if Messer Folco has any hint of sweethearting between his
magnificence's daughter and an insignificant boy."

What Madonna Vittoria said was splendid sense, and I applauded it lustily, and
made her my vows that it should be my business to seek out my Dante and bring

him to her thinking. And then we passed from that matter to talk of love-poems, and from love-poems to lovers, and from lovers to the art of love. I would not for all the world seem indiscreet, so I will say no more than that it was a very pleasant afternoon which I passed in that fair lady's society, the memory of which I treasure very preciously in the jewel-casket of my tenderest recollections.

But when the time came for me to bid her farewell she renewed again and very insistently her warning that Simone of the Bardi meant mischief to Dante of the Alighieri, and her counsel that young Dante should be persuaded, for his dear lady's sake, to fob off suspicion by feigning an affection which indeed had no place in his bosom. To this, as before, I agreed very heartily, and so took my leave of a very winsome and delicious creature, and went my ways wishing with all my heart that it might be my privilege to woo such a lady daily, either for my own safety or the safety of another. Which shows that the fates are very fantastical in their favors, for this exquisite occasion of felicity was offered, not to me who would have appreciated it at its right value, but to Messer Dante, who would not value it at the worth of a single pomegranate seed.

But, however that may be, I did as the lady bade me, and I sought out Messer Dante and found him, and gave him the sum of Madonna Vittoria's discourse, urging him to do as she counselled. In doing this I spoke not at all of the danger there might be to my friend from the rage of Messer Simone, but solely of the need for every true and humble lover to keep his love and service secret enough to avoid either care or offence to his lady. To all of which wisdom Messer Dante agreed very readily, being, indeed, over-willing to reproach himself for heedlessness in the matter of his verses, though, indeed, he named no name in them and kept himself as close and invisible as a cuckoo. And I promised and vowed to tell no man nor no woman the secret of the authorship of the verses that Florence was beginning to love so well.

I kept my word as to this promise, and the time was not yet before other than Monna Vittoria and myself and Messer Simone knew the secret. Dante kept his word to me and followed Madonna Vittoria's advice, and showed himself attentive in her company time and again, and was seen on occasion going to or coming from her house. Which conduct on his part, for all that it was intended for the best, did not, as so often happens with the devices of human cunning, have the best result.

For of course, in a city like Florence, where gossip is blown abroad like thistle-seed, it came soon enough to the ears of Madonna Beatrice that young Messer Dante of the Alighieri was believed by many to be a lover of Madonna Vittoria. Now, Madonna Beatrice knew nothing of Dante's wonder-verses in her honor, nor of Dante's way of life since the day of their meeting in Santa Felicita, for Dante was resolved not to bring himself again to her notice until he considered himself in some degree more worthy to do so. Therefore, Madonna Beatrice was little pleased by the talk that coupled the name of Vittoria with his name to whom she had given the rose. So it chanced that one day when she with her companions met Dante in the street, she refused him her salutation, whereat my poor Dante was plunged in a very purgatory of woe.

Of course, he had no knowledge of how he had offended his sweet lady, for it was no great wonder if a youth of his age were to be friends with Madonna Vittoria, as many of the youths of the city were friends. Besides, his own consciousness that his friendship with the woman was no more than friendship--and indeed would have been no more for him, in those ecstatic hours, had she been the goddess Venus herself--caused him to look at the matter very indifferently, regarding it as no more than a convenient cloak to screen from the prying curiosity of the world his high passion for Madonna Beatrice. But I, that was more in the way of girl-gossips than Dante, got in time to know the truth of the reason why the lady Beatrice had refused her salutation to my friend, and I began to see that Madonna Vittoria's counsel might well prove more mischievous than serviceable in the end.

However, I had no more to do than to communicate to Dante the reason that I had discovered for his dear idol's lack of greeting, and at the news of it he was cast into a great gloom and remained disconsolate for a long while. And I urged him that he should let Madonna Beatrice know what he had done and why, but he would not hear of this, saying that he would never seek to win either her favor or her pity so, by trading on any service he might seem to do her. He added that he hoped in God's good time to set himself right with her again, when he was more worthy to approach her. All of which was very beautiful and devoted and noble, but not at all sensible, according to my way of doing or my way of thinking.

Anyway, Messer Dante would go to visit Madonna Vittoria no more, and she wondered at his absence and sent for me and questioned me, and I told her the truth, how following her advice had brought Dante into disgrace with his lady. Then Vittoria seemed indeed grieved, and she commended Dante for keeping away from her, and vowed that he should be set right some way or other in the eyes of his lady. Indeed, it was a pleasure and a marvel that Madonna Vittoria could show such zeal and heat for so simple a love-business as this of the boy of the Alighieri and the girl of the Portinari.

X
THE DEVILS OF AREZZO

Now, the next page in the book of my memory that is concerned with the fortunes of my friend has to do with the feast that Messer Folco Portinari gave to the magnificoes and dignitaries, the notables and worthies, the graces and the radiancies of Florence--a feast that, memorable in itself, was yet more memorable from all that came of it by what we in our wisdom or our ignorance call chance. It was a very proper, noble, and glorious festival, and I am almost as keen to attend it again in my memory as I was keen to be present at it in the days when Time and I were boys together. Yet for all my impatience I think it good before I treat of it and of its happenings to set down in brief certain conditions that then prevailed in Florence--conditions which had their influence in making Messer Folco's festival memorable to so many lives.

You must know that at this time the all-wise and all-powerful Republic of Florence was not a little harassed in its peace and its comfort, if not in its wisdom and its power, by the unneighborly and unmannerly conduct of the people of Arezzo. These intolerant and intolerable folk were not only so purblind and thick-witted as not to realize the immeasurable supremacy of the city of Florence for learning, statesmanship, and bravery over all the other cities of Italy put together, but had carried the bad taste of their opinions into the still worse taste of offensive action. For a long time past Arezzo had pitted itself in covert snares and small enterprises against the integrity and well-being of the Republic. Were Florence in any political difficulty or commercial crisis, then surely were the busy fingers--ah, and even the busy thumbs and the whole busy hands--of the people in Arezzo sure to be thrust into the pie with the ignoble object of plucking out for their own advantage such plums as they could secure. Florentine convoys were never safe from attack on the highroads that neighbored the Aretine dominion, and if any brawl broke out between Florence and one of her neighbors, a brawl never provoked by Florence, too magnanimous for such petty dealings, but always inaugurated by the cupidity or the treachery of her enemies, the Aretines were sure to be found taking part in it, either openly or secretly, to the disadvantage and detriment of the noble city.

Now, this state of things had endured long enough in the minds of most good citizens, and it was felt that the patience of Florence had been over-abused and her good nature too shamelessly counted upon, and that it was time to teach these devils of Arezzo a lesson in civility and fair fellowship. The time for giving this lesson seemed at this present time the more auspicious because for the moment Florence had her hands free from other external complications, and was perhaps less troubled than was her wont by internal agitations. The jolly Guelphs had it their own way more or less in the city; those that were Ghibelline in principle or Ghibelline by sentiment were wise enough to keep their opinions to themselves. Such exiled Ghibellines as had been permitted to return kept very mum and snug. The Reds and the Yellows wore a show of peace, and the city would have appeared to any stranger's eyes to be a very marvel of union and agreement. Under these circumstances it was thought by many, and indeed boldly asserted by many, that it would be a good opportunity to take advantage of an idle, peaceful time and give the people of Arezzo a trouncing. Wherefore, according to certain wise heads, it became all good citizens to do the utmost that in them lay to further so excellent a cause, the elders by appropriate contributions, according to their means, to the coffers of the state, the younger by volunteering eagerly for service in the ranks of a punitive army to be raised against Arezzo.

Never was such a time of military enthusiasm among the young with whom I frequented, nor did any youth of them all show to me more enthusiasm for the cause of the city than Messer Dante. Ever since that day when he had seen again the fair girl whom he had loved as a fair child he had been, as indeed he had said he would be, a changed man, no longer indifferent to the great concerns of state, no longer absorbed in unproductive studies to the extinction of all sense of citizenship, but a patriotic youth keenly alive to the duties that devolved upon a true-hearted Florentine, and zealous in the practice of all those arts that should make him more worthy to be called her son. If he had surprised me by his quiet and his wiliness on the day of his quarrel with Messer Simone dei Bardi, if he had amazed me by the writing of those verses, the authorship of which Madonna Vittoria had been the first to make known to me, he astonished me still more now by the proofs of his application to military and political science. He would talk very learnedly of the disposition of armies in the field, of the advantages and disadvantages of the use of mercenary troops, and the best way to defend and the best way to assault a well-walled citadel, so that you would think, to listen to him, that he was some gray old generalissimo steeped in experience, and not the smooth-cheeked fellow whom we knew, as we thought, so well, and whom perhaps we knew so little. He showed himself as eager for the affairs of state as for the affairs of war, ever ready to weigh new problems of political administration, and to argue as to the merits or defects of this or that form of government.

In a word, from being a reserved and scholarly lad that seemed to take little or no interest in the busy world about him, he had suddenly become an active, enthusiastic man to whom all living questions seemed exceedingly alive. And with all this he kept on with his sword-practice as if he had not other thought but arms, and kept on at his rhymings as if he had no other thought but love and song. And since I kept the knowledge that Monna Vittoria had given me to myself--yea, kept it even from Messer Guido Cavalcanti--those in Florence that cared for verses still marvelled at the music of the unknown, and wondered as to his identity.

Now, as the natural result of the great ferment and headiness in the city and in the hearts of all men in Florence, there was a mighty desire to come to a proper understanding with these Aretines, the proper understanding having, of course, for its object the placing of the neck of Arezzo under the heel of Florence. But though, as I have said, the bickerings between the two powers had been going on for a long while, Florence did not as yet, in view of the complications that existed, and the new complications that might arise from overt act, feel herself strong enough to take the field in open war and to hazard all, it might be, upon the chances of a single field.

Then it was that there came into the mind of Messer Simone dei Bardi, instigated thereunto, as I verily believe, more for his own purpose than from any pure patriotism, a scheme for sapping the strength of the Aretines by some sudden and secret stroke. It was with this end in view that he went up and down the city, talking with those that were young and inflammable, and baiting his plans with many big words and sounding phrases that were as stimulating to the ear as the clanging of the bells on the war-wagon, so that those who heard them, flushed and troubled by their music, were at little pains to inquire as to the wisdom that lay behind them. When Messer Simone found that there were plenty of young men in the city that were as headstrong and valorous as he could wish, he began to mould his words into a closer meaning and to make plainer what he would be at. This was, as it seemed, no other than the formation of a kind of sacred army, such as he had professed to have read of in the history of certain of the old Greek cities, that was to be entirely devoted to the gain and welfare of the city, and to regard all other purposes in life as of little or no value in comparison. He hinted, then, at the levying of a legion of high-spirited and adventurous gentlemen, whose object was to strike surely and suddenly at the strength of Arezzo, being sworn beforehand never to endure defeat or to know retreat when once they had taken their work in hand. To give their object greater significance, he suggested that this legion should be known as the Company of Death, thereby signifying that those who pledged themselves thereto were only to return victorious or not at all.

You may be sure that a great many gallant youths caught eagerly at such a chance of serving their city, all the more so, it may be, because it offered them no direct reward in the case of success and assured them a self-promised death in the event of failure. Now you shall see wherein this scheme helped to serve the purpose of Messer Simone dei Bardi, for it was his hope that Messer Dante should be tempted to enroll himself in this same Company of Death, whereby there was every possibility of Messer Simone being well rid of him.

XI
MESSER FOLCO'S FESTIVAL

I may say, indeed, to the very extreme of verity, that Messer Folco of the Portinari was an excellent man. I will never say that he had not his faults, for he had them, being mortal. He was, it may be, natived with something of a domineering disposition. Feeling himself worthy to command, he liked, perhaps as often as not, to assert that worthiness. It is very certain that what Messer Guido said of him was true, and that with regard to his own family he was indeed the Roman father, one whose word must be law absolute and unquestionable for all his children. Yet withal a just man whose judgments seldom erred in harshness. Although not acrimonious, he was inclined to be choleric, and he was punctilious to a degree that would never have suited my humor on all matters that concerned what he regarded as the sober conduct of life. Enough of this. Let us turn to the good man's patent virtues.

Though his steadfast adhesion to his own party had earned him many enemies among those of the opposing faction, he was never so hot and desperate a politician as the most of his compatriots. There was in him something of the ancient humor and the ancient sweetness of them that wrote and taught with Cicero, and though he thought as highly as any Roman of them all of the honor and glory of the commonweal, he was so much of a philosopher as to believe that honor and glory to be earned, at least as much, by the welfare in mind and body of the citizens as by the triumph of one party over another party. He was alive with all the delicate and sensible charities, was forever scheming and planning to lessen distress and lighten sorrows, and if he could have had his way there would never have been a sick man or a poor man within the walls of Florence. Toward this end, indeed, he employed the major portion of his considerable wealth with more zeal, and yet at the same time with more prudence, than any other benefactor in the city. Vacant spaces of land, whose title-deeds lay to his credit, were now busy with men laying brick upon brick for this building that was to be a little temple of learning, and that building that was to be a hospital for the hurts and the sufferings of troubled men, and this other that was in time to be a church and sanctuary for the spirit as its fellow-edifices were sanctuaries for the body and the mind.

Messer Folco also gave largely in charities, both public and private, and yet, for all his sweetness of generosity he was so shrewd a man that none ever came to him twice with a lying tale or tempted his beneficence with false credentials. He would say, and, indeed, I have heard him say it, though he spoke not to me indeed, for I was never one of those that he would have chosen for intimate conversation-- he would say that charity, to be of any service in the world, should be as stern and swerveless a judge as ever Minos was. Like all good Florentines, he loved the liberal arts, and no little share of his money went in the encouragement of painters and musicians, and the gravers of bronze and the workers of marble, and those whose splendid pleasure it was to shape buildings that should be worthy of the city.

As the top and crown of all these commendabilities, he had a very liberal and hospitable spirit, loving to entertain, not indeed ostentatiously, but still with so much of restrained magnificence as became so wealthy and so honorable a man. It was in the service of this spirit that Messer Folco, some good while after that lovers' meeting which had been so strangely brought about, and which was to have so strange an issue, made up his mind to give a great entertainment to all his friends and lovers in the city. Because it might be said of him that every man that knew him was his friend, and that many that knew him not loved him for his good deeds and the clarity of his good name, it came about that the most part of Florence that were of Messer Folco's station were bidden to come and make merry at the Palace of the Portinari. Among the number, to his great satisfaction, was your poor servant who tells you this tale.

The Palace of the Portinari was a great and stately building, with great and stately rooms inside it, stretching one out of another in what seemed to be an endless succession of ordered richness, and behind the great and stately house and within the great and stately walls that girdled it lay such a garden as no other man in Florence owned, a garden so well ordained after a plan so well conceived that though it was spacious indeed, it seemed ten times more spacious than it really was from the cunning and ingenuity with which its lawns and arbors, its boscages and pergolas, its hedges and trees, its alleys and avenues were adapted to lead the admiring wanderer on and on, and make him believe that he should never come to the end of his tether.

This garden was, for the most part, dedicated to the service of Monna Beatrice and her girl friends in the daytime. In the evening Messer Folco would often walk there with grave and learned elders like himself, and stir the sweet air with changing old-time philosophies, while Monna Beatrice and her maidens sang or danced or luted or played ball. Messer Folco was a man that cherished the domesticities, and had no desire to see his home distorted into a house of call where all had a right to take him by the hand, and he held that the family life flourished best, like certain plants, in seclusion. But as there is a time for all things, so Messer Folco found a time for opening his doors to his friends and acquaintances, and giving them the freedom of his sweet garden, and bidding them eat and drink and dance and make merry to the top of their desires, always, of course, under the control of such decorum as was due to the noble life.

It was to celebrate the laying of the foundation-stone of his hospital that Messer Folco gave the entertainment of which I have just spoken and whose eventful consequences I have yet to relate. It must, of course, be clearly understood that I was not, and, indeed, could not be, always a witness of the events recorded or a hearer of the words set down in my narrative. But while it was my happy or sad fortune to witness many of these events and to hear many of these words, it was also my privilege, knowing, as I did, those that played their part in my tale, and those that knew them well and loved them well, to gain so close a knowledge of the deeds I did not witness and the words I did not hear as to make me as creditable in the recording them as any historian of old time that puts long speeches into the mouths of statesmen he never saw, and repeats the harangues of embattled generals on fields where he never fought. And so to come back to Messer Folco and his house and his garden and his friends and the festival he gave them.

XII
DANTE READS RHYMES

The great hall of Messer Folco's house where now he received his guests, and me among the number, was a mighty handsome piece of work, very brave with gay color and rich hangings and the costly pelts of Asian beasts, and very splendidly lit with an infinity of lamps of bronze that had once illumined Caesarian revels, and flambeaux that stood in sconces of silver and sconces of brass very rarely wrought. At the farther end the room gave through a colonnade on to the spacious garden which it was Messer Folco's privilege to possess, a garden which, it was said, had belonged in old time to a great noble of the stately Roman days. This colonnade, be it noted, for all it looked so open and amiable, could be shut off, if need were, by sliding doors, so as to make the room defensible whenever the war-cries rattled in the streets and Guelph and Ghibelline or Red and Yellow met in deadly grips together.

When I arrived, and I was among the earliest visitors, for I dearly loved all manner of merry-making, and thought it foolish to stand upon my dignity and seem indifferent to mirth, and so come late and lose pleasure--when I arrived, I say, the musicians were tuning their lutes in the gallery on high, and Messer Folco was standing before the doorway greeting his guests. Those that had forestalled me were moving hither and thither over the smooth floor, and staring, for lack of other employment, at the splendid tapestries, and impatient enough for the dancing and the feasting to begin. And then, because I wished to be courteous as becomes the careful guest, I wrung by his hand Messer Folco, who, as I think, had no notion, or at best the dimmest, of who I was, and I said to him, "Blessed be Heaven, Messer Folco, 'tis good to have such a man as you in Florence."

To which Messer Folco answered, returning with dignity my friendly pressure,

"'Tis good for any man to be in Florence; there is no place like Florence from here to world's end."

And then, as I stood something agape and framing a further speech, another guest pushed by me and clasped Messer Folco's hand and addressed him, saying, "So you have started a-building your new hospital. Will you never have done being generous?"

And because it always amuses me to watch give and take of talk between human beings, I stood off one side, Messer Folco having done with me and forgotten me, and listened to the traffic of voices and the bandying of compliments, and heard Messer Folco respond, "One that is happy enough to be a citizen of Florence should be grateful for the favor."

"Well," said the new-comer, whom I knew very well to be one that made the most of his great monies by usury--"well," says he, "a man cannot spend money better than by benefiting the disinherited."

To which Messer Folco, eying him with gravity, and having, as I make no doubt, his own opinion, answered, "So I think."

Now, by this time the enthusiastic usurer had said his say and had his audience, and was straightway pushed on one side. Then my usurer, not knowing me, though indeed I knew him, or not liking the looks of me, as indeed his looks were distasteful to me, for I think a man's money greed is ever written in bitter ink upon the parchment of his face, passed away into the crowd beyond. Thereafter there accosted Messer Folco a man whose name I knew at the time but for the life of me I cannot recall it now, and all that I can remember of him is that he was fat and affable and a notorious giver and gleaner of gossip, as well as one that aped acquaintance with the arts.

"Messer Folco, your servant," he began, in a voice that was as fat as his abdomen. Then went on, in a splutter of rapture, "Why, what a company! Here is all Florence, from base to apex." He paused for a moment, and said behind his hand, in a loud whisper which came easily to my ears, "Is the mysterious poet of your fellowship?" And he glanced around knowingly, as if he hoped to divine the unknown among the arriving guests.

Messer Folco looked at him gravely. "What poet, friend?" he asked; and I truly think he questioned in all honesty of ignorance as to the man's meaning, and my jolly gossip answered, all agog with his knowledge:

"Why, the poet we in Florence that have an ear for sweet sounds are all talking of; the poet whose name no man knows, whose rhymes are on all men's lips; the fellow that praises fair ladies as never fair ladies were praised before since Orpheus carolled in Arcady."

Then I noted how Messer Folco, with the air of one that did indeed recall some idle rumor, looked at him curiously, as one that is puzzled how busy men can interest themselves in such trifles as love rhymes, and he answered, quietly, "I have given little heed to this wonder; I have been too busy with bricks and mortar. Here comes one who may lighten our darkness."

Even as he spoke my ever beloved friend and the ever beloved friend of all who were young with me and of all good Florentines, Messer Guido Cavalcanti, came into the room.

Messer Folco wrung him heartily by the hand, for he loved him no less than the rest of us. "Messer Guido, ever welcome," he cried, "never more than now. Perhaps you can tell us--"

But before he had time to say what he had to say, Messer Guido Cavalcanti interrupted him, not uncivilly, but as one that wished to spare a good man the pains of saying what his hearer already understood as clearly as words could utter it. "I wager I know what you would say," he declared. "Do I know the name of the unknown poet?"

Messer Folco nodded. "Well, do you?" he asked, and those that were standing about him, and especially my good fat gossip merchant that aired his learning, pricked their ears to hear what Messer Guido might have to say on a matter that tickled them. I, with my wider knowledge, that I had kept steadfastly to myself, stood by and chuckled.

For I had that inside my jerkin against my breast which, though indeed it belonged to Messer Guido, Messer Guido had never yet seen, and I had brought it with me to deliver to him. And it concerned the subject-matter of the speech of Folco and his friends.

But Messer Guido could say little to please them. "Why," he declared, "I know no more than all Florence knows by this time, that some one has written songs which all men sing, sonnets which all women sigh over. There is a ballad of his addressed to all ladies that are learned in love which is something more than beautiful."

My jolly gossip nodded sagaciously. "Aye, but who made it?" he questioned, sententiously, and looked as complacent as if he had said something really wise.

Guido saluted him politely. "Ask some one wiser than I."

As for me, I grinned to think that I was that some one wiser, and that Guido never suspected it.

Messer Folco touched my dear friend lightly on the shoulder. "It was not your honor's self?" he asked, benignly, with his shrewd eyes smiling upon the handsome face.

Messer Guido shook his head. "No, Messer Folco," he protested, "my little wit flies my flag and wears my coat. If I could write such rhymes as those I should never be mum about them, I promise you."

Then, with a gracious gesture, as of apology for having failed to satisfy the curiosity of those that accosted him, he saluted Messer Folco and moved toward the centre of the room. I was on his heels in an instant, for I wished for a word with him before he was unfindable in the thick and press of his friends, and I had somewhat to say to him concerning the very matter on which he had been speaking. I caught him by the arm, and he turned to greet me as he greeted all that knew him and loved him, with a smile, and I whispered him, plucking a paper from my breast.

"Guido, heart, hearken. Here is a new song sent to your house that seems better than all the others. I called at your lodgings and saw a scroll on your table, and knowing what it must be, I made bold to read it, and, having read it, to bear it to you."

And Messer Guido answered me, eagerly: "I have not been home; I have been all day with the cardinal. For love's sake, let me see." He took the paper from me and read it over, and then he said to me, gravely: "Why, this is better than the best we have had yet. This is the finish of the ballad of fair Florentines. Here is the nightingale of Florence singing his heart out for us, and we are at a loss for his name."

Then I, being delighted at my own initiation into this mystery of the nameless singer, and fired by Guido's praises of him, turned to those about me, and the room had filled a little by this time, and I cried out, as indeed I had no business to do in a house where at best I was little more than a stranger. And this is what I said: "Gentles all, squires and dames, loving and loved, here is rose-scented news for you. The unknown poet has sung again, and Messer Guido has the words in his fingers."

Now there came a hush of talking in the room as I said these words, and Messer Guido looked at me something reprovingly, because of my forwardness, and all eyes were fixed upon the pair of us.

Then Messer Folco, moving close up to me, touched me on the shoulder and said, with a quiet irony, "You are very good, sir, to be my major-domo."

Instantly I bowed to the ground in sober recognition of my error. "Forgive me the heat of my zeal," I protested. "I diminish, I dwindle, I wither. Unless your pity forgives me, I shall evaporate into air."

Then Messer Folco laughed good-humoredly, and, turning to Guido, said, "Messer Guido, of your charity, let us hear."

But Guido, the ever obliging, was here unwilling to oblige. "Shall the owl croak the notes of the nightingale?" he asked, extending his open palms in a gesture of emphatic denial.

Now even at that moment, with Messer Guido politely declining, and Messer Folco still in a mood between smiling and frowning on account of my presumption, and I gaping open-mouthed, and the guests that were gathered about us staring eagerly at the parchment which my dear friend held in his hand, something curious occurred. There came a voice from the press hard by me, a voice that I seemed to know very well and yet that I could not on the instant name with the owner's name, and this voice cried aloud, so that all present could hear the cry distinctly: "Let Messer Dante read the rhymes!" Even as the voice spoke I saw the reason for its spending of breath, for at that very moment Messer Dante entered the hall, and was making his way toward Messer Folco with the bearing of one that courteously salutes his host.

I looked about me sharply to right and to left, in the hope that I might by chance catch sight of the guest that thus called upon my friend, but I could see no one to whom I could with any surety credit the utterance. I observed, indeed, a certain youth that was cloaked as to his body and masked as to his face slipping out of the crowd about me who might have been the speaker, but whom I could in nowise identify. It was so much the mode with many of us that were young in Florence to come--and sometimes to come unbidden--to such galas as this of Messer

Folco's in antic habits and to hide our features with vizards, that there was nothing in this costume to single out the youth whom I believed to be the utterer of that call for Dante. There were many other masked and muffled figures within the walls of Messer Folco's house that night as hard to tell apart as one cherry from another. But whoever the speaker may have been, the speech had the desired effect. Coupled as it so timely was with the appearance of Dante under Messer Folco's roof, it caught the fancy of all that heard it, and each hearer echoed readily enough the suggestion: "Let Messer Dante read the rhymes!" Thus it came about that Messer Dante had scarcely gone many paces down the hall toward his host when he became aware that he was the target of all eyes.

Though he was surprised at this unexpected attention on the part of so large a concourse of persons, he was in no sense taken aback or embarrassed, but came quietly to a halt and looked with a curious and composed scrutiny at the crowd of men and women that were all regarding him so intently. As he did so, some one cried again, "Let Messer Dante read the rhymes!" And this time Dante heard the words, and he saw also how Messer Guido stood in the throng hard by to Folco and held in his hands a roll of parchment. For a moment Dante showed some signs of discomposure. He changed his fresh color a little to an unfamiliar paleness, and his eyes meeting mine, they flashed a question at me which I could but answer by a determined shake of the head. For I saw that Dante's had a misgiving that I had revealed his secret, which indeed I had not. Then Dante looked at Guido as if to question him, but before he could speak Messer Folco had paid him a grave salutation and began to address him gravely.

"Messer Dante," he said, "you are very welcome to my house, and I greet you cheerfully. Beyond this it is fit that I should explain to you why, in this instant of your coming, your name is in so many mouths. We were speaking here but now of the unknown poet whose verses have of late at once enraptured and bewildered our city, and many of us were entreating Messer Guido, who holds in his hand the latest verses of the nameless singer, to read them aloud to us. And he declining from, as we think, an over-delicate sense of modesty, it was suggested by him or by another, I know not, on seeing you enter, that you should read to us the rhymes in question."

Here Messer Folco bowed very courteously to Dante, but before Dante, who seemed, as indeed he well might, somewhat at a loss what to say, could utter a syllable in reply, Messer Guido had forestalled him.

"There could not be a better choice," he protested, "though it was none of my proposing. Messer Dante has a sweet and clear voice, and if it will but please him to meet our entreaties we shall be indeed his debtors."

And as he spoke he thrust into Dante's hand the roll of parchment on which the poem was written, and all that heard him applauded, and waited for Dante to begin. Indeed, it was a common thing then, in places where friend met friend, for one that had a voice to read somewhat aloud for the delectation of the others, whether a pleasant tale in prose or a poetic canzonet. But Dante, while he took the parchment from Guido's fingers, looked about him quietly and spoke, and his voice and words were very decided in denial.

"I do not know," he said, "why this privilege should be given to me, and with your good leaves I will ask Messer Guido to find him a worthier interpreter." With that he made as if he would put the parchment back again into the hand of Messer Guido, and I could understand very well, if no one else could, why he should be so unwilling to do this thing. But you know how it is with a crowd: once any mob of men or women, or men and women, gets an idea into its head, it is an adventure that would trouble the devil to get it out again. Ever since the masked youth had voiced his call for Messer Dante to read the poem, it had become the assembly's hunger and thirst, will, desire, and determination that the poem should be read by no other than Messer Dante, though I will dare make wager that any single man or woman of them all, if individually addressed, would as lief any other than Dante should take up the task. I thought I caught a glimpse of my masked youth in another part of the crowd prompting the demand. So Messer Guido, as herald of the general wish, smilingly refused to take back the paper parchment, and Dante, ever too wise to be stubborn for stubbornness' sake, surrendered, where to persist in refusal would have seemed churlish to his host and to his company.

"Since you honor me so far," he said, with the wistful smile of one who feels that chance has penned him in a corner, "I must needs obey." And with the word he began to unroll the parchment carefully. As he did so something moved me to look round, and I saw that Madonna Beatrice had entered the great hall and had come to a halt, observing that something unusual was toward.

Madonna Beatrice stood arrested there among her maidens, pale and fair, as an angel might stand, ranged about by radiant mortality. I never could find then, and I never shall find, though I have tried often enough, Lord knows, the exact word or exact sequence of words that should fittingly convey the effect of her beauty, even upon those who having seen it often seemed on each occasion to behold it for the first time. Of her, as of every beauty that has graced the world since Helen set fire to Troy, and Semiramis sent dead lovers adrift down the river of Assyria, and Cleopatra charmed Caesar and Antony and Heaven knows who besides, it might be said that she had the familiar features of womankind; but what it was that made those features so marvellous, ah! there was the task for a greater poet than I to take upon his shoulders. Even the great poet that loved her--and I keep his love-book on my shelf to this hour, wedged in between a regiment of the Fathers--even Dante has told us nothing that shall serve to make the ages yet to come understand what the woman was like that a man could love with so rapturous a madness of passion. Sometimes I have thought, in my gropings after the phrase to express her, that the word "luminous" was, perhaps, of all single words, the word that seemed to hold shut in its casket the most of the meaning that I sought to convey. There seemed to be about her, even to me that was never her lover, a radiancy, a nimbus, as it were, of celestial light that gave to pulsing flesh and running blood and circumambient skin a quality that was, as it were, flamelike, ethereal, unreal.

Yet though the essence of her bodily being was, as I knew, so frail, there was no show of frailness in her gracious presence. She was tall for a woman, and her coloring was fresh and sane; her bust and limbs were moulded with a wise and restrained generosity that became her youth, and promised nobility of proportion for her maturity. She moved with the smooth and lively carriage of a nymph down the woodland lawns, with her head easily erect and her eyes steadily seeing the world. She might almost have been the youngest of the Amazons or the latest of those strange demi-deities that haunted the hills and woods and waters until the death of the god Pan dealt them, too, their death-blow. Her eyes had the clearness of a clear night in June; her lips were quick with the brisk crimson of a pink quince. Oh, Saint Cupido, what vanity is this, to essay to paint the unpaintable! Enough that she was young and fair and shapely, and that if in her eyes there dwelt the pensiveness of those whose very loveliness suggests a destined melancholy, her lips were always smiling, and her greeting always blithe, yet I seemed to see black care incarnate behind her, and I will tell you why.

Among the girls that were gathered about her, plump, comely, jolly girls that were, I will readily confess it, more in my way of wooing than their radiant mistress, there stood the figure of a thin and withered man in black, with very white hair and very smooth, gray cheeks and very bright, wise eyes. Him I knew to be Messer Tommaso Severo, that had served the Portinari as leech for longer years than many in Florence could count. He it was that had ushered Messer Folco himself into this troublesome world, that is, however, less troublesome at Florence than elsewhere. He had done the like for Madonna Beatrice, and from the hour of her birth he, whom many blamed for a pagan cynicism and philosophic disdain of humanity, had watched over her life with the tenderness that watches the growth of some fair and unfamiliar flower. He was, besides being a master-physician, one that was thoroughly learned in the science of the stars, and I have always heard that the horoscope he drew for my lady Beatrice was the chief cause of his tireless devotion and care. To her service he had dedicated the lees of his life and the ripeness of his knowledge. It was he who had carried her away for so long a space of years from the summer heats and winter colds of Florence to the green temperance and tranquillity of the hills. It was he who at last, still guided by that horoscope of which he alone knew the lesson, sanctioned the maiden's return to the city, to live outside which, though even in the loveliest places thereafter attainable, is to live in exile. I know for sure that he said of his sweet charge that flesh and spirit were so exquisitely poised in her perfect body that it needed but some breath of fate to scatter them irrevocably apart, as a child's breath can scatter the down of a dandelion to all the corners of a field. But though I thought of this now, as I beheld the girl and the elder so close together, I could not, for my life, believe it, seeing how buoyantly she carried her beauty and the nobility of her color.

Messer Dante still had the two ends of the roll of parchment in his fingers as Madonna Beatrice entered the hall, and in the very instant of her appearance he was aware of her presence, and I that was watching all things at once, like Argus in the antique fable, I saw how his hands trembled and how his lips quivered with the knowledge of her approach. But otherwise he showed no sign of the advance of divinity, and holding the parchment well before his face, rolling and unrolling as the duty needed, he began to read what was written on the skin.

The poem, as I already knew, made up the second part of a lengthy ballad in praise of the ladies of Florence. It was cast in an allegorical fashion, aiming to portray a pageant of fair women, each single verse seeking to picture some one of the many lovely ladies that in those days made Florence a very Venus Hill for the ravishment of the senses and the stirring of the blood. I wish with all my heart that I could set the whole of it down here, for it was most ingeniously fancied and handled, and it was not over difficult for the admirers of any particular beauty to pierce the dainty veil of symbolism with which the poet had pretended to envelop her identity. Alas! my memory will not serve me to recall the greater part of it, or, indeed, any but a little, though that little is in truth the very kernel of the whole, and I have no copy of the ballad by me to mend my memory. But, as I say, what I do remember is the centre-jewel of its crown of song.

My Dante read the verses that were his own verses in a voice that was very even, melodious, but so sustained and tamed as to make it seem plain to all that listened that he was dealing with somewhat whose matter he had never seen before. And as he read each stanza, with its laudation of some lovely lady that was one of the living graces and glories of our city, those that spelled the cryptic riddle of its meaning clapped their hands for pleasure and turned their eyes to where the lady thus bepraised stood and smiled at her, and she, delighted, would bridle and fidget with her fan and seek to maintain herself as if she did not care one whit for what in reality she prized very highly. So the river of sweet words ran on, sweetly voiced, and flowing in its appointed course with a golden felicity of thought and phrase.

Very soon the roll of parchment in Dante's right hand was larger by much than the roll of parchment in Dante's left, and it was plain indeed to all present that the reading and the poem were coming to an end. It was also plain to all present that the utterance of the poet was growing more agitated, and his manner more embarrassed and anxious, and it was manifest to me, who watched him keenly, that he was trembling like a cypress in a light wind. As he came to the last verse it seemed as if some irresistible compulsion compelled him to turn his head in the direction where Madonna Beatrice stood apart with her women and her leech. As he did so the parchment fell from his suddenly parted fingers and lay in two rolls at his feet. But, as if he were unaware of what had happened, Dante went on with his recitation of the poem. I could see very clearly that the madness of love was wholly upon him, the madness that makes a man lose all heed of what he does and be conscious of naught save the presence of the beloved. He stood there rigid, as one possessed, with his face turned in the direction where the lady Beatrice stood amid her women, and his hands, newly liberated from the control of the parchment that lay at his feet, were clasped together in a tight embrace. And when I turned my gaze from him to her whose beauty he so passionately regarded, I was aware that she too was under the spell of his words, and was conscious of the adoration in his eyes. Truly that boy and that girl, as they stood there in the clean springtide of their youth and comeliness, seemed to me to be a pair very properly and lovingly made by Heaven one for the other. "Here," said I to myself, "if there be any truth in Messer Plato's theory of affinities, here is a living proof of the Grecian whimsy. And here," I said to myself, "if folk must needs marry--a thing I never could understand--here, as I think, is an instance in which a man and a woman might really be happy together, making true mates, lovers, and friends, finding life sweet to share, and finding nothing in their union that was not noble and pure." So I thought while my Dante was betraying his secret by repeating his lesson without his book.

These were the words that he spoke with his eyes fixed upon the lady Beatrice, and they live in my memory as fresh as they seemed on the day when I first read them in Messer Guido's lodging, and the evening when I first heard them in Messer Folco's hall. Here is what they said:

> "Blessed they name the lady whom I love,
> Even as the angelic lips in Paradise
> At last shall bless her when she moves above
> The sun and all the stars. But while mine eyes
> Regard her ere she numbers the Nine Skies,
> Immortal in her mortal loveliness,
> Can I be scorned if to my soul of sighs
> Earth's blessing seems the greater, Heaven's the less?"

Even as he came to an end in the great quiet that reigned over the place, I saw how Dante grew of a sudden strangely pale, and how his body swayed as if his senses were about to drown themselves in a swoon, and I truly think that he would have fainted away and fallen to the ground in the transport of his passion if I had not sprung forward from amid the throng where I stood and caught him in my arms.

XIII
GO-BETWEENS

To most of those that were present in Messer Folco's house that night it was little less than impossible to misunderstand the meaning of those latest rhymes that Messer Dante had read. Even if none had taken into account the agitation that had come over my friend, and which at least identified him in spirit with the substance of what he read, if it did not patently proclaim him the author, at least it was staringly evident that the stanza was a public tribute to the loveliness of Madonna Beatrice. Did not her name of Beatrice imply blessedness, and was not blessedness, terrestrial and celestial, the intimate theme of the octave? Further, since I speak of the octave, were not those that had nimble judgments and sprightly memories able to recall that Madonna Beatrice's name was made up of eight letters, and then, following on this pathway of knowledge, to discover that the first letter of each line of the stanza corresponded in its order with the like letter in the name of the daughter of Folco Portinari.

In the face of such an amazing revelation a kind of heavy silence brooded awhile over the company, and lasted, indeed, as long as the time, which was indeed but brief, that Dante lay in my arms in his stupor. While some believed that in Dante they beheld--as in very truth they did--the author of the poem, and in consequence the body of the unknown poet that had haunted their imaginations, others merely appreciated that the unknown poet, whoever he might be, had declared himself very patently the adorer of Monna Beatrice, wherefore it was to be inferred that all those other love-songs, which the golden youth of Florence loved to murmur to the ears of their ladies, were so many roses and lilies and violets laid on the same shrine.

Whoever misunderstood the true meaning of what had happened, I think that

Messer Folco understood well enough, and was mightily little pleased in the understanding. Though Dante had, indeed, the right to claim nobility of birth, neither his station in the city nor his worldly means were such as to commend him to Messer Folco's eyes as a declared lover of his daughter. Whatever annoyance Messer Folco may have felt at the untoward occurrence, he was too accomplished a gentleman to allow any sign of chagrin to appear in his voice or countenance or demeanor. He did no more than thank Dante, who had by this time quite overmastered his passing weakness, for his courtesy in reading such very pleasing verses. Then, turning to the guests that stood about, somewhat disconcerted and puzzled by what had taken place, he addressed them in loud tones, telling them that a slight banquet was set forth in the adjacent room, and begged them to enjoy it before the dancing should begin.

At these pleasant tidings the most of Messer Folco's company were greatly elated, and hastened to pair themselves off very merrily, and to make their ways toward the banqueting-room, where, indeed, a very delectable feast was spread, such an one as might have tickled the palate and flattered the appetite of any of the high-livers and dainty drinkers of old Rome. As our jolly Florentine lads and winsome Florentine lasses ate and drank, they chattered of what they had just heard, of what they had just seen, and were all agreed to a man Jack and a woman Jill that Madonna Beatrice was a very flower of women, and that if Messer Dante laid his heart at her feet it was no doubt a piece of great presumption, but otherwise an act highly to be applauded. We were very young in Florence in those days, and our hearts were always quick to beat time to the drum-taps of love or any other high and generous passion. If we have changed since, it is the fault of the changing years and the loss of the Republic.

I make no doubt that there were some who grumbled and carped and cavilled; said this and said that; grunted porcine over the pretty pass things were coming to in the city when a nobody or a next-to-nobody like young Dante of the Alighieri could presume to lift his impudent eyes to a daughter of a man like Folco Portinari, one of the first citizens of Florence, and a man that builded hospitals and basilicas at his own expense. But the growls of these grumblers and carpers and snarlers did not count in the general and genial applause that our youth gave to mellifluous numbers and lovely love, and the thousand beautiful things and thoughts that make this poor life of ours seem for a season Elysium. So they feasted and prattled, and I turn to another theme.

If the meaning of what Messer Dante said and the meaning of what Messer Dante did was plain and over-plain to Messer Folco, it was surely in the very nature of things no less plain to his daughter. To her, at least, there can have been no riddle to read in the young man's words, in the young man's actions. Love, splendid and fierce and humble, reigned in the glowing words that he read, ruled his failing voice, swayed his reeling figure. She could not question the identity of the Blessed One whose beauty made the singer sacrilegious in the white-heat of his devotion. She could not misinterpret the significance of the abandoned parchment lying discarded where it had fallen on the floor while the reciter, with his sad eyes fixed upon her face, repeated so familiarly the words which he was supposed never to have seen. For Beatrice, Dante of the Alighieri was the author of the ballad in praise of fair Florentines; for her he was the unknown poet whose fame had flamed through Florence, and she was the lady that was praised with words of such enchanting sweetness in his songs.

While the guests were going toward the banquet as brisk as bees to blossoms, Dante caught me by the hand and drew me apart, and entreated me to seek speech with Beatrice, and to entreat her to grant him an interview in private that very night. He dared not, so he said, approach her himself, in the first place because the doing so might prove too noticeable after what had occurred, and, in the second place, because he feared that she had some cause of complaint against him, seeing that she had of late refused him her salutation. He bade me urge her very strenuously to grant his prayer, for his soul's sake and his body's sake, that he might live and not die.

Since I was ever willing to serve my friend, I agreed to do this thing, and so left him to the care of Messer Guido, who came up on that instant and addressed him in very loving terms, charging him with being indeed the poet whose name they had sought so long. Dante not denying this, as indeed denial would have been idle, even if Dante had been willing, as indeed he never was, to utter such a falsehood, saying that he had not done that which he had done, Messer Guido began to praise him in such glowing words as would have made another man happy. But for Dante happiness lay only in the kind thoughts of his lady, and the very shaft of his ambition was only to please her. He listened very quietly while Messer Guido praised him so highly, and I, for my part, set about performing the task with which he had intrusted me.

I did not know at the time, though I learned it later, that my mission, if not forestalled, had in very truth been rendered much easier by the action of another. That masked youth I told you of, who would needs have Dante read his own poem that none there knew for his, was no other a person than Monna Vittoria. Vittoria had ever a freakish humor for slipping into man's apparel, which some of her friends found diverting and others not, as the mood took them. Madonna Vittoria took it into her head that she would be present at Messer Folco's festival, and to do so was easy enough for her when once she had clothed her shapely body in the habit of a cavalier, and flung a colored cloak about her, and curled her locks up under a cap, and clapped a vizard upon her face. She went to Messer Folco's house for this reason most of all, that she meant to speak with Madonna Beatrice, a thing not ordinarily very easy to come at for such as she. Indeed, there was no risk for her of discovery, doing what she did in the way she did, with a man's jacket on her back and a man's hose upon her legs.

She came, as it seems, upon Beatrice in the early hours of the festival, having bided her time till she should find Folco's daughter alone or nearly so, and then and there addressed her earnestly with a request for some private speech. In such a season of merry-making the request did not come so strangely from a masked youth as to seem either insolent or unfitting. But Beatrice knew at once that the voice was a woman's, and so said, smilingly, as she drew a little apart with her challenger. Then it appears that Vittoria unmasked and named herself, and that Beatrice looked at her very steadily and gravely, and said no more than this: "I have heard of you. You are very beautiful," the which words, as Vittoria told me later, gave her a greater pleasure than any she had ever tasted from the praises of men's lips.

Vittoria said, "If you have heard of me, perhaps you will think that I should not be here and seeking speech with you."

To which Beatrice answered, very sweetly, that it was no part of the law of her life to deny hearing to one that wished for speech with her, and while she spoke she was still smiling kindly, and there was no anger in her eyes and no scorn, but only a kind of sad wonder. Then Vittoria said that she had made bold to do what she did for the sake of a friend and for the sake of Beatrice herself. Thereat the manner of Beatrice, albeit still courteous, grew colder, and she answered that she did not know how the doings of any friend of Vittoria's could concern her, and Vittoria knew that she guessed who the friend was.

Vittoria said, "The friend of whom I speak, the friend whom I would serve with you, is not and never has been more than my friend."

At this Beatrice made a gesture as if to silence her and a movement as if to leave her.

But Vittoria barred her way and delayed her entreatingly, saying, "Do not scorn me because I am what I am."

Whom, thus entreated, Madonna Beatrice answered, very gently: "Indeed, I do not scorn you for being what your are. I will not even say that I do not understand you, for I have it in my heart that a woman must always understand a woman, however different the way of the one may be from the way of the other. And it might very well have happened, if our upbringings had been other, that you were as I am and I as you."

Vittoria answered: "I think not so, for God has so made you that you would never care for the things I care for, and God has so made me that I should always care for them."

Beatrice replied: "Very well, then; let us leave the matter with God, who made us, and say to me what you wish to say."

Then Vittoria told Beatrice of Dante, how he was devoted soul and body to Beatrice, and how it was only in consequence of Vittoria's well-meant but ill-proving advice that he at all sought her society. She told how she had given that advice to save the youth from the hatred of Simone, but had not told him this, telling him rather that by so doing he would keep his love for Beatrice a secret from the world. Then the paleness of Beatrice changed for a little to a soft red, and Vittoria saw that she believed, and kissed her hand and left her. Thus it came about that my labor was already lightened, though I knew it not when I set out to seek for Beatrice on behalf of my friend.

The good chance that sometimes favors the ambassadors of Love served me in good stead very presently by affording me occasion to approach Madonna Beatrice and engage her in speech, for she was ever courteous in her bearing toward her father's guests. After we had discoursed for a brief while on trifles, I, finding that where we stood and talked I might speak with little fear of being overheard, straightway disclosed my mission to her, and delivered my errand, putting it, as I think, in words no less apt than choice, and making a very proper plea for my friend, presenting, indeed, his petition so well that, though I say it who, perhaps, should not say it, I do not think that he could have done it any better himself. I made bold to add that my friend went in fear that he had in some way offended her, but that I was very sure he would be able to excuse himself to her eyes if only she would afford him the opportunity to do so.

Madonna Beatrice listened to me very quietly while I delivered myself of my message and of such embroideries of my own as I saw fit to tag on to its original simplicity, and though I thought I could discern that she was affected not unkindly toward my friend, in spite of whatever fault he might have committed, she did not in any way change color or display any other of those signals by which ladies are accustomed to make manifest their agitation when any whisper of love business is in the air. When I had finished, she did no more at first than to ask me if, indeed, Messer Dante was the unknown poet who had so delighted Florence.

To which question I made answer that the truth was indeed so, at which assurance she seemed to me at first to smile, and then to look sad, and then to smile again. But when I was beginning to utter some golden words in the praise of my friend's verses, she very sweetly but very surely cut my compliments short, and gave me the answer to my embassy.

"Tell Messer Dante," she said, "that he is so great a poet that it were scarcely gracious for me to refuse him the favor he asks, though, indeed, he must know as well as I know that it is no small favor. It is not perhaps fitting, and it certainly is not easy, for a maiden to accord a lonely meeting to a youth, even when that youth has some reason to call himself the maiden's friend. But I shall retire before this festival comes to an end, and I shall walk awhile on the loggia above in the moonlight and the sweet air before going to my sleep. If he will come to me there I will speak with him and hear him speak for a little while. Tell him I do this for the sake of his verses."

Therewith she made me a suave salutation and turned to speak to another, and I, finding myself thus amiably dismissed, and being very well satisfied with the fruits of my enterprise, bowed very lowly before her, and turned and went my ways, seeking my friend. Soon I found him with many youths and elders about him, all as eager as Guido had been to congratulate him on what he had done. But if Dante seemed pleased to hear their praises, as it was only right he should seem pleased, he showed still greater pleasure in beholding me and reading the message of my smiling face.

He made some excuse for quitting his company and drawing apart with me, and when he had heard what I had got to say, I think that he looked the happiest man that I had ever seen. "Heaven bless my lady Beatrice for her sovereign grace," he said, very softly and earnestly, and then he wrung me very hard by the hand, and left me and went back to his admirers, and thereafter, during the progress of the night's pleasures, I saw him move and take his share with an unwonted brightness of countenance and mirthfulness of bearing, and I was glad with all my heart to see him so cheerful.

Indeed, that was a cheering time, and the man or woman would have been hard to please who found nothing to delight or to amuse at Messer Folco's festival. To speak for myself, I had never known better diversion. There was a whole world of pretty women assembled within Messer Folco's walls, and I may as well confess here, if I have not confessed it already, that I take great delectation in the companionship of pretty women. How many little hands, I wonder, did I press that night, with the tenderest protestations? How many kisses, I wonder, did I venture to steal, or, rather, pretend to steal? for I swear the dainty rogues met me half way in the matter of the robbery. Well, well, it was all very merry and pleasant, and we feasted very gayly, and we danced very nimbly, and we wandered in the green glooms of the garden, and then we feasted anew, and after that we set to work to dancing in good earnest. Save for a few, we all danced and danced and danced again, as if we could dance the world back into its young-time.

XIV
MESSER SIMONE SPOILS SPORT

The dance was at the very top of its progress; all the youths and maidens were bright and smiling; the musicians scraped and plucked like mad, and the strings quivered with happy melody. All about against the wall the elders ranged at gaze, recalling wistfully or cheerfully, according to their temperaments, the days when they, too, tripped lightly to music and made love in a measure, and some old toes ached for a caper. While the mirth was at its blithest there suddenly came an interruption to the gayety, and in a twink, one knew not how, the dance that had been so jovial and harmonious seemed suddenly resolved into its individual elements, so many youths and men, and so many maids and matrons staring at the thing that had thus suddenly marred their pleasure. I, that had been placed by chance at a post in the dance the most removed from the main door of the apartment, was not at first aware of what had caused the commotion among the dancers; I was only aware of the commotion and the pause in the dancing and the knowledge that the faces of those near to me showed surprise or fear or wonder, according to their instinct. Meanwhile the musicians in their gallery, knowing nothing of any reason why they should stop, were still twitching their strings busily, though no one marked them and no one danced to their music. But I, being resolved to argue, as it were, from the effect to the cause, pushed my way through the men and women that were huddled together in my neighborhood, and then I came to an open space of the floor, and face to face, at a distance, with the cause of the disturbance.

This cause was Messer Simone dei Bardi, who was standing in the centre of the room with Messer Folco Portinari and other grave elders about him, and he was talking in a loud voice, as it were, to them in particular, but also in general to the assembled company. Now, I had never in all my life felt any kindly liking for Messer Simone, but I had to confess to myself that he cut something of a flourishing figure just then and just there. While all of us that were gathered under Messer Folco's roof were habited in our best bravery of velvets and soft stuffs and furs and such gold trinkets and jewels as it were in our power to display, and so looked very frivolous and foppish and at ease, Messer Simone dei Bardi came among us clad as a soldier-citizen of a great Republic should be clad in time of danger to his nation. His huge bulk was built about in steel, a great sword swung at his side, and though his head was bare, a page in his livery stood close behind him resting his master's helmet in the bend of his arm. So lapped in mail, so menacing in carriage, Simone might have seemed some truculent effigy of the god Mars suddenly appearing from the riven earth in a pastoral gallantry of shepherds and shepherdesses.

What he was saying he was saying very clearly with the purpose that all should hear, and I among the rest benefited by what he said. It was to this effect: that our enemies the Aretines were planning a secret stroke at Florence, knowledge of which had come to his patriotic ears; and according to the estimation of his mind, it was no time for Florentine citizens to be singing and dancing and making merry when there was a stroke to be struck with a strong hand against her enemies.

These bellicose words of Messer Simone found their immediate echo in the hearts of all men present; for to do us Florentines justice, we have never loved frolicking so much that we did not like fighting a great deal better, and we have never had private business or private pleasure which we were not ready at a moment's notice to thrust on one side when the great bell of the city sounded its warning of danger to the Republic. So for the immediate time Messer Simone was the hour's hero, and dancing and banqueting and laughing and love-making were clean forgotten, and every youth and every mature man there present, and, for that matter, every elder, too, was eager to ring himself in steel and to teach the devils of Arezzo of what stuff a Florentine citizen was made. I must honestly and soberly confess that I myself was so readily intoxicated with the heady wine of the excitement about me that I found myself cheering and shouting as lustily as the rest, for the which I do not blame myself, and that I found myself for the moment regarding Messer Simone dei Bardi as a kind of hero, for the which I severely blame myself even now, after all this lapse of years.

When Messer Simone found that he had got the company, so to speak, in the hollow of his hands, he was silent for a little while, looking about him sharply, as if he were making sure of the courage and enthusiasm of his fellow-citizens, and seeking to find in the press of flushed and eager faces any countenance that seemed unwilling to answer to his call. All about him the elders of the city were gathered giving and taking counsel, giving, I think for the most part, more readily than taking, and hurriedly revolving in their minds what were best to do for the city in the crisis that Messer Simone had made plain to them. While these deliberations went on, we that had been dancing danced no longer, nor had desire to dance, and though some talked among themselves, the main kept silence, for the most part waiting upon events. By this time, my wits having grown cooler and my old distrust of Messer Simone being resuscitated, I scrutinized him closely as he stood there in his steel coats, the centre figure of the assembly.

As I looked at Messer Simone where he stood there, girt with strength in every line of his body, in every curl of his crisp hair and short beard, in the watchful ferocity of his eyes, he seemed to me a kind of symbol of what man may be who is unlifted by any inspiration of divinity or tincture of letters from the common herd. In him brute strength, brutish desires, brutal passions were presented, so it seemed to my fancy, as a kind of warning to others of what man may be that is content to be merely man, with no higher thought in him than the gratification of his instincts and his impulses. I have heard tell in travellers' tales of strange lands, beneath fiercer suns than ours, where naked savages disport themselves with the lawless assurance of wild beasts, and it seemed to me--being always given to speculation--that Messer Simone, if he found himself in such a company, would never be at a loss, but would straightway be admitted to their ruffian fellowship. I think, indeed, he would be better suited for such companionship than for citizenship of the fair, the wise, the gifted, the civilized queen-city of Florence. But even as such savages are reported to have, in place of a higher wit, such natural craft as Providence has implanted in the hearts of foxes and hyenas and other such wild beasts, so Messer Simone, for all his bestiality, could be cunning enough when it served his ends, as you shall presently learn.

In a little while Messer Simone began to speak again, and to tell his hearers of the plan which he had formed for the service of Florence and the confusion of her enemies. This plan, as you already know, was to be furthered by the enrollment of all such among the youth of Florence as desired to prove themselves true patriots into a body which was to be known by the high-sounding name of the Company of Death, the meaning of this title being that those who so enrolled themselves were prepared at any moment to give their lives for the advantage of the mother-city. Messer Simone's plan had, as we now learned, been applauded by all the magnates, such as Messer Corso Donati and Messer Vieri dei Cerchi, and had received the approval of the priors of the city. As the scheme was due to Messer Simone, it was agreed on all hands that he should be its leader so long as the Republic of Florence was in a state of war. Whoever had taught him his lesson, Messer Simone had learned it creditably enough. He talked well, and while you listened to him it was hard not to feel that the Company of Death was indeed a very noble and hopeful thought, and that it might very well be the duty of all honorable patriots to join it. But such thoughts might have cooled off under reflection and deliberation if Messer Simone had not been at the pains to prevent reflection and deliberation by a cunning stroke of policy.

So he pitched his loud voice some notes higher, bellowing like a bull of Bashan as he rolled off sonorous sentences very deftly learned and remembered, in which glory and the service of the state and the example of old Rome were cleverly compounded into a most patriotic pasty. Even as he was in the thick of his speaking there came a flourish of trumpets at the door, and to the sound of that music there came into the room a brace of pages that were habited in cloth of gold, and that bore on their breasts the badge that showed them to be the servants of Messer Simone. This pair of pages carried between them a mighty gold charger, and on this charger lay a huge book of white vellum that was bound and clasped in gold. These pages were followed by other two pages, one of whom carried ink in a great golden ink-horn and sand in a golden basin, while the other bore a kind of golden quiver that was stuffed full, not indeed of arrows, but of quills of the gray goose. When this little company of pages had come anigh to Messer Simone, who seemed to greet their approach with great satisfaction, the pages that carried the book stood before their master, and Simone, stooping to the charger, unclasped the great book and flung it open and showed that its leaves were white and fair. The book-bearers supported the book so open, on the charger, making themselves into a living desk, and he that carried the ink and sand and he that carried the quills came alongside of them, and stood quietly, waiting for their work to begin.

Then Messer Simone struck with his open palm upon the smooth, fair parchment, and cried aloud that in time to come this book would prove to be one of the city's most precious possessions, for it was to be the abiding record of those noble-souled patriots who had enrolled their names upon the roll-call of the Company of Death. And he said again that such a book would be, indeed, a catalogue of heroes; and after much more talk to this purpose, he called upon all those present that had high hearts and loved their mother-city to come forward and inscribe their names, to their own eternal honor, upon the pages of the there presented volume.

Now at this there came a great shout of applause from many that listened to Messer Simone, and because men in such an assemblage, at such an hour, in such a mood of merry-making, are little likely to prove thoughtful critics of what may be said by a big voice using big words, it seemed to many of those there standing that Messer Simone's scheme of the Company of Death was the best that had ever been schemed for the salvation of the city, and that to write one's name on the pages of Messer Simone's book was the noblest duty and proudest privilege of a true citizen.

There was a great hurrying and scurrying on the part of those that stood around to get to the book and borrow quill and ink from the attendant pages, and be among the earliest to deserve the honorable immortality that Messer Simone promised. There were certain restrictions, so Messer Simone explained, attendant upon the formation of the Company of Death. Its members must be young men of no less than eighteen and no more than thirty years of age. You will bear in mind that Messer Dante was but just turned eighteen, and that Messer Guido was in his eight-and-twentieth year. But no one thought of that at the time, not even I, though it showed plain enough to me afterward. Furthermore, the Companions were to be all unmarried men, such as therefore were free to dedicate their lives to the cause of their country with a readiness that was not to be expected or called for from men that had wives and families.

While Messer Simone thus explained, youth after youth of the young gentlemen of Florence, both of the Reds and of the Yellows, came forward and wrote their names with great zeal and many flourishes on the smooth, white parchment, and soon the white leaves began to be covered thick with names, and still the would-be votaries came crowding about the ink-bearer and the pen-bearer, and catching at the quills and dipping them in the ink. As fast as a sheet was filled the attendant would spill a stream of golden sand over the wet inscription and make ready a fresh sheet for the feverish enthusiasm of the signatories.

After a while Messer Simone called a halt in the business of signing, and now he began to speak anew, and though his voice was rough and harsh from all the talk that he had talked before, and though he rather growled his words than gave them liberal utterance, yet what he said was what he wanted to say, and came from his black heart with a very damnable aptness. He was speaking in the praise of those Florentine youths that had first enrolled their names in the book of the Company of Death, and he was praising them ostentatiously for their valor and their patriotism, and yet while he praised, I, listening, thought that his praises were not very good to get, though some share of them was due to me who had written my name on the pages of the big book, partly because I had drunk much wine, and partly because I could never resist the contagion of any enthusiasm, and partly because the pretty girl that was by my side--I forget her name now--egged me on to the folly.

After Simone had made an end of his laudations, he came to speak with a rough scorn of those that were content to show their devotion to their mother-city by no greater sacrifice than the serving to defend her in case of an attack. While he spoke I could see that his eyes were fixed upon the face of Dante, where he stood a little apart and watched and listened. I had lost thought of Dante in my merry-makings and lost sight of him in the hurly-burly, and now suddenly I saw him leaning against a pillar a little apart, and looking at the eager crowd of youths and Simone that was its central figure. If I had been a painter like Messer Giotto it would have pleased me to paint in the same picture the faces of those two men, the one no more than beastly flesh, and the other, as it seemed to me, the iron lamp in which a sacred spirit burned unceasingly, purifying with its glowing flame the human tabernacle. Then Messer Simone gave a short laugh, and said, mockingly, that such stay-at-home tactics were well enough for puling fellows that liked to lie snug behind city walls and write puling sonnets, and would rather be busy with such petty business than risk their fine skins in brisk adventures.

Now, as for the taunt in Messer Simone's speech, it was, as who should say, an arrow that might have been aimed at the heart of many there, even at my own poor heart, for I was myself an indifferent poet, as you know by this time if you have not known it before. But I knew that Messer Simone had no thought of me when he spoke, for indeed I do not think he thought of me at all, and for my part I thought of him as little as I could help, for I have no love for ugliness. Messer Guido Cavalcanti, who was also there, he, too, was a poet, and a great poet, but it was not of him that Messer Simone spoke, and if it had been it would not have mattered, for Messer Guido would have cared no whit for what Messer Simone said of him or thought of him, and now as Simone spoke, Guido only stood there and laughed in his face, swaying gently with the laughter.

Messer Guido despised Simone dei Bardi, thinking him, what indeed he was, a vulgar fellow, and making no concealment of his thought, and what Messer Guido thought counted in Florence in those days, for he came of a great race and was himself a very free-hearted and noble gentleman, against whom no man had anything to say save this, that it was whispered that he did not believe as a devout man should believe. This tale, for my part, I hold to be exaggeration, thinking that Messer Guido, in the curious clarity and balance of his mind, was less of a sceptic than of a man who should say, standing in a strange country, "I do not know whither my road shall lead me, and therefore I will not say that I do know."

Anyway, it was not with Messer Guido Cavalcanti that Messer Simone dei Bardi would have chosen to quarrel, unless the quarrel were forced upon him, and then I will do him the justice to say that he would have fought for his cause like the untameable male thing he was. But he had set his eyes evilly upon Messer Dante while he had been speaking, and he kept them fixed on Messer Dante's face now that he had made an end of speaking. I saw that Dante's face flushed a little, even to the hair above the high forehead, and his eyes for a moment seemed to widen and brighten like those of some fierce, brave bird. Then he pushed his way to the front of the company and looked up at Simone steadfastly, and his arms were still folded across his body and his sharp-featured face was tense with suppressed rage, and he spoke very quickly but clearly, too, for all the quickness of his words.

What he said was to this effect: "Messer Simone, I thank Heaven that it may be possible for a man to write verses in the praise of his sweet lady and to draw sword in the service of his sweet city. Because I think that no man can honor his lady better than in honoring the city that is blessed in giving her birth and blessed in sheltering her beauty, I hereby very cheerfully and joyously give my name to be written on the list of the Company of Death."

Thereat there was a great cheering and shouting on the part of the younger men, and they gathered about Dante, hotly applauding him. My heart was heavy within me, for I looked at the face of Simone dei Bardi and saw that it shone with pleasure, and I looked at the face of Guido Cavalcanti and saw that it was gray with pain, and I knew that Messer Simone had gained his purpose. As I looked from face to face of the two men that made such ill-matched enemies, Messer Guido Cavalcanti came forward, and, taking a quill from him that held them, wrote his name on the book of the Company of Death, just below the name of Dante.

XV
A SPY IN THE NIGHT

Messer Simone had in his service, as you know already who have read this record of mine, a fellow named Maleotti that was of great use to his master--a brisk, insidious villain that was ever on good terms with all the world, and never on such good terms with a man as when he was minded to do him an ill turn, assuming, of course, that such ill turn was to his own advantage or in the service of his master, Messer Simone dei Bardi. To Messer Simone this fellow Maleotti was altogether devoted, as, indeed, he had a right to be, for Simone was a good paymaster to all those that served him, and he knew the value of Maleotti's tongue when it had a lying tale to tell, and Maleotti's hand when it had a knife in it and a man to be killed standing or lying near to its point.

This Maleotti wisely, from his point of view, made it his business not merely to serve Messer Simone to the best of his ability in those things in which Messer Simone directly demanded his obedience and intelligence, but he also was quick to be of use to him in matters concerning which Messer Simone was either ignorant or gave no direct instructions. It was Maleotti's pleasure to mingle amid crowds and overhear talk, on the chance of gleaning some knowledge which might be service-able to his patron, and, indeed, in this way it was said that he had heard not a few things spoken heedlessly about Messer Simone which were duly carried to Messer Simone's ears, and wrought their speakers much mischief. Also he would, if he could find himself in company where his person and service were unknown, in the wine-house or elsewhere, endeavor to engage those about him in conversation which he would ever lead deftly to the subject of his master and his master's pur-pose, and so win by a side wind, as it were, a knowledge of Florentine opinion that more than once had been valuable to Simone.

Now it had occurred to this fellow, since the beginning of the feud between Simone dei Bardi and Dante dei Alighieri, that it would be to his master's advantage, and to his own, if thereby he pleased his master, that he should set himself to spy upon Messer Dante and keep him as frequently as might be under his eye. It was thus that Messer Simone came to know--what, indeed, was no secret--that our Dante had devoted himself very busily to the practice of arms, and was making great progress therein. But this information, as I learned afterward, did little more than to tickle Messer Simone and make him grin, for he believed that he was invincible in arms, and that no man could stand against him, in which belief he was somewhat excused by his long record of successes, and it seemed to him no more than a sorry joke that a lad and a scholar like Dante should really pit his pigmy self against Simone's giantship. It was no information of Maleotti's that told Simone the truth about the unknown poet. That, as you know, he found out for himself, and if he did but despise any skill that Dante might attain in arms, he had the clumsy man's horror of the thing he could not understand, of the art of weaving words together to praise fair ladies and win their hearts. Maleotti did not know what his master knew, therefore, about Dante, but he came to know it on this night. For Maleotti was among the hearers when Dante, yielding to Messer Guide's insistence, consented to read the verses of the unknown poet, and his quick eyes had been as keen as Messer Guido's to understand the meaning of Dante's change of voice and color when Madonna Beatrice came into the room.

Now this fellow Maleotti, having, as it seems, nothing better to do with his petty existence, must have judged, after this discovery, that it might please his master in some fashion to keep an eye upon Messer Dante what time he was the guest of Messer Folco of the Portinari on that evening of high summer. And I believe it to be little less than certain that he must have observed the meeting and the greeting between Monna Beatrice and me, although it is no less certain that he could have heard none of our speech. So when our speech, whatever it was, for it was all nothing to Maleotti, had come to an end, and I had glided quietly away from Madonna Beatrice and carried her message to my friend, the Maleotti rascal still continued his observation of Messer Dante and his actions.

As I learned afterward from one to whom Maleotti told the matter, he saw at a later hour Messer Dante linger for a while in the garden as one that is lost in thought. Maleotti swore that he seemed all of a sudden to stiffen where he stood, even as a man in a catalepsy might do, and that he stood so rigid and tense for the space, as it seemed to Maleotti, of several minutes, though why he stood so or what the cause of his immobility this Maleotti could in nowise conjecture. I, of course, know very well that this was one of the moments when the God of Love made itself manifest to him. But after a while, as he affirmed that told it to me, Messer Dante seemed to shake off the trance or whatever it was that held him possessed, and then, moving with the strange steadiness of one that walks in his sleep, made through the most lonely part of the garden for that wing of the house of Messer Folco where Madonna Beatrice was lodged. Maleotti, creeping very stealthily at his heels, saw how he came, after a space, to a little gate in the wall, and how, as it seemed to Maleotti, the gate lay open before him, and how Messer Dante straightway passed through the open gateway and so out of his sight.

Now Maleotti, who was as familiar with the house of Messer Folco as he was with his own garret in the dwelling of Messer Simone dei Bardi, knew that this gateway gave on a winding flight of stairs that led to an open loggia, on the farther side of which lay the door of Madonna Beatrice's apartments. Whereupon it pleased this Maleotti, putting two and two together, after the manner of his kind, and making God knows what of them, to be quick with villanous suspicions and to be pricked with a violent desire to let his master know what had happened, partly, as I believe, knowing the vile nature of the man, because he thought the knowledge he had to impart might prove a little galling to his master. However that may be, for in his damnable way he was a faithful servant to his lord, he waited awhile until he saw that Beatrice walked on the loggia and that Dante came to her, and that she seemed to greet him as one expected. Now it taxes no more the wit of a rogue than the wit of an honest man to guess that when two young people stand apart and talk, it is God's gold to the devil's silver that they talk love-talk. So as Maleotti had seen enough, and durst not go nearer to hear aught, he made his way back as swiftly as he could through the green and silent garden to the noisy rooms within the house where folk still were dancing and singing and eating and drinking and making merry, as if they knew not when they should be merry again.

High at the table Maleotti spied his master, Messer Simone. He had now disarmed, and sat, very big with meat and drink and very red of face, talking loudly to a company of obsequious gentlemen who thought, or seemed to think, his utterances oracular. A good way off, at the head of his own table, sat Messer Folco, grave and gray and smiling, his one thought seeming to be that those that came under his roof should be happy in their own way, so long as that way accorded with the decorum expected of Florentine citizens. I fancy that his glance must have fallen more than once, and that unadmiringly, upon that part of the table where Messer Simone sat and babbled and brawled and drank, as if drinking were a new fashion which he was resolved to test to the uttermost. Messer Simone, being such a mighty giant of a man, was appropriately mighty in his appetites, and could, I truly believe, eat more and drink more, and in other animal ways enjoy himself more, than any man in all Italy. But though he would, and often did, drink himself drunk at the feasts where he was a guest, as very notably in that case where he made his wager with Monna Vittoria, he could, if need were, and if occasion called for the use of his activities, shake off the stupor of wine and the lethargy of gluttony and be ready for any business that was fitted to the limitations of his intelligence and the strength of his arms.

Such ways as Messer Simone's, however, were distasteful to the major part of our Florentine gentry, who always cherished a certain decorum in their bodily pleasures and admired a certain restraint at table, and what they approved was naturally even more highly esteemed and commended by Messer Folco Portinari, who was very fastidious in all his public commerce with the world, and punctilious in the observance of the laws and doctrines of good manners. How such a man could ever have consented to consider Messer Simone for a single moment as a suitor for his daughter passes my understanding. But Messer Simone was rich and powerful and of a great house, and Messer Folco loved riches and power and good birth as dearly as ever a woman loved jewels.

However that may be, our Maleotti got near to Simone, and after trying unavailingly to catch the attention of his eye, made so bold as to come hard by him and to pluck him by the sleeve of his doublet once or twice. This failing to stir Messer Simone, who was thorough in his cups, Maleotti spurred his resolve a pace further, and first whispered and then shrieked a call into Messer Simone's ear. The whisper Messer Simone passed unheeded, the shriek roused him. He turned in his seat with an oath, and, gripping Maleotti by the shoulder, peered ferociously into his face.

Then, for all his drinking, being clear-headed enough to recognize his henchman's countenance, he realized that the fellow might have some immediate business with him, and, relaxing his grip, he asked Maleotti none too affably what he wanted. Thereupon, Maleotti explained that he needed some private speech with his master, and very anxiously and urgently beckoned to him to quit the table and to come apart, the which thing Messer Simone very unwillingly, and volubly cursing, did.

But when he had risen from the table and quitted the circle of the revellers, and stood quite apart from curious ears, if any curious ears there were, his manner changed as he listened to the hurried story that Maleotti had to tell him. The news, as it filtered through his wine-clogged brain, seemed to clarify his senses and quicken his wits. He was, as I guess, no longer the truculent, wine-soaked ruffian, but all of a sudden the man of action, as alert and responsive as if some one had come to tell him that the enemy were thundering at the city's gates. He asked Maleotti, as I understand, if he were very sure of what he said and of what he saw, and when Maleotti persisted in his statement, Messer Simone fell for a while into a musing mood that was no stupor of intoxication. Once or twice he made as if to speak to his fellow, and then paused to think again, and it was not until after some minutes that he finally decided upon his course of action.

I think it would have pleased Messer Simone best if this spying creature of his had waited for Dante when he came from his meeting, and stabbed him as he passed. But he thought, as I believe, that what had not been done by the man might very well be done by the master, and with that, as I conceive, for his most immediate intention, he had Maleotti wait for him in the garden. There in a little while he joined him, and the two went together toward the part of the palace where Beatrice had her dwelling. But when they came to the gateway beneath the loggia where Beatrice had talked with Dante, the lovers had parted, and Dante had gone his ways and Beatrice had returned to her rooms. Then Messer Simone turned to his follower and bade him hasten to Messer Folco, where he sat at his wine, and get his private ear, and tell him that a man was having speech with his daughter on the threshold of her apartments. Messer Simone knew well enough how great an effect such a piece of news would have upon the austere nature of his host, and I make no doubt that his red face grinned in the moonlight as he dispatched his fellow upon his errand. When Maleotti had gone, Messer Simone slowly ascended the staircase that conducted to the loggia, and concealed himself very effectually behind a pillar in a dark corner hard by the door of Beatrice's rooms.

I have stood upon that loggia in later years, and looked out upon Florence when all the colors of summer were gay about the city. I know that the prospect is as fair as man could desire to behold, and I know that there was one exiled heart which ached to be denied that prospect and who died in exile denied it forever. I dare swear that his latest thoughts carried him back to that moon-lit night of July when he made bold to climb the private stair and seek private speech with Madonna Beatrice. I can guess very well how the scene showed that night in the moonbeams--all the city stretched out below, a harlequin's coat of black and silver, according to the disposition of the homes and the open spaces with their lights and shadows. I can fancy how, through the gilded air, came the cheerful sounds of the dancing and the luting and the laughter and the festival, and how all Florence seemed to be, as it were, one wonderful, perfect flower of warmth and color and joy.

It is all very long ago, this time of which I write, and it may very well be that I exaggerate its raptures, as they say--though in this I do not agree--is the way with elders when they recall the sweet, honey-tinted, honey-tasting days of their youth. It would not be possible for any man to overpraise the glories and beauties of Florence in those days. Those glories, as I think, may be said to have come to an end with the Jubilee of His Holiness Pope Boniface the Eighth, the poor pope who was said to be killed by command of the French king, but who, as I have heard tell, escaped from that fate and died a nameless hermit in a forest of Greece.

However that may be, I am glad to think, for all that I am now so chastened, and for all that I have learned patience, that I can recall so clearly that pillared place with the moonbeams dappling the marble, and can rekindle in my withered anatomy something of the noble fire that burned in the heart of Dante, as he stood there in his youth and his hope and his love, and looked into the eyes of his marvellous lady. Also, I am glad to think that I know much of the words that passed between the youth and the maid in that hour, and if not their exact substance, at least their purport. For though Dante never made confidence to me of a matter so sacred as the speech exchanged at such an interview, yet he spoke of it to Messer Guido, whom, after he had entered into terms of friendship with him, he loved and trusted, very rightly, better than me. Also--for that was his way--he set much of that night's discourse into the form of a song which he gave to Messer Guido. Messer Guido, before his melancholy end, over which, as I believe, the Muses still weep, knowing how great a concern I had in the doings of Messer Dante, told me with great clarity the essence of what Dante had told to him, and showed me the poem, not only allowing me to read it, but granting me permission, if it so pleased me, to take a copy. This, indeed, I should have done, but being, as I always have been, a lazy knave, I neglected to do, thinking that any time would serve as well as the present, and being, as I fear, entangled in some pleasant pastime with a light o' love or two that interfered with such serious interests as I owned in life, and of which certainly none should have been more serious than any matter concerning my dear friend and poet. Then, when it was too late for me to amend my error, came Messer Guido's death, and no man knows now what became of those verses.

As for me, I cannot remember them, try I never so hard to cudgel my brains for their meaning and sequence. Sometimes, indeed, at night, in sleep, I seem to see them plain and staring before me on a smooth page of parchment, every word clear, every rhyme legible, the beautiful thoughts set forth in a beautiful hand of write; but when I wake they have all vanished. Sometimes on an evening of late summer, when the winds are blowing softly through the roses and filling the air with odors almost unbearably sweet, it seems to me as if the sweet voices of lovers were chanting those lines, and that I have only to listen heedfully to have them for my own again. But it is all in vain that I try to remember them to any profit. A few phrases buzz in my own brains, but they are no more than phrases, such as I, or any man that was at all nimble in the spinning of words, might use about love and a sweet lady, and there are not enough of them left to build up again the noble structure of so splendid a vision.

Well, as I say, Messer Dante, having quitted the festivity, made his way into the garden, where he lingered a little while. Then it seemed to him that the God of Love appeared to him in the same form as before, only more glorious, and bade him follow, and he went, guided, as it seemed to him, ever by that strange and luminous presence through this path and that path, till he came to the appointed staircase and climbed it, following ever the winged feet of Love. When he came to the top of the stairway he passed through a little door on to the open, moon-drenched loggia, and straightway his first thought was that he beheld the stars, seeing that they seemed to him to shine so very brightly in heaven after the blackness of the darkness through which he had passed. And I think it must be some memory of that night which has made him thrice record with much significant insistence his beholding of the stars.

In the mingled moonlight and starlight of the loggia the figure of the God of Love showed, he said, as clearly to his eyes as when he had ascended the winding stair, albeit differently, for whereas in the darkness the shape of Love had appeared to him luminous and fluttering, as if it had been composed of many living and tinted fires, now in the clear light of that open space it showed more like a bodily presence, not human indeed, but wearing such humanity as it pleased the gods of old time to assume when they condescended to commune with mortals. I remember how he said, in the poem which I spoke of, that he could have counted, had he the leisure, every feather in Love's wings. But the god, or the vision which he took to be a god, gave him no such leisure, for he came to a halt, and he had his arrow in his hand, and with that arrow he pointed before him, and then the image of the God of Love melted into the moonlight and vanished, and the glory of the stars was forgotten, and Dante knew of nothing and cared for nothing but that his lady Beatrice stood there awaiting him.

XVI
THE TALK OF LOVERS

When Dante came to the loggia it was very white in the moonlight, save where the shadows of the marble pillars barred it with bands of black. Amid the moonlight and the shade Beatrice walked, and waited for his coming. When she heard his footsteps she came to a halt in her course, and he, as he advanced, could see the shining of her eyes and the quickened color of her cheeks; and it seemed to him in his rapture that he did not move as mortals do, but that he went on winged feet toward that vision of perfect loveliness. But when he came nigh to her, so near that if he had stretched out his arm he could have touched her with his hand, he stopped, and while he longed with all his soul to speak, the use of words seemed suddenly to be forbidden to him, and his members began to tremble again, as they had trembled before, when he came to an end of reading the poem.

Madonna Beatrice saw the case he was in, and her heart pitied him, and, per-chance, she marvelled that Dante, who carried himself so valiantly and could make songs of such surpassing sweetness, should be so downcast and discomfited in the presence of her eighteen years. However that may be, she addressed him, and the sound of her voice fell very fresh and soft upon his ears, enriching the summer splendor of the night with its music as her beauty enhanced its glory with the glory of her bodily presence. "What have you to say to me," she asked, "that is so urgent that it cannot wait for the day?"

At this question Dante seemed to pluck up some courage--not much, indeed, but still a little; and he made bold to answer her after the manner that is called sym-bolic, and this, or something like this, is what he said:

"Madonna, I may compare myself to a man that is going on a journey very instantly, and since no man that rides out of a gate can say to himself very surely that he will ride in again, I have certain thoughts in my heart that clamor to make themselves known to you, and will not by any means be gainsaid if I can at all compass the way to utter them."

Beatrice smiled at him very kindly in the moonlight, for the youth in his voice appealed very earnestly to the youth in her heart, and it may be to a gaingiving that had also its lodging in her body and warned her of youth's briefness.

While she smiled she spoke. "Many would say that I lacked modesty if they knew that I talked with you thus belated and unknown, but I think that I know you too well, though I know you so little, to have any doubt of your honesty and well-meaning."

At the kindness in her voice and the confidence of her trust Dante carried himself very straight and held his head very high for pride at her words, and he was so strangely happy that he was amazed to find himself even more happy than he had hoped to be in her presence.

With that blissful exaltation upon him, he addressed her again. "Lady, when a traveller takes the road, if he has possessions, and if he be a wise man, he makes him a will, which he leaves in safe hands, and he sets all his poor affairs in order as well as may be. And he leaves this possession to this kinsman, and that gift to that friend, till all that he has is properly allotted, so that his affairs may be straight if evil befall. But I, when I go upon a journey, have no greater estate than my heart to bequeath." He paused for a moment, watching her wistfully, and seeing that her face was changeless in the moonlight, showing no sign either of impatience or of tolerance, he spoke again, in a very low voice, asking her, "Have I your leave to go on with what I am hot to say?"

"You may go on," Beatrice answered him, and her voice seemed calm as she spoke.

But if Dante had known women better--if he had been like me, for instance--he would have known that, for all her show of calm, she was no less agitated than he who stood before her and adored her. But he only saw her divinely aloof and himself most humanly mortal. Yet he took courage from her permission to speak again. "Madonna, ever since that sacred day when you gave me the rose that I carry next my heart, my mind has had no other thought but of you, and my life no other purpose than to be worthy, if only in a little, of your esteem. Yet, for some reason unknown to me, you have of late, in any chance encounter, chosen to withdraw from me the solace of your salutation, and I grieve bitterly that this is so, though I know not why it is so."

"Let that pass," said Beatrice, gently, "and be as if it had not been. I had heard that you kept light company. Young men often do so, and it is no part of my duty to judge them. But you yourself, Messer Dante, invited my judgment, challenged my esteem, told me that for my sake you meant to do great things, prove yourself noble, a man I must admire. When, after all the fine-sounding promises, I found you counted by gossip as the companion of Vittoria, you need not wonder if I was disappointed, and if my disappointment showed itself plainly on my averted face."

"Madonna," Dante began, eagerly, but the girl lifted her hand to check interruption, and Dante held his peace as the girl continued to speak.

"I know now that I was wrong in my reading of your deed; that what you did, you did for a reason that you believed to be both wise and good. Though I do not think that it is ever well for a true man to play an untrue part, yet I know that you acted thus in the thought of serving me. So let it pass, and be as if it had not been."

She was silent, and for a little while Dante was silent too, staring at her beautiful face and clasping his hands tightly together, as one that has much to say and knows not how to say it. Once and again his lips that parted to speak closed again, for if he rejoiced greatly to stand there in her presence and be free to speak his mind unimpeded, yet also he feared greatly lest the words he might utter should prove unworthy of this golden chance given him by Heaven.

But at length his longing conquered his alarm, and he spoke quickly. "Hear me, Beatrice," he pleaded. "My heart is young, and I will never be so vain as to swear that it is untainted by the folly of youth, or free from the pride of youth, or clean of the greed of youth. But now it is swept and garnished, made as a fair shrine for a divine idol, for a woman, for a girl, for an angel--for you!"

Beatrice looked very steadfastly upon the eager face of her lover while she listened to his eager words, and when he paused she began to murmur very softly the opening lines of one of the sonnets that Dante had written in those days of his secrecy:

> "The lady that is angel of my heart,   She knows not of my love and may

not know--"

She stopped and looked at Dante as if she questioned him, and Dante answered her by carrying on the lines:

"Until God's finger gives the sign to show   That I to her the secret may impart."

He paused for a moment, rejoicing to think that she had so far cherished his verses; then he went on, eagerly: "God's finger gives me the sign to-night, and I will speak, lest I die with the message of my soul undelivered. I love you." It seemed to him that she must needs hear the fierce beatings of his heart as he spoke these words.

Beatrice looked at him with a melancholy smile. "Is that the message of your soul?" she asked.

And Dante answered: "That is my soul itself. All my being is uplifted by my love for you. It has made a new heaven and a new earth for me: a new heaven whither you shall guide me, a new earth where I shall walk more bravely, and yet more warily, than of old, fearing nothing, for your sake, save only to be found un-worthy to say, 'I love you.'"

If Dante spoke with a passionate happiness in thus setting free his soul, there was happiness too, in Beatrice's voice as she answered him. "I am, indeed, content to hear you speak, for your words seem, as words seldom seem in this city and in this world, to be quite true words. So when you say you love me, I feel neither agitation, nor flattered vanity, nor amazement--all which feelings, as I have read in books and heard of gossips, are proper to maidens in these hours. Only I know that I believe you, and that I am glad to believe you."

Dante interrupted her, crying her name with passionate eagerness--"Beatrice!" But he kept the place where he stood.

The girl spoke again, finishing her thought. "And I think you will always be worthy to offer love and to win love."

Dante moved a little nearer to her, and he stretched out his hands as one that begs a great gift. "Beatrice," he entreated, "will you give me your love?"

The smile that was partly kind and partly wistful came again to the girl's face. "Messer Dante, Messer Dante," she said, "how can you ask, and how can I answer? A raw youth and a green girl do not make the world between them, nor change the world's laws, nor the laws of this little city, nor the laws of my father in my father's house. And my father's law is like a hand upon my lips, forbidding them to speak, and like a hand upon my heart, forbidding it to beat."

Dante protested very vehemently, in all the zeal and freshness of his youth. "The law of Love is greater than all other laws. The strength of Love is stronger than all strength. The sword of Love is stronger than the archangel's sword, and conquers all enemies."

Beatrice shook her head at her lover's fury, and her eyes shone very brightly in the moonlight. "Oh, Dante! Dante!" she said, softly, "if this were indeed so, the world would be an easier world for lovers. If you were to tell my father what you have told me, or if I were to tell my father what I have told you, he would twit us for a pair of silly children, and take good heed that we were kept apart. If you were to ask my father for me, he would deny you, and laugh while he denied; for my father is a proud man, and one that loves wealth and power very greatly, and will not give his child save where wealth and power abide. If he were to come upon us here, now, where we talk alone in the moonlight, he would raise his hand to slay you, and he has not a neighbor nor a friend but would say he did right. You know all this, even as I know it. Why, then, do you ask me to give what I cannot give?"

She was very calm and sad as she spoke, and the truth that was in her mournful words was not to be denied by Dante. But all the ardors of his being were spurred by his consciousness that he had made known his love for her, and that she, surely, had scarcely done less than confess her love for him, and while such sweet happenings hallowed the world, it did not seem to the poet possible that any mortal power could come between them. And in this confidence he addressed his beloved again, all on fire.

"Dear woman," he urged, "not all the fathers in Florence can bind our spirits. I love you now, I shall love you while I live--in hunger and thirst, in feasting and singing, in the church and in the street, in sorrow and in joy, in cross or success. My life and every great and little thing within my life is sanctified to a sacrament by my love for you. Cannot your spirit, that is as free as mine, uplift my heart with a word?"

So he petitioned her, ardently, and his warmth found favor in the girl's grave, watchful eyes.

"I have heard you praised highly of late," she said, "and men give you great promise. But, truly, I judge you with the sight of my own eyes, not with the sound of others' words. And I think you are indeed a man that a woman might be happy to love."

Dante's heart leaped to hear such sweet speech, and for very joy he was silent awhile. Then he said: "If I be indeed anything worth weighing in the scales of your favor, it is for your sake that I have made myself so, Madonna."

Beatrice laughed a little, very gently, at his words, and pretended to frown, and failed. "My cold reason," she asserted, "tells me that I would rather you bettered yourself just for the sake of being better, and with no less unselfish intention; but, to be honest, my warm heart throbs at your homage."

Dante would have come closer, but she stayed him with a gesture. "You make me very proud," he murmured.

Beatrice went on. "Yet I know well that men have done greatly to please women that were not worth the pleasing, or merely for the lure of some grace of hand or lip. I should like to think that my lover would always live at his best for my sake, though he never won a kiss of me."

"Then here I swear it," Dante said, proudly, "to dedicate my life to your service, and to make all honorable proof of my devotion. But you, beloved, will you not give me some words of hope?"

Beatrice extended her hands to him, and he caught those dear hands in his, and held them tightly, and Beatrice was smiling as she spoke, although there were tears in her eyes. "So far," she said, "as a woman can promise the life that is guided by another's law, I give you my life, Dante. But my love is my own, to hold or to yield, and I give it all to you with all my heart, knowing that because you think it worth the winning, you will be worthy of what you have won."

Now, as I think, here my Dante made to take his lady in his arms, but she denied him, very delicately and gently, pleading with such sweet reason that the most ardent lover in the world could not refuse her obedience. For she would have it thus, that until their love could be avowed, as in time it might be, if Dante won to fame and honor in the state, until their love could be avowed there should be no lover's commerce between them, not even to the changing of a kiss. For she would not have him nor her act otherwise than in perfect honorability as befitted their great love. Because Dante did, indeed, cherish a great love for her, that was greater than all temptings of the flesh, he let it be as she wished. So this pair, that were almost as the angels in the greatness of their love, pledged their troths with the simplicity of children, and parted with the innocence of children, as gentle and as chaste.

XVII
A STRANGE BETROTHAL

What happened now happened after I had left the festival, but I heard all the facts later from eye-witnesses, so that I honestly think I can make it as plain a tale as if I had seen the things myself. Messer Maleotti, doing as he was told and rejoicing in the thought that he was making mischief, came into the feasting-hall where Messer Folco sat apart with certain old friends and kinsfolk of his, sober gentlefolk of age and repute, that made merry in their grave way and laughed cheerfully over the jests of yesteryear, and one of them was Master Tommaso Severo, that was Madonna Beatrice's physician. Now Maleotti, catching sight of a certain ancient servant of Messer Folco's, whom he knew well to be an honest man and one much trusted by his master, made for him and drew him a little apart, and whispered into his ear that very amazing message with which Messer Simone had intrusted him.

This message, bluntly and baldly stated, came to this: that Maleotti, taking his ease in the garden and wandering this way and that, came at last by chance beneath the walls of that part of the palace where Madonna Beatrice dwelt. There, on the loggia, very plain in the moonlight, he saw Madonna Beatrice in discourse with a man. Though the moonlight was bright and showed the face of Madonna Beatrice very distinctly, the man stood at an angle, as it were, and he could make nothing of him, face or figure. Such was the story which Maleotti, primed thereto by Simone, had to tell. At first the man to whom he told it seemed incredulous, as well he might be, albeit it chanced the tale was true, and then he became doubtful--for, after all, youth is youth and love love--and finally, upon Maleotti's insistence, he did indeed consent to go toward his master, and, plucking him by the sleeve, solicit the favor of a private word with him. Messer Folco, who was always very affable in his bearing to those that served him, and who had a special affection for this fellow, rose very good-humoredly from the table and the converse and the wine, and going a little ways apart, listened to what his old servant, who seemed so agitated and aghast, had to tell him.

When Messer Folco heard what it was that his man had to say, Messer Folco frowned sternly, and expressed a disbelief so emphatic and so angry that there was nothing for the poor servitor to do but to call Maleotti himself, who, with great seeming reluctance and with many protestations of regret, that must have made him seem like a particularly mischievous monkey apologizing for stealing nuts, repeated, with a cunning lack of embellishment, the plain statement that he had made to the retainer. Thereupon, Messer Folco, in a great rage which it took all his boasted philosophy to keep under control, called to him two or three of his old cronies that were still lingering about the deserted tables. These folk were, indeed, also his kinsfolk, and it was from one of them that I had the particulars which I am about to set forth with almost as much certainty as if I had seen them myself.

Making hurried excuses to those few that remained at the table, Messer Folco and his friends quitted the room upon their errand of folly. And Maleotti, having done his devil's work, departed upon other business of his master's, that was no less damnable in its nature and no less threatening to Simone's enemies.

Messer Folco and his friends hurried swiftly and in silence through the still, moon-lit gardens till they came to the gateway that Dante had opened and the little staircase whereby Dante had ascended. Passing through this gateway and mounting those steps, Messer Folco and his friends came to the loggia and stood there for a moment in silence. Had they been less busy upon a bad and unhappy errand, they must needs have been enchanted by the beauty of all that lay before and around them in that place and on that night of summer.

The air was very hot upon the loggia, and the night was very still. All over the field of the sky the star-candles were burning brightly, and it scarcely needed the torches that certain of Messer Folco's companions carried to see what was to be seen. Those of Messer Folco's kinsfolk that stood huddled together about the entrance of the loggia, curious and confused at the suddenness of the unlovely business, could see that their leader looked very pale and grave as he crossed the pavement and struck sharply with his clinched hand at the door which faced him. In a little while the door opened, and one of Madonna Beatrice's ladies peeped out her head, and gave a little squeal of surprise at the sight of her lord and the rest of the company, the unexpected presence, and the unexpected torches. But Messer Folco bade her very sternly be still, and when Messer Folco commanded sternly he was generally obeyed. Then he ordered her that she should summon her mistress at once to come to him there, where he waited for her. When the sorely frightened girl had gone, there was silence for a little while on the loggia, while the perplexed friends stared at each other's blanched faces, until presently the little door opened again and Monna Beatrice came forth from it, and saluted her father very sweetly and gravely, as if nothing were out of the ordinary, though some thought, and Messer Tommaso Severo knew, that there was a troubled look in her usually serene eyes.

Messer Folco addressed her calmly, with the calmness of one that, being consciously a philosopher, seeks to restrain all needless, unreasonable rages, and he said, slowly: "Madonna, I have been told very presently by one that pretends to have seen what he tells, that you talked here but now with a man alone. The thing, of course, is not true?"

The question which went with the utterance of his last words was given in a very confident voice, and he carried, whether by dissimulation or no, a very confident countenance.

The look of confidence faded from his face as Madonna Beatrice answered him very simply. "The thing is true," she said, and then said no more, as if there were no more to say, but stood quietly where she was, looking steadily at her father and paying no heed to any other of those that were present.

The voice of Folco was as stern as before, though harder in its tone as he again addressed his daughter. "The thing is true, then? I am grieved to hear it. Who was the man?"

Madonna Beatrice looked at him very directly. She seemed to be neither at all abashed nor at all defiant, as she answered, tranquilly, "I cannot tell you, father."

For a little while that seemed a great while a dreary quiet reigned over that moon-bathed loggia. Father and daughter faced each other with fixed gaze, and the others, very ill at ease, watching the pair, wished themselves elsewhere with all their hearts.

While those that assisted reluctantly at this meeting wondered what would happen next, seeing those two high, simple, and noble spirits suddenly brought into such strange antagonism--before they, I say, could formulate any solution of the problem, a man stepped out of the shadow of the doorway and advanced toward Folco boldly, and the astonished spectators saw that the man was none other than Messer Simone dei Bardi. However he may have revelled at the now ended festival, there were no signs of wine or riot about him now. He stood squarely and steadily enough, and his red face was no redder than its wont. Only a kind of ferocious irony showed on it as he loomed there, largely visible in the yellow air.

"What is all this fuss about?" he asked, with a fierce geniality. "I am the man you seek after, and why should I not be? Though why you should seek for me I fail to see. May not a man speak awhile in private to the lady of his honorable love, and yet no harm done to bring folk about our ears with torches and talk and staring faces?"

As he spoke those present saw how Madonna Beatrice looked at him, and they read in her face a proud disdain and a no less proud despair, and they knew that somehow or other, though of course they could not guess how, this fair and gracious lady was caught in a trap. They saw how she longed to speak yet did not speak, and they knew thereby there was some reason for her keeping silence. Messer Folco looked long at Messer Simone dei Bardi as he stood there clearly visible in the mingled lights--large, almost monstrous, truculent, ugly, the embodiment of savage strength and barbaric appetites. Then Folco looked from Simone's bulk to his daughter, who stood there as cold and white and quiet as if she had been a stone image and not a breathing maid.

Folco advanced toward Beatrice and took her by the hand and drew her apart a little ways, and it so chanced that the place where they came to a pause was within ear-shot of one of those that Messer Folco had brought with him, one who stood apart in the darkness and looked and listened, and this one was Tommaso Severo, the physician. Messer Simone kept his stand with his arms folded and a smile of triumph on his face, and I have it on good authority--that, namely, of Messer Tommaso Severo--that at least one of the spectators wished, as he beheld Simone, that he had been suddenly blessed by Heaven with the strength of a giant, that he might have picked the Bardi up by the middle and pitched him over the parapet into the street below. But as Heaven vouchsafed this spectator no such grace, Severo kept his place and his peace, and he heard what Messer Folco said to his daughter Beatrice.

And what he said to her and what she answered to him was very brief and direct.

Messer Folco asked his daughter, "Was this the man you talked with but now?"

And Beatrice, looking neither at her father nor at any other one there present, but looking straight before her over the gilded greenness of the garden, answered, quietly, "No."

Then Folco questioned her again. "Will you tell me who the man was that you talked with here?"

And again Beatrice, as tranquil, resolute to shield her lover from danger, with the same fixed gaze over the green spaces below her, answered as before the same answer, "No."

Then there came a breathing-space of quiet; Messer Folco looked hard at his daughter; and she, for her part, looking, as before, away from him, because, as I guess, she judged that there would be something irreverent in outfacing her father while she denied his wishes and defied so strangely his parental authority. Messer Simone stood at his ease a little apart with the mocking smile of conquest on his face, and the guests, kinsfolk, and friends, that were witnesses of the sad business, huddled together uncomfortably.

Then Messer Folco, seeing that nothing more was to be got from the girl, turned round and addressed himself to those of his kin that stood by the entrance to the loggia. "Friends," he said, and his voice was measured, and his words came slow and clear--"kinsmen and friends, I have a piece of news for you. I announce here and now the betrothal of my daughter Beatrice to Messer Simone dei Bardi, and I bid you all to the wedding to-morrow in the church of the Holy Name."

Then, in the silence that greeted this statement, Messer Folco held out his right hand to Simone and took his right hand, and he drew Simone toward him and then toward Beatrice, and he lifted the right hand of Beatrice, that lay limply against her side, and made to place its whiteness on the brown palm of Messer Simone. Messer Simone's face was flushed with triumph and Monna Beatrice's face was drawn with pain, and those that witnessed and wondered thought a great wrong had been wrought, and wondered why. But before Messer Folco could join the two hands together Beatrice suddenly plucked her hand away from her father's clasp.

"No! no! no!" she cried, in a loud voice, and then again cried "No!" And even as she did so she reeled backward in a swoon, and would have fallen upon the marble pavement if Messer Severo, that was watching her, had not sprung timely forward and caught her in his arms.

XVIII
A WORD FOR MESSER SIMONE

I must, in the fulness of my heart, agree with those that speak in favor of Messer Simone dei Bardi. It is the native, intimate, and commendable wish of a man to abolish his enemies--I speak here after the fashion of the worldling that I was, for the cell and the cloister have no concern with mortal passions and frailties--and Messer Simone was in this, as in divers other qualities, of a very manly disposition. He thought in all honesty that it would be very good for him to be the ruler of Florence, yet, also, and no less, that it would be very good for Florence to be ruled by him. This is the way of such great personages, as indeed it is the way of meaner creatures: to persuade themselves very pleasantly that what they desire for themselves they are justified in desiring on account of the benefit their accomplished wishes must bear to others.

Messer Simone, having the idea once lodged in his skull--a dwelling-place of unusual thickness, that was well made for keeping any idea that ever entered it a prisoner--that it would be well for him to take charge of Florence, had no room in his pate for tender or merciful consideration of those that sought or seemed to seek to cross him in his purpose. They were his enemies; there was no more to be said about it, and for his enemies, when it was possible, he had ever a short way. Now, Messer Guido Cavalcanti, and those of his inclining, were very curiously and truly his enemies, and he had been longing for a great while to get them out of the way of his ambitions and his purposes, yet could find no ready means to compass their destruction. But of late he had found a new enemy in the person of my friend Dante, and a formidable enemy for all his seeming insignificance; and if Simone sought to crush Dante, I cannot blame him for the attempt, however much I may rejoice in his failure.

I believe Messer Simone to have been as much in love with Monna Beatrice as it was humanly possible for such a man to be in love with such a maid. He was in love, of course, with the great houses that Messer Folco owned, with the broad lands that fattened Messer Folco's vineyards; for though he had houses of his own and broad lands in abundance, wealth ever covets wealth. But I conceive that whatever of god-like essence was muffled in the hulk of his composition was quickened by the truly unearthly beauty of that pale face with its mystic smile and the sweet eyes that seemed to see sights denied to the commonalty. I think Messer Simone was in love with Beatrice very much as I might have been, out of very wonder at a thing so rare and fair and unfamiliar. I was never, as I have said, in love with Folco's daughter; my tastes are simpler, more carnal; give me an Ippolita in my affectionate hours, and I ask nothing better. Love for me must be a jolly companion, never squeamish, never chilly, never expecting other homage than such salutations as swordsmen may use for preliminary to a hot engagement. Messer Dante has written a very beautiful book on his business, its words all fire and golden air, but I wrote my rhymes in a tavern with red wine at my elbow and a doxy on my knee. I wonder which of us will be remembered longest.

Yet if I was never in love with Beatrice, I could understand the matter, and feel how the thick-headed, thick-hearted, thick-fingered giant must shiver at the unfamiliar twinges and rigors. When a man of such a kind finds himself in such a dilemma, he is in much such a case as if he were sick of some childish ailment more dangerous to maturity than to youth. The thought that another should challenge his right or traverse his desire galled him to a choler little short of madness. Wherefore, if he had hated the Cavalcanti faction before, he hated them a thousand times more now, seeing that Dante was of their number, this Dante that had gained a rose of lady Beatrice, and wore it next his heart no doubt, and had denied him and defied him with such cheer and cunning, and dared to make verses in praise of his lady. If Simone had wished ere this that the Cavalcanti party was ruined, now he was resolved upon its ruin, and for no reason more strongly than because it included Dante in its company. In this resolve, I say again, I cannot honestly blame Messer Simone. He only acted as most of us would have acted if we had been in his place.

Messer Simone, I must cheerfully admit, had calculated his plans cleverly enough. Long before his magnificent appearance at Messer Folco's house he had been at the pains to make himself aware that the bulk of the youth of the city were with him hand and heart in his desperate adventure. To do the youth of Florence the merest justice, it was every ready to risk its life cheerfully for the advantage of the city, and, furthermore, for the sheer lust of fighting. What Messer Simone had hoped to gain at Folco's house, and, indeed, had succeeded in gaining, was the allegiance of certain young men of the Cavalcanti inclining, adherents of the Reds, that were not in the natural way of things affected over kindly to him. All this he had accomplished very successfully. The heady enthusiasm upon which he had cunningly counted, the presence of fair women whose sweet breaths are ever ready to fan the flame of the war-like spirit, the stimulating influences of wine and light and laughter and dancing--all these had played their parts in furthering Messer Simone's aims by spurring the Florentine chivalry to a pitch of exuberance, at which any proposal made in a sounding voice in the name of the God of War might be relied upon to carry them away. As you know, it did so carry them away, and Messer Simone's book was scrawled thick with hurried signatures, and, best of all for his pleasure, it carried at last the name of Messer Dante, and best of all, perhaps, for his personal advantage, it carried the name of Messer Guido Cavalcanti.

I know very well, looking back on those old days, that were so much better than these new days, that if Messer Simone had failed to lure Messer Dante into that immediate scheme of his, and had so compelled a postponement of his revenge, he would still have carried out his purpose of sending the others that were his enemies to their deaths. But, in his piggish way, Messer Simone had a kind of knowledge of men. He that was all ungenerous and bestial--he, this most unknightly giant--he could realize, strangely enough, what a generous and uplifted nature might do on certain occasions when the trumpets of the spirit were loudly blowing. And it was a proof of his mean insight that he had spread his net in the sight of the bird and had snared his quarry.

Having won so briskly the first move in his game, Messer Simone lost no time in making the second move. Fortified, as he was, by the friendship and the approval of certain of the leaders of the city, he could confidently count upon immunity from blame if any seeming blunder of his delivered to destruction a certain number of young gentlemen whose opinions were none too popular with many of those in high office. So, while still the flambeaux of the festival were burning, and while still a few late guests were carousing at Messer Folco's tables, the emissaries of Messer Simone were busy in Florence doing what they had to do. Thus it was that so many of the fiery-hearted, fiery-headed youths who had set their names in Messer Simone's Golden Book found, as they returned gay and belated from Messer Folco's house, the summons awaiting them--the summons that was not to be disobeyed, calling upon them at once to prove their allegiance to the Company of Death and obey its initial command. It is well to recollect that not one single man of all the men so summoned failed to answer to his name.

It is in that regard, too, that I can scarcely do less than extend my admiration to Messer Simone. For, in spite of the fact that he was a very great villain, as he needs must be counted, being the enemy of our party, he had in him so much as it were of the sovereign essence of manhood that he could read aright men's tempers. And he knew very well that such words as "patriotism" and "service of the sweet city" and "honorable death for a great cause" are as so many flames that will set the torch of a young man's heart alight. There was no generosity in Messer Simone, yet--and this I think is the marvel--he could guess at and count upon the generosity of others, and know that they would be ready to do in an instant what he would never do nor never dream of doing. He was not impulsive, he was not high-spirited, he was not chivalrous; yet he could play upon the impulses, the high spirits, and the chivalries of those whom he wished to destroy as dexterously as your trained musician can play upon the strings of a lute. Of course it is impossible not to admire such a cunning, however perverted the application of that cunning may be. For there is many a rascal in the broad world that has no wit to appreciate anything outside the compass of his own inclinations, and takes it for granted that because he is a rogue with base instincts, that can only be appealed to by base lures, all other men are rogues likewise, and only basely answerable to some base appeal.

Nor can I do otherwise than admire him for the ingenuity of the means by which he sought to attain his end. It was in its way a masterpiece of imagination, for one that throve upon banking, to conceive that scheme of the Company of Death, with its trumpet-call to youth and courage and the noble heart. It was excellently clever, too, of Messer Simone so to engineer his contrivance that while he seemingly included in its ranks the young bloods of every party in the state, he was able, by the wise adjustment of his machinery, to deal, or at least to intend, disaster only to those that were opposed to him. Caesar might well have been praised for so intelligent an artifice, and yet Messer Simone of the Bardi, for all that he was brave enough, was very far from being a Caesar. However, he planned his plan well, and I praise him for it all the more light-heartedly because it came to grief so signally, and all through one whose enmity he rated at too light a price.

It is ever the way of such fellows as Simone, that are of the suspicious temperament and quick to regard folk as their enemies, to overlook, in their computation of the perils that threaten their cherished purposes, the gravest danger of all. Simone had plenty of enemies in Florence, and he thought that he had provided against all of them, or, at the least, all that were seriously to be reputed troublesome, when he swaddled and dandled and matured his precious invention of the Company of Death. But while he grinned as he read over the list of the recruits to that delectable regiment, and hugged himself at the thought of how he would in a morning's work thoroughly purge it of all that were his antagonists, he suffered his wits to go wool-gathering in one instance where they should have been most alert. Either he clean forgot or he disdained to remember a certain wager of his, and a certain very fair and very cunning lady with whom he had laid it, and to whose very immediate interest it was that she should win the wager. Messer Simone seemed either to think that Madonna Vittoria was not in earnest, or that she might be neglected with safety. Whichever his surmise, Messer Simone made a very great mistake.

It proved to be one of the greatest factors in the sum of Messer Simone's blunder that he should have been tempted by ironic fortune to turn for aid in the ingenious plot he was hatching to the particular man upon whom he pitched for assistance. Already in those days of which I write, far-away days as they seem to me now in this green old age--or shall I, with an eye to my monkish habit, call it gray old age?--of mine, those gentry existed who have now become so common in Italy, the gentry that were called Free Companions. These worthy personages were adventurers, seekers after fortune, men eager for wealth and power, and heedless of the means by which they attained them. Italian, some of them, but very many strangers from far-away lands. It was the custom of these fellows to gather about them a little army of rough-and-ready resolutes like themselves, whom they maintained at their cost, and whose services they were always prepared to sell to any person or state that was willing to pay the captain's price for their aid. And these captains, as their fortunes waxed, increased the numbers of their following till they often had under their command as many lances as would go to the making of a little army. Of these captains that were then in Italy, and, as I have said, they were fewer in that time than they are to-day, the most famous and the most fortunate was the man who was known as Messer Griffo of the Claw. He was so nicknamed, I think, because of the figure on the banner that he flew--a huge dragon with one fiercely clawed foot lifted as if to lay hold of all that came its way.

Messer Griffo was a splendid fellow to look at, as big every way as Messer Simone, but built more shapely, and he had a finer face, and one that showed more self-control, and he was never given to the beastly intemperances that degraded the Messer Simone. Messer Griffo and his levy of lances lived in a castle that he held in the hills some half-way between Florence and Arezzo. He was, as I believe, by his birth an Englishman, with some harsh, unmusical, outlandish name of his own that had been softened and sweetened into the name by which he was known and esteemed in all the cities of Italy. He had been so long a-soldiering in our country that he spoke the vulgar tongue very neatly and swiftly, and was, indeed, ofttimes taken by the people of one town or province in our peninsula for a citizen of some other city or province of Italy. So that his English accent did him no more harm in honest men's ears than his English parentage offended their susceptibilities. For the rest, he was of more than middle age, but seemed less, was of amazing strength and daring, and a great leader of Free Companions.

At the time of which I tell he was in command of a force of something like five hundred lances, that were very well fed, well kept, well equipped, and ready to serve the quarrel of any potentate of Italy that was willing to pay for them. He had just captained his rascals very gallantly and satisfactorily in the service of Padua, and having made a very considerable amount of money by the transaction, was now resting pleasantly on his laurels, and in no immediate hurry to further business. For if Messer Griffo liked fighting, as is said to be the way of those islanders, he did not like fighting only, but recognized frankly and fully that life has other joys to offer to a valiant gentleman. His long sojourn in our land had so civilized and humanized him that he could appreciate, after a fashion, the delicate pleasures that are known to us and that are denied to those that abide in his frozen, fog-bound, rain-whipped island--the delights of fine eating, fine drinking, fine living, fine loving. Honestly,

I must record that he took to all these delectations very gayly and naturally, for all the world as if he had the grace to be born, I will not say a Florentine, but say a man of Padua, of Bologna, or Ferrara. In a word, he had all the semblance of a very fine gentleman, and when he was not about his proper business of cutting throats at so much a day, he moved at his ease with a very proper demeanor.

When Messer Simone began to hatch his little conspiracy of the Company of Death, he bethought him of Messer Griffo, that was then at liberty and living at ease, and he sent to the Free Companion a message, entreating him to visit Florence and be his guest for a season, as he had certain matters of moment to communicate to him. Now if this Griffo liked idling very well, he did not like it to the degree that would permit him to push on one side a promising piece of business. This is, I believe, the way of his country-people, that are said to be traders before all, though thereafter they are sailors and soldiers. When the message of Messer Simone reached him, he appreciated very instantly the value of Messer Simone's acquaintance, and the probability of good pay and good pickings if he found reason to enter the Bardi's service. So with no more unwillingness than was reasonable, considering that he was passing the time very happily in his house with pretty women and jolly pot-companions, he made answer to the message that he would wait upon Messer Simone very shortly in the fair city of Florence. In no very long time after he kept his word, and came to Florence to have speech with Messer Simone and drink his wine and consider what propositions he might have to make.

It was, perhaps, unfortunate for Simone dei Bardi that while there were many points of resemblance between himself and the Free Companion that was his guest, the advantages were on the side of the stranger rather than of the Florentine. Both were big men, both were strong men, both were practised to the top in all manner of manly exercises. But while there was a something gross about the greatness of Simone of the Bardi, the bulk of the Englishman was so well proportioned and rarely adjusted that a woman's first thought of him would be rather concerning his grace than his size. While Messer Simone's face betrayed too plainly in its ruddiness its owner's gratification of his appetites, Messer Griffo's face carried a clean paleness that commended him to temperate eyes, albeit he could, when he pleased, eat and drink as much as ever Messer Simone.

Messer Simone's plan had one great merit to the mind of a foreigner denied the lucidity of our Italian intelligence--it was adorably simple. I can give it to you now in a nutshell as I learned it later, not as I knew it then, for I did not know it then. Nobody knew it then except Messer Simone of the one part, and Messer Griffo of the other part, and one other who was not meant to know it or supposed to know it, but who, in defence of special interests, first guessed at it, and then made certain of it, with results that were far from satisfactory to Messer Simone, though they proved in the end entirely pleasing to Messer Griffo.

Here and now, in few words, was Messer Simone's plan. Messer Griffo was to enter his, Simone's, service at what rate of pay he might, weighed in the scale of fairness and with a proper calculation of market values, demand. At least Messer Simone was not inclined to haggle, and the five hundred lances would find him a good paymaster. In return for so many stipulated florins, Messer Griffo was to render certain services to Messer Simone--obvious services, and services that were less obvious, but that were infinitely more important.

In the first place, the Free Companion was ostensibly to declare himself Messer Simone's very good and zealous subaltern in the interests of the city of Florence, and very especially in those interests which led her to detest and honestly long to destroy the city of Arezzo. For this proclaimed purpose he was to hold himself and his men in readiness to march, when the time came, against Arezzo. This was the first page of the treaty. But there was a second page of the treaty that, if it were really written out, would have to be written in cipher. By its conditions Messer Griffo bound himself to wait with his fellows on a certain appointed night at a certain appointed place some half-way between Florence and Arezzo. What his business was to be at this appointed time and place makes pretty reading even now, when almost all that were concerned in the conspiracy have passed away and are no more than moth-like memories.

When Messer Simone dei Bardi contrived to chain upon the Company of Death that law which bound every member of the fellowship to unquestioning obedience to its founder, he had in his mind from the start the goal for which he was playing. At a certain given hour a certain given number of the Company of Death would be called upon to foregather outside the walls of Florence, bent on a special adventure for the welfare of the state. By a curious chance those that were thus summoned were all to be members of the party that was opposed to Messer Simone, and would include all those youths who, like Guido Cavalcanti and Dante Alighieri, had incurred the special detestation of the would-be dictator.

The rest of the scheme was as easy as whistling. The hot-headed, hot-hearted gallants of the Company of Death were to ride swiftly in the direction of Arezzo, carrying with them the information that they would be reinforced half-way upon their journey by a levy of mercenaries under the command of Griffo. It was, however, privately arranged between Simone and Griffo that when the young Florentines made their appearance they were to be very promptly and decisively put to the sword, after which deed Messer Griffo and his followers were to betake themselves to Arezzo, declare themselves the saviors of that city, and insist on entering its service at a price. After a little while Messer Griffo was to make his peace with indignant Florence by offering to betray, and, in due course, by betraying, the town of Arezzo into the hands of her enemies. By such ingenious spider-spinnings of sin did Messer Simone of the Bardi promise himself that he would within a very little space of time cleanse Florence of the pick of his enemies, and also earn the gratitude of her citizens by placing Arezzo within their power. This was a case of killing two birds with one stone that mightily delighted Messer Simone, and he made sure that he had found the very stone that was fit for his fingers in the excellent, belligerent Free Companion.

It is whimsical to reflect that all would probably, nay, almost certainly, have gone as Messer Simone desired if only Messer Simone had not been so bullishly besotted as to leave the name of a certain lady out of his table of calculations; for Messer Griffo liked the scheme well enough. Though it was, as it were, a double-edged weapon, cutting this way at the Florentines of one party and that way at Arezzo, it was a simple scheme enough that required no feigning to sustain it, no dissimulation--qualities these apparently repugnant to the English heart. Griffo also liked the florins of Messer Simone that were to be spent so plenteously into his exchequer, and he liked exceedingly the prospect of the later plunder of Arezzo. That he did not like Messer Simone very much counted for little in the business. It was no part of his practice to like or dislike his employers, so long as they paid him his meed. Still, perhaps the fact that if Simone had not been his employer he would have disliked him may have counted as an influence to direct the course of later events.

Certainly Messer Griffo had no compunctions, no prickings of the conscience, to perturb or to deflect the energy of his keen intelligence from following the line marked out for it. That he was to dispatch without quarter the flower of the youth of Florence troubled him, as I take it, no whit. He was too imperturbable, too phlegmatic for that. Had he been of our race he might, perhaps, have sighed over their fate, for we that are of the race of Rome have some droppings of the old Roman pity as ingredients in our composition. Messer Griffo was no such fantastico, but a plain, straightforward, journeyman sword-bearer that would kill any mortal or mortals whom he was paid to kill, unless--and here is the key to his character and the explanation of all that happened after--unless he was paid a better price by some one else not to kill his intended victims. In this particular business he was, maugre Messer Simone's beard, paid a better price not to do what Simone paid a less price to have done. What that price was you shall learn in due course.

XIX
THE RIDE IN THE NIGHT

Through all the quiet of that divine night the minions of the Messer Simone had slipped hither and thither through the moon-lit streets of Florence, bearing the orders of the captain of the Company of Death to certain of his loyal lieutenants and faithful federates. And the order that each man received was to report himself ready for active service and properly armed at the gate of the city which gave upon the highroad that led in the fulness of time to Arezzo. It was a curious fact, though of course it was not realized until later, that no one of these summonses was delivered to any man other than a man known to be a member of the Red party, and, therefore, by the same token, one that was an opponent of Messer Simone dei Bardi and his friends of the Yellow League. The call to each man told him that at the tryst he would find a horse ready to carry him to his destination.

Each man that received that summons had but a little while before been feasting blithely at the house of Messer Folco. Each man hastened to obey his summons without a sinister thought, without a fear. Each man hastily armed himself, hurriedly flung his cloak about him, and sped swiftly from his abode or lodging across the night-quiet streets to the appointed meeting-place. Each man, on arrival at the indicated gate, found the warders awake and ready for him, ready on his production of his summons to pass him through the great unbolted doors into the liberty of the open country. The later arrivals found those that had answered earlier to the call waiting for them in the gray vagueness between night and dawn, each man standing by a horse's head, while a number of other horses in the care of a company of varlets waited, whinnying and shivering in the shadow of the walls, to be chosen from by the new-comers. Every man that crossed the threshold of the gateway that night found Maleotti waiting for him on the other hand with a smile of welcome on his crafty face, and whispered instructions on his evil lips.

Those instructions were simple enough. The little company of gallant gentlemen, citizens, for the most part, in the flower of their youth, and certainly the very flower of the Red party, was to fall under the temporary command of Messer Guido Cavalcanti. Messer Guido was to conduct the party, which numbered in all some two hundred souls, to a designated place, a thickly wooded spot some half-way between Arezzo and Florence. Here the adventurers were to find waiting for them a company of Free Companions, some six hundred lances, under the command of the very illustrious *condottiere*, Messer Griffo of the Claw, to whom, at the point of conjunction, Messer Guido was instantly to surrender his temporary leadership of the dedicated fellowship. After that it was for Messer Griffo to decide the order of the enterprise and the form in which the attack upon Arezzo was to be made. These were very plain and simple instructions, very simple to follow, very simple to understand, very easy to obey. No man of all the some two hundred men to whom they were confided by Maleotti, or one of Maleotti's comrades, required to be told them a second time or felt the need to ask a single explanatory question.

It was true enough, as Messer Simone had said, that the rogue Ghibellines of Arezzo had a mind to deal Florence an ugly stroke, if ever they could, and that the hope of the Aretines was to trap the Florentines in a snare. As you know, Messer Simone had hatched a double-edged plot, though we young hot-heads of the Company of Death knew of but one-half of its purpose. He had caused information to be sent to Arezzo that there was a traitor within their walls who was prepared on a certain night to let in a certain number of Florentines, who thus would seize and hold one of the gates until reinforcements came from Florence to secure the weakened city. He schemed all this with the aid of a Guelph that dwelt in Arezzo as a red-hot Ghibelline. Now, it would have been simple enough for him after this to send the little handful of Florentines against a warned Arezzo and have them cut to pieces by an Aretine ambuscade. But his purpose went further than merely demolishing a number of his enemies. He wanted to win Arezzo, if he could, as well. So, by his machinations, he arranged that the forces of Arezzo should be out to meet and overthrow the adventurous Florentines, whereafter they might march on Florence and take the city unawares. But, to counteract this, he made his arrangements with Messer Griffo, who was, in one and the same job, to massacre the Florentines of the Red and give battle to the Aretines unaware of his presence, and so, at a stroke, rid Simone of his enemies, and cover him with patriotic glory.

It will be seen by this that Messer Simone, if treacherous to his enemies within the city, was in nowise treacherous to the city herself. But we were ignorant of his wiles that night, as we gathered together outside the gates.

In an amazingly short space of time we were all a-horseback, and riding quietly through the night on the road toward Arezzo, with Messer Maleotti, on a high-mettled mount, shepherding us as we rode, as if we were so many simple sheep and he our pastor. I, that had come late to the meeting-place, had sought for and found Messer Dante, after a little seeking hither and thither through the press of eager, generous youths that were bestirring themselves to strike a good stroke for Florence that night. I found him standing quietly alone, with his hand resting in a kindly command upon the neck of the steed that he had chosen, and a look of great happiness softening the native sternness of his regard. I stood by him in silence till we rode, for after our first salutation he chose to be taciturn, and that in no un-friendly seeming, but as one might that had great thoughts to think and counted very certainly upon the acquiescence of a friend. And I was ever a man to respect the humors, grave or merry, of my friends.

So I stood by him and held my peace until the muster-roll of our fellowship was completed, and it seemed good to Maleotti that the signal should be given for our departure upon our business. But while I waited I looked hither and thither through the moon-lit gloom to discern this face and that of familiar youth, and as I noted them and named them to myself, I was dimly conscious of a thought that would not take shape in words, and yet a thought that, all unwittingly, troubled me. I seemed like a child that tries, and tries in vain, to recall some duty that was set upon it, and that has wickedly slipped its memory. Man after man of the figures that moved about me in the darkness was well known to me. Those faces, those figures, were the faces and figures of intimates whose pleasures I shared daily, companions with whom I had grown up, playfellows in the days when we gambolled in the streets, playfellows now in the pleasant fields of love and revelry. What could there be, I asked myself, almost unconscious that I did so question--what could there be in the presence of so many well-known, so many well-liked, so many well-trusted gentlemen, to make me feel so inexplicably ill at ease? Where can a man stand better, I seemed to ask myself, than in the centre of a throng of men that are all his friends? Thus I puzzled and fumed in the silent minutes ere we started, struggling with my unaccountable misgivings, not realizing that it was the very fact that all about me were my friends which was the cause of my most natural disquiet. It was not until we were all in the saddle and well upon our way to Arezzo, that with a sudden clearness my muffled thought asserted itself, and I must needs make it known at once to Dante, at whose side I rode.

"Friend of mine," I said to him, in a low voice, "I would not willingly seem either suspicious or timorous, and I hope I am neither. But I think I have reason for some unquiet. I have noticed something that seems curious to me in the composition of our company."

To my surprise he turned to me a smiling face, as of one that was too well contented with his star to be fretted by wayward chances. "I think I know what you would say," he answered me, cheerfully, "and indeed I have noticed what you have noticed--that we who ride thus to-night are all the partisans of one party in Florence. There is not, so far as I have been able to see, a single man of the other favor among us."

Now this was exactly the fact that I had at last been able to realize, the portentous fact which had thrilled my spirit with significant alarms, the fact to which I wished to call his attention, and, behold, he had anticipated my observation and seemed to draw from it an agreeable and exhilarating deduction.

"Is it not a compliment," he went on, "to us that are of the Red party, to be thus signalled out for an errand of such great danger, and, in consequence, of such great glory, by the head man of the Yellow faction? I do not suppose," he said, with a smile, "that Messer Simone has planned the matter solely to pleasure us. Doubtless he has reasoned it somewhat thusly: if we fail in our enterprise, why then he has very cleverly got rid of a number of his adversaries."

He paused for a moment, and I caught at the pause to interrupt him somewhat petulantly. "And if we succeed?" I said, in a questioning voice, for I was in that happy age of youth and that sanguinity of temperament which makes it hard to realize that failure can associate its grayness or its blackness with one's own bright colors of hope. "If we succeed?"

"If we succeed," Dante echoed me, slowly, "why, if we succeed, then will not Messer Simone appear indeed to be a very generous and perfect gentleman, who was willing to give this great opportunity for honor and conflict to those that were so hotly opposed to him and his people in the brawls of the city?"

I could not, for my own part, see Messer Simone in this character of the high-minded and chivalrous knight, and Madonna Vittoria's words of warning buzzed in my ears with a boding persistence. To be frank, I felt qualmish, and though I did not exactly say as much, having a sober regard for the censure of my friend, yet, in a measure, I did indeed voice my doubts.

But my dear friend was not to be fretted by my agitations, and much to my surprise and something to my chagrin, would indeed scarcely consider them as, to my thinking, they deserved to be considered.

"I feel very sure," he said, tranquilly, "that we shall succeed in what we are set to do to-night, though I could give you no other reason for my confidence than the certainty that reigns so serenely in my heart. Have you not already noted, comrade, for all that you are young and the way of the world before you, how there sometimes comes to one, although rarely, such a magic mood in which the liberated spirit seems to swim in an exalted ether, and the body seems to move uplifted in a world made to its liking?"

It was at a later time that I learned the great cause of Messer Dante's contentment and serenity displayed in our journey. It came, in the main, from the fact that he had that night given and taken troth with Madonna Beatrice, and that he esteemed himself, as most men esteem themselves in such a case, though not all as rightly, the man the most happy in all the world. But this joy of his had its complement and sustainer in a marvel, a portent vouchsafed to him, as he believed and averred, that same evening and journey. For as himself told me thereafter, he was, or thought himself, companioned through all that night-riding by a youth clad after the fashion of the Grecians, that wore a crimson tunic and that rode a white horse. Ever and anon this youth turned a smiling countenance upon Dante, as one that bade him be of cheer, for again he should see his lady. Dante knew that strange and beautiful presence, seen of him alone, to be the incarnation of the God of Love that had already appeared to him before this, time and again, ever since that morning on the Place of the Holy Felicity, where he beheld for the second time the lady Beatrice. It is one of my regrets that I have never been favored, on my own account, with any such celestial apparitions, but I am glad that Dante was so graced, and I wish I had known at the time that Love was riding by our side. The presence of Love in the Company of Death: what an allegory for a poet!

It was very beautiful to hear Messer Dante talk as he talked, and his calm reasoning, together with the sweetness and serenity of his confidence, cheered me mightily. In such company, and hearkening to such speech, it was impossible to be downhearted, and as the brave, hopeful words fell from him, I that had been not a little in the dumps grew blithe to whistling-point--not that I did whistle, of course, seeing that such an ebullition of high spirits would be something out of place on a night march toward an enemy's country, and scarcely to be commended by your strategists. Some may say, when they learn the leave of my tale, that it makes an ironic commentary on Messer Dante's speech and Messer Dante's conviction, to learn, after all, that what saved us from the destruction that was spread for our feet was no more and no other than the craft of a woman and a light o' love. But methinks the answer to that is, that the instruments whereby it may please Heaven to work out its purposes are not of our choosing, but of Heaven's; and those that cavil may recall, to their own abashment, how one that was of the same way of life as our Vittoria was permitted by celestial grace to be a minister unto holiness. I will not venture to say that Monna Vittoria did that which she did do with any very conscious thought of serving Heaven. Nay, more, I am very sure that, as far as she knew, her main purpose was to serve herself; but it is the result we must look to in such instances as these. After all, the Sybil, when she uttered her words of wisdom to all Greece, was as ignorant of what she communicated as a jug is of the liquor it contains, and yet what a mighty service the jug renders to your true toper!

Now, while we thus wiled away the journey in such profitable conversation, the tide of the night had turned, the glory of the summer stars had paled and faded and departed from the lightening skies. Behind the hills dawn, in its cloak of unearthly colors, was beginning to fill the cup of heaven, and the multitude of small birds, waking from their slumbers, unwinged their heads and started to utter their matins like honest choristers. The world that had been all black and silver, like the panoply on a knightly catafalque, was now flooded with a gray clearness in which all things showed strange, as if one dreamed of them rather than saw them. Below and beyond us lay a great stretch of wooded land, and here it was that we knew we were to meet our reinforcement; here we realized that from this point the adventure might veritably be said to begin. Our spirits rose with the rising day to the blithest altitudes; already we seemed to savor the taste of brisk campaigning; I think we all longed boyishly for action. Pray you, remember that the most of us were very young, that to most of us the events of life had still something of the zest that a schoolboy finds in robbing an orchard and glutting himself with its treasures.

But while most of us were thus brimful of eagerness, he that had been until now our guide and leader, even Simone's man Maleotti, was all of a sudden retarded in his progress by the ill conduct of his nag. It was always a mettled beast, but now it turned restive and took to all kinds of bucking and jibbing and shying, that seemed strangely disconcerting to its rider, albeit he was known as a skilful cavalier. So Maleotti must needs dismount and look to his girths and gear, to see what ailed his steed, while we rode merrily forward, eager to join hands with those that we knew were awaiting us behind the mask of yonder clump of trees. What was it to us if Maleotti could not handle an unmanageable horse? Behind that brown wood Messer Griffo of the Dragon-flag waited for our coming--Messer Griffo, the famousest soldier of fortune in all Italy. Who could be more lucky than we to be thus chosen as sharers in an enterprise that was honored by the alliance of so astonishing a **condottiere**? If I were to judge of all our fellowship by myself, as I fairly think I may judge, then I can assure you that all our pulses were drumming, that we were hungry and thirsty to get to grips with the devils of Arezzo.

How exquisitely vain is youth! We who rode and thought that we were going to do great deeds and win endless applause, how little we dreamed that we were no more than the toys of chance, the valueless shuttles between a rich man's gold and the kisses of a courtesan. We that likened ourselves to the conquerors of worlds were no better than petty pawns on an unfriendly chess-board, making moves of which we knew nothing, in obedience to forces of which we were as ignorant as children. All we knew, all we cared to know, in our then mood, was that we had come to the point where it was ordained that we were to meet and join forces with Messer Griffo of the Dragon-flag.

XX
THE FIGHT WITH THOSE OF AREZZO

This was what was to have happened at this point; this is what caused Messer Maleotti to have so much show of trouble with his steed. The little company of Florentine gentlemen were to have joined their forces with those that rode under the Dragon-flag of Messer Griffo, were to have ridden with them into the darkness of the wood, and were then and there incontinently to have been cut to pieces by the mercenaries. Maleotti, lingering behind to look after that troublesome horse of his, saw that much of this came very properly to pass. As the Florentines of the Company of Death came within view and hail of that midway wood, there rode out to greet them a number of Free Companions, with Messer Griffo at their head. In the gray of the growing dawn Maleotti could recognize him very clearly by his height on horseback and his burly English bulk, and Maleotti, still busy with his horse, could see how the two forces joined hands, so to speak, and how the free-lances gathered around the little company of youths from Florence, and, as it were, swallowed them up in their greater number, and how the whole force, thus united, disappeared into the darkness of the wood, as the children in the fairy tale disappear into the mouth of the giant.

Then Maleotti made up his mind that he had seen enough, and congratulated himself upon his wisdom in holding aloof from that meeting, for, as he very sensibly reflected, in a scuffle of the sort that was arranged to follow, your mercenary who is paid to kill is not always clear-headed enough to distinguish between his properly appointed victims and a respectable individual like Maleotti, who was a firm friend and faithful servant of the master butcher. So Maleotti mounted on his horse, which, now that we were out of sight, had very suddenly and unexpectedly grown quiet again, and rode off at an easy walking pace toward Florence, congratulating himself and his master upon a night's work well done.

Yet Maleotti had to learn that it does not always follow in life that because the first portion of a carefully prepared plan goes as it was intended to go, the rest of the plan must necessarily move with equal success along its appointed lines. Though Maleotti was as sure as if he had seen it of our slaughter in the forest shambles, there came no moment in that journey of ours through the darkness of the wood when Messer Griffo, drawing his sword, thundered an appointed order, and forces of destruction were let loose upon the Company of Death. On the contrary, Messer Griffo rode very quietly and pleasantly by the side of Messer Guido, chatting affably of the affairs of Florence and the pleasures and advantages of a morning attack, when you take your enemy by surprise, and ever and anon, to Messer Guido's surprise, leading the conversation craftily to the name of Monna Vittoria, and dwelling enthusiastically on her manifold charms and graces. I, still by the side of Dante, trotted on in the most blissful unconsciousness that if things had gone as they were intended to go, we should all be lying on the carpet of the wood with our throats cut.

It was only later that I learned, partly from the lady herself that was the main cause of the change, and partly from Messer Griffo, in a moment of confidence over a flask of Lacrima Christi, when all those things that I am speaking of were as ancient as the Tale of Troy. Julius Caesar! what that morning's business might have been, and was meant to be, by our friend Simone! It seems that Monna Vittoria, being a woman, and shrewd, and knowing her Simone pretty well, saw clearer through the device of the Company of Death when it was first hinted at than any of the feather-headed enthusiasts who were eager to swell its levy. And being a watchful woman and a cunning and a clever, she soon found out that Messer Simone was in treaty with Messer Griffo of the Dragon-flag, and feeling sure that what she might fail to elicit from Simone she could get from Messer Griffo, she was at pains to make herself acquainted with that gallant adventurer, and to show him certain favors and courtesies which won his English heart. So that in a little while Madonna Vittoria knew all about Simone's purposes, and very pleasantly resolved to baffle them.

In her opinion, it was a very important point in her game that Dante should be alive and well, and the wooer of lady Beatrice. So long as Dante lived to love and be loved, as she, with her cunning intuition, guessed him to love and be loved, so long there was little likelihood that Messer Simone would win the girl's hand and his wager, and leave her, Vittoria, very patently in the lurch. She reasoned rightly that such a maid as Beatrice would not yield her love while her lover lived, and she hoped that Messer Folco, for all he liked to play the Roman father, was in his heart over fond of his daughter to seek to compel her to a hateful marriage by force. It was, therefore, of the first importance to Vittoria to thwart the devices of Simone having for their object the death of Dante, and, to a woman like Vittoria, it was by no means of the first difficulty to carry out her purpose.

The winning over of Messer Griffo was no very difficult business. He was paid so much by Messer Simone; it only remained for Monna Vittoria to pay him more to secure at least a careful consideration of her wishes. She pointed out to the ***condottiere*** that all the advantage lay for him in doing what she desired and leaving undone what was desired by Messer Simone. Messer Griffo would serve Florence by preserving the lives of so many of her best citizens; he would serve Florence by aiding those citizens in that raid upon Arezzo, from which so much was hoped; he would serve Florence by saving Messer Simone from the stain of such unnecessary blood-guiltiness; above all, which to her, and indeed to the Free Companion, seemed perhaps the most important point in the argument, he would serve Monna Vittoria.

Messer Griffo had ever an eye for a fine woman, and he was mightily taken with Monna Vittoria, and made his taking plain in his bluff, simple, soldierly fashion with a fine display of jewels and gold, which only served to move Monna Vittoria to laughter, for she had as much as she cared to have of such trifles, and was not to be purchased so. But she clinched her bargain with him by assuring him, when she paid into the hands of a sure and trusted third party the overprice agreed upon, which was to make Messer Griffo false to Messer Simone, that after the return to Florence of the Company of Death uninjured by him or his, he would be a very welcome visitor at her house, and might consider himself for a season the master of everything it contained. Messer Griffo was in his way an amorist and in his way an idealist, to the extent of regarding one pretty woman as more important than another pretty woman, so he took Monna Vittoria's money and fooled Messer Simone, and spared the lives of the young Florentine gentlemen, and rode with them and fought with them, as you shall presently hear.

It is no part of my intention to rehearse all that happened as the result of our little raid. You can read all about it at great length elsewhere. It was, as it proved, a very successful little raid. The Aretines, marching out of their stronghold in good force to assault us, whom they expected to find marching in all innocence to our doom, were very neatly and featly taken in ambuscade by us. For, by the advice and orders of Messer Griffo, who knew his business if ever a soldier of fortune did, we that were of the Company of Death, we that the men of Arezzo expected to see, we rode the latter part of our ride alone, as if indeed we were the only attacking force, the while Messer Griffo dissimulated his lances easily enough in the woods and valleys adjacent. And when the Aretines perceived us, they shouted for satisfaction and made to fall upon us pell-mell, having no heed of order or the ordinances of war. Then it was, while they were in this hurly-burly, that Messer Griffo launched his men upon them from the right and from the left, and that the real business of the day began. For what seemed to me quite a long space of time, though indeed the whole business lasted little more than an hour, there was some very pretty fighting, with the solution of the war-like riddle far from certain. For the Aretines were more numerous than we expected by a good deal, and, for all they were taken by surprise, they carried themselves, as I must confess, with a very commendable display of valor.

To be entirely honest, I must confess that I remember very little about the skirmish or scuffle or battle or whatever you may please to call it. There was a great deal of charging and shouting, and though there were a good many of us engaged on both sides on that field, it seemed to me, at the time, as if I enjoyed a kind of isolation, and had no immediate, or at least dangerous, concern with all those swords and lances that were hacking and thrusting everywhere about me. I have since been told by tough soldiers that when they were tender novices they felt much the same as I felt in the clash of their first encounter, felt as if the whole thing were a business that, however serious and significant to others, was of no more moment than a pageant or a play to them themselves that were having their first taste of war. Though I gave and took some knocks as the others did, and shouted as they shouted, I had at the time no fear, not because of my valor, but because of a sudden numbing of my wits, which left me with no intelligence to do otherwise than charge and shout and lay about me like the rest.

I am glad to record that Dante carried himself valiantly; not, indeed, that I saw him at all till the tussle was over and such of our enemies as were left taking to their heels as nimbly as might be. But I had it on the word of Messer Guido, who could see as well as do, and who told me the tale, that our friend bore himself most honorably and courageously in the skirmish, which ended by beating back the discomfited and diminished Aretines within the shelter of their walls. It was, indeed, but a petty engagement, yet to those concerned it was as serious as any pitched battle, and afforded the same chance of a wreath of laurel or a broken head. And it seems certain that our Dante deserved the wreath of laurel. He showed a little pale at first, according to Guido, when the moment came to engage, and it may be that there was a little trembling of the unseasoned members that was not to be overmastered. But in a twinkling our Dante was as calm as a tempered veteran, and in the thickest of the scrimmage he urged himself as indifferent to peril as if, like Achilles in the old story, he had been dipped in Styx.

What he told me himself later, as we rode for home, though he spoke but little of the business and unwillingly, in reply to my eager and frequent questionings, did but confirm what Guido related. He had, he admitted frankly, been somewhat scared at first, but instantly he had thought of his lady, and with that thought all terror fell away from him, and his one desire became so to carry himself in that encounter as to be deserving of her esteem. Afterward he told me that while he was in the tremors of that first and unavoidable alarm he was cheered by a miracle. You know already how the God of Love, in very person, had ridden, visible only to the eyes of Dante, by Dante's side that night, though the vision vanished at the time when the lances of the Dragon-flag rode out of the sheltering wood to welcome our coming. Well, now it seems that, when Dante was assailed by that very human, pitiable, and pardonable pain and frailty, he suddenly became aware again of the God of Love that was riding hard by him, but this time a little in front, and this time on a great black war-horse. It seemed to Dante that the wonderful youth turned a little in his saddle as he rode, and showed his comely face to Dante and smiled, and it appeared to Dante as if Love said to him, "Where I go, will not you go too?" And at the sound of those words, Dante's heart was as hot as fire within his body, and he carried himself very valiantly in the battle, as every man should that serves his city and loves a fair woman.

Now if you that read me be at all inclined to wonder why we rode back so rapidly to Florence on the very top of our victory, I am very ready to tell you the why. It was Messer Griffo's doing, which is as much as to say that it was Monna Vittoria's doing, who had laid her commands upon her trusty Free Companion for her own ends. When the battered Aretines had scurried back within the shelter of their walls, we would have been ready and willing enough, we of the Company of Death, to stay and besiege them. But Messer Griffo would not have it so, and Messer Griffo was our captain. His orders were that as soon as we were breathed after our battle--for I like to call it a battle--and had eaten and drunk of the food and wine with which the mercenaries were plentifully provided, we should ride back to Florence as briskly as might be, and uplift the hearts of our fellow-citizens with our joyful tidings of triumph. Which is why we got back to Florence on the morning of our engagement, as Monna Vittoria wished, but not so early as Monna Vittoria would have wished if she had known what was happening in our absence--known what you are about to know.

XXI
MALEOTTI BEARS FALSE WITNESS

On that summer morning which saw us riding homeward, all flushed and triumphant over our little victory, all Florence was early astir. Florence was ever a matutinal city, and her citizens liked to be abroad betimes to get at grips with their work, which they did well, and earn leisure for their pleasures, which they enjoyed as thoroughly. But on this especial morning the town seemed to open its eyes earlier than usual, and shake itself clear of sleep more swiftly, and to bestir itself with an activity unfamiliar even to a town of so active a character. The cause for this unwonted bustle was not easy to ascertain with precision. Somehow or other rumors, vague, fantastic, contradictory, perplexing, irritating, bewildering, had blown hither and thither as it were along the eaves and through chinks of windows and under doorways, as an autumn wind carries the dried dead leaves. These were rumors of some event of moment to the Republic that either had happened, or was about to happen, or was happening at that very instant of time. What this event of moment might precisely be, few, indeed, could say, though all could make a guess and all availed themselves of the power, and many and varied were the guesses that men made, and very confident was every man that his particular guess was the only right and true one.

It is, indeed, strange how often, when some subtle move of statecraft is being made whereof secrecy is the very vital essence, though those that be in that secret keep their lips truly sealed, some inkling of what is going on seems by some mysterious intuition to be given to folk that have neither need of such knowledge, nor right nor title to it. So it certainly proved in Florence on the morning after the ride against Arezzo. Every man that came out into the streets--and the streets were soon full of people, as a pomegranate is full of seeds--was positive that something had happened of importance, or no less positive that something of importance was going to happen, or that something of importance was actually happening. In some occult manner it had leaked out that a number of the youths of Florence were absent from their dwellings. It gradually became known that all those that were thus absent were members of the same party, and that party the one which was held in no great affection by Messer Simone, the party of the Reds. Furthermore, the story of the formation of the Company of Death had become known, and it needed no very elaborate process of speculation to assume that the youths whose lodgings lacked their presence had overnight, in Messer Folco's palace, inscribed their names in Messer Simone's great book of enrollment.

It being established, therefore, definitely, beyond doubt or cavil, that something had happened, the next great question for the expectant Florentines was, What thing had happened? But the answer to this question was not yet, and in the meantime the expectant Florentines had another matter of interest to consider and to discuss. Through all the noise and babble and brawling of that agitated morning there came a whisper, at first of the very faintest, which breathed insidiously and with much mystery a very amazing piece of news. Men passed the whisper on to men, women to women, till in a little while it had swelled into a voice as loud as the call of a public crier, carrying into every corner of the quarter where Messer Folco lived, and from thence into every other quarter of the city its astonishing message of amazing wedlock. Gossip told to gossip, with staring eyes and wagging fingers, that Messer Folco's daughter, Monna Beatrice, she that had been the May-day queen, and was so young and fair to look upon, she was to be married at nine of that morning to Messer Simone dei Bardi, the man that so few Florentines loved, the man that so many Florentines feared. It had, of course, long been known in Florence, where the affairs of any family or individual are for the most part familiar to all neighbors, that Messer Simone wished to wed Monna Beatrice. It was known, too, that Messer Folco was in nowise opposed to the match. Yet, for the sake of the girl's sweetness and loveliness, all were ready to hope that such ill nuptials would never come to pass. Thus, when the news of the immediate marriage fluttered through Florence streets, it was the cause of no little astonishment to those that first heard it, and they carried it on the very edge of their lips to the nearest ears, and so made the circle of astonishment greater.

I am proud to say it, to the credit of my fellow-citizens, that the greater part of those that heard the tidings shook their heads and sighed. And, indeed, it needed no very great niceness of feeling or softness of heart to recognize that a marriage between a man like Messer Simone and a maid like Monna Beatrice was no admirable marriage, however much the wish of a parent was to be respected. Every one recognized that Beatrice was a maid as unusual in her goodness as Simone was a man, thank Heaven, unusual in his badness. Wherefore, all detested the undertaking. Yet disbelief in the story, a disbelief that was popular, had perforce to change into unpopular belief when the very church was named in which the ceremony was to take place--the Church of the Holy Name; and those that hastened thither did indeed find all preparations being made for a wedding, and learned from the sacristan that Messer Simone did, indeed, upon that very morning, mean to marry the daughter of Folco Portinari. Yet, as I learned afterward, for all these assurances and all these preparations, the marriage was, up to a certain moment, no such sure a matter as Messer Simone wished and Messer Folco willed and the good-hearted folk of Florence regretted.

I have always accepted the customs of my time, and found them on the whole excellent, and it has ever been our custom for us to wed our daughters as we will, and not according to their wishes, our view being that elders are wiser than youngsters, and that it is more becoming and orderly that a maid should marry to please her father than that she should marry to please herself. For there may be a thousand reasons for a certain marriage, very obvious to a prudent parent, such as land, houses, plate, linen, vineyards, florins, and the like, all of which are of the utmost importance in the economy of a well-domesticated household, but are unhappily little calculated to attract the dawning senses of a nubile girl. Yet in a little while, when she has become a matron and got used to her husband, with what a complacent, with what a housewifely approving eye she will behold her treasures of gold and silver and pewter and fine linen and the rest of her possessions. So, for the most part, it should always be; but there is no rule that has not its exception, and if ever there were a case in which a daughter might be justified for resisting the will of her parent in the matter of a marriage, I think the case of Folco's daughter is the case, and I for one can never be brought to blame her in the slightest degree for her conduct, or call it misconduct.

It seems that when the morning came Madonna Beatrice showed herself unexpectedly and unfamiliarly opposed, not merely to her parent's wish, but to her parent's commands. Messer Folco, who had not seen his daughter since the previous night, when she fell swooning in the arms of Messer Tommaso Severo, at first could not believe in her opposition. She told him, astonished as he was at this amazing mutiny, that she could not and would not wed Messer Simone, because her heart was pledged to another, and that other one whom she would not name. Madonna Beatrice kept silence thus rigorously the identity of her lover, because of her certainty that the swords of her kinsmen would be whetted against him the moment that his name was known. In this she was right, for Dante was everything that the Portinari scorned, being poor with a poverty that tarnished, in their eyes, his rightful nobility, being of the Reds, being of no account in the affairs of Florence. That he was a poet would no more hinder them from killing him than the gift of song would save a nightingale from a hawk. Messer Folco was at first very stern and then very angry at his daughter's attitude, but he was stern and angry alike in vain. The more Messer Folco stormed, the less he effected. Though Beatrice seemed to grow paler and frailer at her father's nagging, she grew none the less stubborn, and Messer Folco's fury flamed higher at her unwonted obstinacy. His naturally choleric disposition got the better of his philosophic training and his habitual self-restraint, and he threatened, pleaded, and commanded in turns without making any change in Beatrice's frozen resistance. The pitiable struggle lasted until Messer Maleotti, having ridden leisurely through the cool of the morning, chose, when within sight of Florence, to spur his horse to a gallop and to come tearing through the gates, reeling on his saddle, as one that bore mighty tidings, which must be delivered to Messer Simone dei Bardi without delay.

What these tidings were Folco was soon enough to learn. Messer Simone hastened to Messer Folco's house and demanded audience of the lady Beatrice. He found her and her father together, Messer Folco still fuming, Madonna Beatrice still pale and resolved. Simone stayed with a large gesture Messer Folco's protestations of regret at having so unmannerly a daughter, and, addressing himself to Beatrice, asked her if it was true that her affection for another stood in the way of her obedience to her father's wishes. She seemed to be almost past speech after the long struggle with her father, but she made a sign with her head to show that this was so. Thereupon Simone, making his voice as gentle and tender as it was possible for him to make it, went on to ask her if by any chance the man she so favored was young Messer Dante of the Alighieri. Madonna Beatrice would not answer him this question, either by word or sign. Then Simone, allowing his voice to grow sad, as one that sorrows for another's loss, assured her that if that were so, there could be no further obstacle to her father's wishes, because he was at that moment the bearer of the bad news that Messer Dante and all those that were with him had been killed that morning by treason in a wood half-way to Arezzo. While Messer Simone was telling this tale to Beatrice, the same story was running like fire through the streets of Florence, for Messer Maleotti was very willing to tell what had happened, or rather what he thought had happened, to whomsoever cared to ask or to listen, and I take it that there was not a man or woman in all Florence who did not seek to have news at first hand of the disaster.

It seems that at this news the unnatural resistance of Madonna Beatrice to her father's orders broke down entirely. I use the term "unnatural" as one in no-wise implying any censure of Madonna Beatrice for her resistance to her father's wishes, but rather as describing the strength beyond her nature which she put into that resistance. For I hold that the dominion of parents on the one side, and the obedience of children and the deference of children to that dominion on the other side, may be made too much of and thought too much of, and in no case more so than when a controversy arises concerning matters of the heart. All this wisdom by the way. If Madonna Beatrice had been pale before, she was paler now, and for a breathing-while it seemed as if she would swoon, but she did not swoon. They sent for her physician, Messer Tommaso Severo, who could do nothing, and said as much. Madonna Beatrice, he declared, was very weak; it were well not to distress her over-much. Beyond that he said little, partly because he was naturally enough in agreement with Messer Folco in his views as to the rule of parents over children, and partly because he was aware how frail a spirit of life was housed in her sweet body, and knew that no art of his or of any man's was of avail to strengthen it or to hinder its departure when the time must be.

While all this was toward, Madonna Beatrice seemed to come out of the silent fit into which the false news of Dante's death had cast her, and when her father asked her again, something less sternly than before, but still peremptorily, if she would have Messer Simone for mate, she did no more than incline her head in what Messer Folco took to be a signal of submission to his will. At this yielding he, being by nature an authoritarian, seemed not a little pleased. For the death of Dante, and the effect that death might have upon his daughter's welfare, he did not care and did not profess to care in the least. Dante as a human being was nothing to him--nothing more, at least, than a young man who belonged to an opposite party, had no money or family backing, and owed what little esteem he had gained in the public mind to his writing some clever verses and making a mystery about their authorship, the said verses being particularly offensive to him, Folco Portinari, because they had the insolence to be aimed at his daughter. So having carried his point and enforced his authority, Messer Folco straightway sent a messenger to the church chosen for the ceremony to have all in readiness for the immediate nuptials.

As for Beatrice, though she still seemed like a woman that was stricken with a catalepsy, she was, by her father's orders, girded in a white gown and girdled and garlanded with white roses, and in such guise Messer Folco and Messer Simone between them--with my curse on them for a fool and a knave--led their helpless victim from the Portinari house into the open air. There a litter awaited her, into which she went unresisting, and so with the people of her father's household about her, wearing her father's crest upon their coats, she went her way to the Church of the Holy Name.

I do not think that in all the tragic tales of old time there is one more lamentable than this of lady Beatrice. Monna Iphigenia, so piteously butchered in Aulis, that the Greek kings might have a soldier's wind toward Troy, was not more sadly sacrificed, and in the case of Beatrice, as in that of the Greek damsel, a father was a consenting party to the crime. The case of Jephthah's daughter was less pathetic, for there at least the parent was deeply afflicted by the darts of destiny, whereas old Agamemnon and our Folco were, whatever their reluctance to dedicate their daughters to an uncomfortable fate, quite prepared to do so. All of which goes to show that humanity is the same to-day as it was yesterday, and will, in all likelihood, be the same to-morrow. There will always be good and bad, kind and unkind, wise and foolish, always sweet lovers will be singing their songs in the praise of their sweethearts that are walking in the rose-gardens, and sour parents will be scowling from the windows. For my own part, I am always on the side of any lover, young or old, straight or crooked, gentle or simple, for to my mind, in this muddle of a world, the state of being in love is at least a definite state, and, whenever and however gratified, a pleasant state.

I can honestly say, in looking back over the book of my memory, that I can find no page therein which is not overwritten with the name of some pretty girl. And though I will not be such a coxcomb as to assert that I was always favored by any fair upon whom it might please me to cast an approving eye, yet I must needs admit that I found a great deal of favor. This I attribute largely to a merry disposition and a ready desire to please, together with a very genial indifference if, by any chance, the maid should prove disdainful. For it may be taken as a general principle that maids are the less tempted to be disdainful if they guess--and they are shrewd guessers--that their disdain will be met with a blithe carelessness. Speaking of carelessness and disdain and the like, reminds me that I have never done what I meant to from the beginning, and tell you how I fared in my love-affair with Brigitta, the girl that gave me the cuff and had such strange eyes. But I fear now that I am too deeply embarked upon the love-affairs of another to have the leisure to digress into my own adventures. The world is more interested in love's tragedies than in the comedies of love, wherein I have ever played my part, and so I will go back to my Dante and his sad affairs, and leave my little love-tale for another occasion. But at least I may be suffered to set down this much in passing--that Brigitta was a very attractive girl, and that I was really very fond of her.

XXII
THE RETURN OF THE REDS

The Church of the Holy Name was filled as full as it could hold, and those outside were grumbling at their hard case in being cut off from so much solemnity or jollification, according to their opinion of the ceremony inside. But it came to pass that the lot of these outsiders proved, from the point of view of those that like to assist, if only as spectators, at the making of history, to be more fortunate than that of those who had gained admittance to the church. For suddenly, from far away, there came a shouting, meaningless at first, but momentarily growing in meaning, till at last men shrieked into their neighbors' ears that the supposed lost and slaughtered of the youth of Florence were not lost nor slaughtered at all, but were alive and well, and were riding in triumph through the city gates, having inflicted innumerable woes upon the devils of Arezzo.

Such tidings were unbelievable, were not to be believed, were not believed, were believed--all in the winking of an eyelid. The insolent chivalry of the Company of Death were, as it seemed, all, or almost all, to hand with Messer Guido Cavalcanti at their head. With them came the news that the Aretines had been beaten in battle, and that the ever illustrious **condottiere**, Griffo of the Claw, was flying his Dragon-flag in the very face of the scared burghers of Arezzo, huddled behind their naughty walls. Here was a mighty change in the fortunes of Florence, its full significance understood by few then, and not by many until long after that day.

At first the news seemed incredible to those that had not ocular proof of its verity, but these soon were convinced. Was not Messer Guido Cavalcanti riding through the city gates, whither all were now running, and was not Messer Dante by his side, and your humble servant who writes these lines, and many another youth well known to the Florentine populace? So that, in a little while, the space before the church, that had been so thickly crowded, was as empty as my palm, and Messer Guido and his fellowship of the Company of Death were like to be unhorsed and swallowed up in a wave of popular enthusiasm. Messer Guido restrained the kindly intentions of the crowd with some difficulty, and thereafter harangued them at some length, and with eloquence worthy of a Roman patrician of old days. He told them how the fortunes of Florence were again, as ever before, triumphant, how the devils of Arezzo had been taught a lesson they would not be likely to forget in a hurry, and, furthermore, how much Florence owed to the splendid assistance given to her arms by Messer Griffo of the Dragon-flag and his Free Companions.

Now, at every pause in Messer Guido's speech, the air was shattered with deafening huzzas, some echo of which would, one must surely think, find its way into that solemn and sombre church where the fairest lady in Florence was being given to Florence's greatest knave. How great a knave none of us realized at that moment, for we, of course, were ignorant of the intention of Messer Simone with regard to us, and the narrow escape we had from being annihilated by those very Free Companions whose praises Messer Guido was so generously voicing. Even while Guido was speaking, those of us behind and about him heard many things hurriedly from the citizens that pressed against us. One of them was the news of our own supposed slaughter at the hands of the people of Arezzo, and the other--more terrible, indeed, to one of us--was that on that very instant Madonna Beatrice was being wedded to Simone dei Bardi in the Church of the Holy Name.

It was just when Messer Guido had made an end of speaking that the ill news came to Dante's ears, and when he heard it he gave a great cry and urged his horse forward through the throng, crying to the people in a terrible voice to let him pass, and there was something in his set face and angry eyes, and in the manner of his command, which made the people yield to them, and so he rode his way, slowly, indeed, because of the press, but as quickly as he could, and still calling, like one possessed, for free passage. When Guido knew what had happened, for the tale was soon told to him, he foresaw what trouble might come to pass, and he resolved to stand by Dante and lend him a hand in case of need. So he called upon his friends to keep with him, and we all followed hard upon Dante's heels, and, as rapidly as was possible for the crush in the streets, we made our way to the open space in front of the church, the open space that now lay so vacant under the noontide sun. There

Messer Dante flung himself from his horse and made to run at full speed toward the church door, and we, too, dismounting hurriedly, made after him, for we feared greatly what he might do or say in his anger, even within the precincts of the sacred place. Messer Guido, though I fear he had no great regard for the sanctity of such shrines and temples, made haste to restrain him, for he knew very well how it would hurt his friend in the eyes of devout Florentines if he were to cause any scandal in a church.

But before Dante could reach the blessed house its great doors yawned open, and many of those that were inside came tumbling out and down the steps to form a hedge on either side, and through the human lane thus made the wedding party came out into the fierce sunlight. They stood for a moment on the threshold, very plain for all to see. Messer Simone showed very large and gorgeous, shining in some golden stuff like the gilded image of a giant, his great face flushed with triumph. Hard by him stood Messer Folco, looking very anxious and haughty and stern, grimly conscious, I suppose, that he had played the Roman father very properly, and yet, as I take it, not without some tragic aches and pinches at his heart for the consequences of his deed. Between him and Simone stood his doomed daughter, Beatrice, resting a little on the arm of her physician, Messer Tommaso Severo, and pale with such a paleness as I never yet saw upon the face of a woman, living or dead. It was, as who should say, a kind of frozen paleness, the pallor of a marble statue, the outward sign of a sorrow so great that time could never soften its sting. Behind these three stood the friends and kinsfolk of Simone and the friends and kinsfolk of Messer Folco, and made a brave background for the tragedy. So, for a moment, the three stood looking straight into the square before them, and then it was plain that they suddenly became conscious of untoward events, and Messer Simone forgot his triumph, and Messer Folco his pride, and Madonna Beatrice her misery, when they saw Dante standing all armored in front of them, and behind him the triumphant faces of the Company of Death. Then Madonna Beatrice gave a great cry and ran quickly forward to Dante, and Dante caught her in his arms.

"They told me you were dead," she sobbed, and then lay very quiet in his embrace, whispering to him what had been related to her.

Messer Simone gave a great bellow of rage, and bent his head like an angry bull, and he wrenched his sword from the hand of the serving-man that carried it, and plucked its blade from its house. Very plainly he must have seen that his damnable plan had miscarried, and that in some unfathomable manner the men he had devoted to destruction, and of all these men most notably Dante, had escaped the fate he had arranged for them. Messer Dante, still holding Beatrice in his arms, had his sword drawn, and stood very steadfastly awaiting Simone's onslaught, looking, as it seemed to me, like some young saint from a Book of Hours abiding the attack of some pagan monster. But before Simone could move, Messer Guido and the rest of us had swarmed up beside and about Dante, and all our victorious swords were bare, and we seemed a menacing body enough to any that chose to oppose us. So those of Messer Simone's friends immediately about him flung themselves upon him, persuading him by words and restraining him with difficulty by force, for he dragged them hither and thither, clinging to him as a wounded bear plays with a huddle of dogs.

Then Messer Folco, very gray in the face and stately of bearing, advanced in front of Messer Simone, where he struggled with his friends, and addressed us. "Sirs," he said, gravely, "what has come to the city of Florence, so famous for its decorum and its dignity, when the marriage of one of her citizens is thus rudely interrupted by roysterers in arms?"

XXIII
THE PEACE OF THE CITY

While Messer Folco spoke, he did not look at Messer Dante at all, but seemed to address himself solely to Messer Guido, as being the man of most standing present among his antagonists, and he began to reprove Messer Guido very sharply for such brawling and riotous conduct. But Messer Guido answered him very plainly and courteously that he was there present merely as a friend of his friend, and that it was for Messer Dante and not for him to speak as to the reasons for what he had done.

Then Dante cried out in a loud voice to those about him, saying: "Oh, Florentines, I am here to demand justice of the Republic! For this lady and I were troth-pledged, and she has only been persuaded to marry my enemy through a lying tale of my death."

At these words of Dante's, the clamor and tumult that had lulled for a moment broke out afresh, every man striving to say his say at the same time, with the result that no man was anywise audible in the great din that followed. It seemed likely that Florence would see again enacted one of those bloody public feuds such as had not now, for some time, desolated her hearths and distracted her streets. People were beginning to divide on this unexpected quarrel and take this side or that, as their fancy or their allegiance might lead them, and I think that the most part of the public took sides with Dante, partly because he was young and a lover, and partly because he was one of the victors in the fight against the Aretines, and fresh from the field of triumph, and partly, too, out of a very general dislike to Messer Simone. But Simone had plenty of followers too, that were very ready to draw sword and to strike for him, and Messer Folco Portinari had his friends and his kinsfolk, who shared his indignation at the wrong which, as they conceived, was thus publicly put upon him.

The object of Messer Folco's friends was to take away Beatrice from Dante, by whose side she now stood, very pale and calm and determined. The object of Messer Simone was now, if by any means he could compass it, to kill Dante where he stood, and as many of his friends as were with him, and so get rid of this troublesome young opponent once for all. Therefore, many swords were raised in the air, and many voices screamed old war-cries that had not vexed the winds of Florence for long enough, and enemy taunted enemy, and antagonist challenged antagonist, and it needed but a little thing to set fire to the torch of civic war. But before any sword could strike against another, and before those zealous champions of peace, that were running as fast as they could to the Signory to summon the city authorities to intervene and stay strife, could gain their end, there came an unexpected interruption to the threatened conflict.

It was Beatrice herself who held back the hostile forces and stayed the lifted swords. She moved from her place by the side of her lover and stood a little ways apart from him, at about an equal distance between him and her father, and she raised her voice to speak to the people of her city; and those about her, seeing what she meant to do, were instantly silent, and the silence spread over all the assembled crowd; and when Beatrice spoke she was heard by all who were present. It was a rare and a strange thing for a Florentine woman thus to address a turbulent assemblage of citizens that seemed bent on immediate battle. Yet the lady Beatrice spoke to all those fierce and eager people as sweetly and as quietly as if she had been welcoming her father's guests in her father's house. What she said was to the effect that she entreated all those that were about her to have patience, even as she would have patience. She further said that a great wrong had been done to her, for it was indeed true that she had plighted her troth to Messer Dante there present, though this had been done in secret, for which secrecy she now asked her father's forgiveness, but that when her father desired her to marry Messer Simone, she had refused to wed another than the man she loved, whatever might come of it. Then she said she had been told of Dante's death, and had no further strength left in her to disobey her father's wishes, seeing that if her lover were indeed dead, she had no care for what might become of her. Now she appealed to her father and to the people of her city to take her strange and sad case into their hands, and to protect her until it was made plain that she had been wrought upon by fraud and cunning, and forced by false representations into a marriage that should never have taken place and should now be annulled.

All the people marvelled to hear her speak so calmly and so wisely, and the most part of them applauded her when she had done speaking, and Messer Folco, for all his anger and his wounded pride, was touched by her words, and extended his hand to her, and she came to him and stood by his side. But Messer Simone and Messer Simone's people would have none of the proposal, and shouted loudly against it, and it seemed as if the brawl were likely to begin again on the instant, and I am very sure it would have done so had it not been for the arrival of the Priors of the city with an armed following. These kept the two opposing parties asunder, and the Captain of the People of the city demanded to know the meaning of what had happened, and Messer Guido Cavalcanti began to tell him the tale.

Now, while he did so, and while all were listening to him in silence, Messer Dante, who was standing very still and stern, with his hands resting upon the hilt of his sword, felt that one plucked him by the garment, and, turning, found that a woman stood at his side with a hood drawn closely over her face. This woman told him, in a low voice that seemed to him familiar, that if he was alive in that hour it was no thanks to Messer Simone, who had sold him to Griffo, and had, as he believed, sent him and his companions to a certain and treacherous death, and that he would have perished if Messer Griffo had not been persuaded to play an honorable part and be faithful to the city of Florence. When the woman had done speaking she slipped away from Dante and disappeared into the crowd, and Dante, with that strange story humming in his brain, waited with little patience till Messer Guido had finished saying his say to the listening authorities. Then he sprang forward toward the Captain of the People, declaring, in a loud voice, that Messer Simone was a traitor to the city, inasmuch as to gratify a private hate, he had sent him and his fellows to perish in an ambuscade.

Now at these words, of course, the brawling was renewed a thousandfold worse than before, every man screaming at the top of his voice and gesticulating, as if in the hope that pantomime might succeed in conveying his opinions where words indeed must fail in the hubbub. Under cover of the clamor, men of the Red party and men of the Yellow party challenged one another to the arbitrament of steel, and what with the shouting and counter-shouting and the clatter of weapons, and the stamping of many feet on the cobbles, there was such a din set up as seemed to some of us, in our bewilderment, likely to last forever. Words would speedily have become blows and blows brought blood, and all the place become a battle-field very presently, if it had not been for the presence of the Captain of the People and the Priors of the city, whose dignity indeed counted for nothing to allay the tumult, but whose strong escort of armed men served the turn better by keeping the would-be combatants apart, that were so lusting to be upon one another. After a while, for want of a better settlement, this composition was agreed upon, or, rather, was decided upon by the Priors, that were enabled to enforce their authority by their showing of armed force.

What they did was to put the Peace of Florence, as the custom was in those days, upon the belligerent disputants. According to this custom, each of the parties to any quarrel that threatened to become such a public brawl as might cause distur-bance to the state was called upon to clasp the hand of the Captain of the People, and swear to keep the Peace of the City. If he did this, he was suffered to go to his own house, where for a while, as I think, authority kept a wary eye upon him. If he would not do this, then the Captain of the People had the right to clap him into prison and keep him there till he was of a more reasonable and pacific mood of mind. All of which serves to show how excellent were our laws and customs, and how intelligently and discriminatingly they were administered.

Well, our Captain and Priors put the Peace of the City upon Messer Simone dei Bardi, that was on one side of the quarrel, and on Messer Dante dei Alighieri, that was on the other side of the quarrel. Messer Simone took the peace because he could not very well help doing so at that time and in that place, being, as it were, in a tight corner. He was outnumbered for the moment; the feeling of the fickle public was against him, taken, as it naturally was and rightly was, by the love-tale and Dante's youth and daring, and Beatrice's beauty and her sadness and her courage. So, with a sour smile enough, the bull-faced fellow flung out his right hand to the Captain of the People and gave the clasp of peace, and then drew back a little, very sullen and scowling, yet for the nonce tame enough. Then Dante in his turn came forward to give and take the pressure of peace, and all we that looked upon him and loved him, Messer Guido and I and others of our age and company, thought that we had never beheld him show more noble. His spirit, that had been tempered in conflict, gave an elder's dignity to his youth; his anger had set him in a splendid sternness, while his love had invested him with the raiment of a no less splendid serenity. It was a brave and chivalrous soldier that stood there in the sight of all Florence, a figure infinitely better to my eyes than the scholar who dogged the footsteps of Brunetto Latini, or even than the poet whose songs had enchanted the city. For a scholar is often a thing of naught, and a poet, as I know, may be little enough, but our Dante, as he stood there and gave the pledge of peace, was indeed a man.

So it was for the time arranged and settled. Madonna Beatrice, she that was a wife and yet no wife, went with her father to her father's house, there to abide until such time as a decision might be come to as to her case. Messer Simone, in high dudgeon, withdrew to his dwelling-place with his friends about him. As for Messer Dante, he was for going to his lodging, very lonely and stern and silent, but I would not have it so. For I could guess, being, after all, no fool, how bad it might be for one of so sensitive a disposition as my friend to fret his spirit in isolation. So I persuaded him--and indeed I think in the end he was not sorry to be so persuaded--to take up his quarters with me.

Mine were merry rooms in a merry house of a merry neighborhood, and therein I installed him, and did my best to cheer him, and in the end persuaded him to talk a little, but not much. For he was one of those that will spin out the secret of his heart in rhymes for all the world to read, but is inclined to be sullenly mumchance if invited to open his bosom to a sympathetic listener. But anyways I sang to him; I had a mellow voice in those days, and even now, though I ought not to say it, Brother Lappentarius is as good as another, and perhaps better, when it comes to chanting a hymn. I pressed food and wine upon him, of which, however, he would taste but little, for the which lack of good-fellowship I was obliged to make amends myself, that was ever a good trencherman, by eating and drinking for the pair of us. Which I did, as I am pleased to believe, very honestly and thoroughly. But I think, on the whole, I was glad, as I sat and watched him sitting there by my hearth, with the brooding look on his face that was already so eagle-like, that my love-affairs had not conducted me to such great stresses of the soul. I had enjoyed myself very much. I was, as I am pleased to record, to enjoy myself even more in the years that followed. But my pastimes had never cost me, and never did cost me, an hour's sleep for any cares that they brought me, and I never had to strive with the great ones of the earth for the smiles of any she. While here was my Dante, very unhappy, in a position of great danger, menaced by mighty enemies, threatened by an infinity of perils, and all for a woman. "All for *the* woman!" he would have answered me, rebuking me, if I had been so unwise as to set my views of life and love before him on that day.

I was not so unwise. I merely babbled and chanted to divert him from his distress, and was careful to keep my thoughts to myself. In my heart I wondered how it was all to end for him, that was so young and so little rich, pitted against such powerful interests. At least I could read in his face, and in those lines which destiny was already tracing with iron pencil on his springtime's flesh, that he would face his dangers and his difficulties with a dauntless spirit, and that no enemy or bunch of enemies would ever get the better of that so long as it still held a lodging within the carnal house. If I was glad, on the whole, that I was not in Messer Dante's shoes, I may say very truly that I did not think any the better of myself then, and do not think any the better of myself now, for being so glad. But it is well to know one's own boundaries, and I knew very well that I was never made for Dante's loves or Dante's hates or Dante's adventures on life's highway. Well, if there must be knights-errant, there must also be more easy-going, flower-picking pilgrims in the pageant of life.

XXIV
BREAKING THE PEACE

Now, of course, it is one thing to put the Peace of the City upon a man, and another thing to make him abide by his peaceful promise. Messer Simone had put his pledge, with his palm and fingers, into the hand of the Captain of the People, but he had done so because at the given instant he could not very well see that there was anything else for him to do--as, indeed, there was not. But Simone was never a man to give undue weight to the words or forms of a foolish ceremony if the ceremonial stood in the way of anything he wished to accomplish and saw the chance of accomplishing. Therefore, Messer Simone did not intend to keep the Peace of the City a moment longer than was convenient for him. But before deciding to break it he had other things to do which he set about doing with all possible dispatch.

In the first place, he was very wild to know how he had been baffled and bubbled in the business of the Aretine expedition, and who had played him false in that matter. Interrogation of Maleotti made it plain to him that Maleotti had acted in good faith if Maleotti had acted foolishly. He had been confident, and, as Simone could not but admit, reasonably confident, that when he saw the little fellowship of the Company of Death ride into the wood with Griffo's lances about them and Griffo's Dragon-flag above them, that they would never emerge alive from the wood, but would leave their bones to whiten amid its leaves. Why, then, had Messer Griffo been untrue to his promise? Simone could not admit that any arguments or promises of his intended victims would have had power to stay his lifted sword, for there was no one in all their number who could pay down the money that Simone could pay down; and as to argument, Griffo of the Dragon-flag was too busy a man to bother about other people's arguments. Yet Griffo left the

Company of Death a misnomer, as far as he was concerned. Griffo had let the Reds ride onward to Arezzo and back to Florence, very much to Simone's annoyance and discomfiture. What, then, was the cause of Griffo's defalcation, and who had inspired him to this signal piece of treachery?

Simone shrewdly suspected Madonna Vittoria to be at the back of the matter, a suspicion that was plentifully fed by Maleotti, who was eager enough to get his patron's angry thoughts directed against any other than himself. Luckily, however, for Madonna Vittoria, she very shrewdly suspected that Simone would shrewdly suspect her, and she laid her plans accordingly. After she had whispered into Dante's ear, in the square before the Church of the Holy Name, the secret of Simone's treason, she decided that it might be as well for her to change the air of Florence for one which she could breathe in greater security. Simone of the Bardi, never a pleasant man in his best moods, would be very far indeed from proving a pleasant man to any crosser of his purpose, even if that crosser were a woman as fair as Monna Vittoria. The woman's imagination could feel the grip of Simone's fingers about her throat, and she shivered at the thought in the warm air. She could see Simone's eyes glaring wolfishly down upon her, and she lowered her own lids at the fancied sight and shuddered. When she had a little shaken off the effects of this most disagreeable vision, she took her precautions to prevent its becoming a reality.

When, therefore, Simone came in a rage to Vittoria's villa with a tale of his trustiest ruffians at his heels, he found no Madonna Vittoria waiting to receive him, to be questioned, to be forced to confess, to be punished. Far away on the highroad toward Arezzo a youth was riding furiously, a comely youth that seemed not a little plump in his clothes of golden brocade, a youth with a scarlet cap on a crown of dark hair, a youth that kept a splendid horse galloping at full speed toward Messer Griffo's encampment outside Arezzo. If Messer Simone could have known of that riding figure he would have been even angrier than he was. All he did know was that Monna Vittoria was nowhere within the liberties of her villa, and as he realized this fact he stood for a while closing and unclosing the fingers of his great hands with an expression on his face that would have made Vittoria sick could she but see it.

Though his business with Monna Vittoria was thus, and thus far, proved a failure, Simone had another matter to attend to which yielded a more successful issue.

Messer Simone wished to ascertain how far his standing in the city had been injured by recent events, and how far he might count on the support of those that had always hitherto been reckoned as his friends. As to the first horn of the dilemma, he really felt little anxiety. There was never a man of all the men in the party of the Yellows that could be found to utter disapproving word of a plan that had promised to annihilate at a single stroke the majority of those that were most important among their opponents. Some few, indeed, might be inclined, on general patriotic grounds, to protest against a course of action which slaughtered one's private foes--however commendable the slaughter might be under ordinary circumstances--while engaged in military operations against an enemy of the city, and under the very eyes, as it were, of that enemy. But here Messer Simone had his comfortable answer in reserve. The very wiping out of his private enemies was to be an important factor in the later wiping out of the public enemy. Was not Arezzo, deceived by this action of private justice, to take Messer Griffo to her arms, only to find that she had cuddled a cockatrice? Up to this point Messer Simone felt fairly sure of himself and of his ground.

He received no goring from the second horn--nay, not so much as a prick to break the skin. His friends were as plentiful, his friends were as zealous as ever, as ready to serve Messer Simone with enthusiasm so long as Messer Simone had the millions of his kinsmen and the bank behind him. Simone made sure, and very sure, that a very respectable army would rise behind him if he chose to cry his war-cry, and season that utterance with the relish of the added words, "Death to the Reds!"--words that were always in Simone's heart, and would now, as he believed, be very soon upon his lips, to the discomfiture of his adversaries. In a word, Messer Simone was ripe, and overripe, for a breach of the peace, and could barely be persuaded to wait for opportunity and a pretext. He did wait, however, and he soon got both.

With the next morning there came one to my abode asking to have speech with me, and when I went to see who it was I found that my visitor was none other than Messer Tommaso Severo, that was so long physician to the Portinari family. He told me that he heard that Messer Dante was for the time dwelling with me as my guest, and when I told him that this was so he went on that he had come the bearer of a message to my friend, asking him to come very instantly to the Portinari palace. When I showed some surprise at this, Messer Tommaso Severo told me that

Madonna Beatrice desired most earnestly to speak with Dante, and that her father had consented to this out of his great love for his child, which seemed suddenly to have grown stronger in the midst of all these ill-happenings. He further told me that Messer Folco had long been bound to Simone because of large sums that ruffian had lent him from time to time for the building of his hospitals and the like, which had swallowed up the mass of Messer Folco's own fortune. Not that Messer Simone cared for any such good works, but because, by doing as he did, he laid Messer Folco under heavier obligations to him. Now, however, according to Messer Tommaso, Folco saw more clearly the character of the man that he had made his son-in-law, and also the character of his own daughter that he had never understood till now, and he was now resolved to repay Messer Simone all he owed him if he sold everything he possessed to do so, and thereafter use all his credit among his friends at Rome, and he had many there, to get the marriage annulled by the Holy See. Then I went and summoned Dante, and he came out and greeted Messer Tommaso and went away with him, going like one that moves in the grave joy of some fair dream.

Now what chanced to Dante when he went his ways to the Portinari palace I shall set down presently as it has come to me, seeing that I was not present, but giving, as I believe, the substance and the truth. But when he and Messer Tommaso had left me, I thought to myself that I would busy my leisure with writing a sonnet or so to some merry jills of my acquaintance. But when I had got me ink and parchment, I found, to my surprise, that I was in no fit mood for wooing the muses, and that the rhymes that were wont to be so ready to jig to my whistle were now most fretfully rebellious, and would not come, for all my application. So there I sat and stared at the unstained whiteness of my sheets and grumbled at the sluggishness of my spirit, and presently I applied myself pretty briskly to the wine-flask, in the hope of quickening my spirits. But the wine proved as hostile to my rhyming as the muses had been, and after a little while, when I had drunk a toast to some half a dozen sweetnesses that were then very dear to me, what must I do but fall into the depths of a very profound sleep.

How long I lay in that lethargy I do not know; only I remember dreaming incoherent and distorted dreams, because, after all, a chair is no proper place in which to seek slumber. I thought I was wandering in a wood where satyrs grinned at me and nymphs eluded me, and where I was mightily vexed at my ill fortune. Then suddenly all the trees began to talk at the tops of their voices, and though it did not surprise me in the least that trees could talk, yet it annoyed me that I could not hear what they said, because of their all talking together, and in my indignation I awoke to find that the trees were still talking as it seemed, and that the sound of their voices filled the chamber where I sat uncomfortably enough, staring about me with drowsy eyes. All of a sudden I realized that the noises I heard were the voices of no trees, but the clamor of human voices in the streets outside, and that they swelled to a great roar of menace and alarm and anger.

You may believe that I was up and awake in a twinkling, and that I caught up my sword as a wise citizen does when there is brawling abroad in the streets of Florence, and in less time than I take to tell it I was out of my house and in the open, looking eagerly about me. The street was all full of people running and shouting as they ran, and man caught at man as they ran and asked questions and was answered, and I heard the name of Simone dei Bardi and of the Portinari palace, and that was enough for me. If I had borne wings on my heels, like Hermes of old, or carried a pair on each shoulder, like Zetes and Calais of pagan memory, I could scarcely have sped swifter than I did along the streets of Florence, threading my way with amazing dexterity through the throng that hurried, like me, in the same direction. In a few wild minutes I found myself in the Place of the Holy Felicity, which was now no other than a camping-ground for two opposing forces under arms. As I began to realize what these opposing forces were, I also realized that the time of the day was long past noon, and that I must have slept my heavy, dream-disturbed sleep for some hours that were eventful hours to many that were familiar to me.

Let me try and present a picture of what I saw that afternoon in the Place of the Holy Felicity. In front of the house of Messer Folco Portinari, that seemed to me more grim and solemn than ever that day, were ranged a number of the soldiers of the authorities of the city, that had evidently been set there to protect Messer Folco's house from attack, and that were far too few for the purpose, considering who was the assailant and what his powers of aggression. For the assailant was Messer Simone dei Bardi, that strode a big horse and was girt with a big sword, and looked for all the world like the painted giant of a puppet play. Behind Messer Simone was massed a mighty following, that took up much of the space in the square and flowed off into the other streets adjacent, which his men held, that no assistance might be sent to the soldiers of the authorities. It was not these soldiers, indeed, that stayed Messer Simone from his purpose of forcing an entrance to the Portinari palace, but the presence of other elements in the struggle that was to be striven that day.

One of these elements was represented, to my wonder and delight, by my dear Dante, who stood on the steps of the Portinari palace with a great sword in his hand. So standing, he looked like some guardian angel of the place, appointed to protect it from desecration. His face was very calm, and he kept his gaze ever fixed most steadily upon Simone of the Bardi, and he seemed eager for the conflict that must surely be. Below him were gathered many of his friends, many of the Reds, many of the fellowship of the Company of Death, that had fought and beaten the Aretines but yesterday, and among these, of course, and of course in the foremost place, was Messer Guido Cavalcanti. But though the friends of Dante were many, they were but few in comparison with the numbers that were led by Simone dei Bardi, and Simone could have swept his enemies away from the threshold of the Portinari palace were it not for the existence of a further element in the struggle. That element was represented by a multitude of armed men on horseback that were ranged in front of the palace in manifest antagonism to Messer Simone and his supporters. Over the helms of these horsemen floated the Dragon-flag that I now knew so well, and at their head, mounted on a great gray horse that he held well reined in, Messer Griffo of the Claw, that made a fine opposition to Messer Simone, both in bulk and bearing.

By the side of Messer Griffo, on a high bay, rode one that at the first glance I took for a youth, and that at the second glance I knew for Madonna Vittoria in the habit of a youth. It became her plumpness very lovingly, and, indeed, she looked very well with a scarlet cap set atop of her twisted-up tresses and her eyes all fire with excitement. She kept very close to Messer Griffo's side, and looked at him every now and then as if she loved him, which, as I gathered thereafter, was exactly what she did. It seems that well-nigh from the first the big Englishman won her demi-Roman, semi-Grecian heart, and that while he was so smitten with her as to do her will in that business of Arezzo and Messer Simone, she, on her side, was so won by his willingness and his bulk and his blunt love-making, that she cared no longer for the winning of that wicked old wager, and had but one thought in her head, which was to become the lawful wife of Messer Griffo of the Claw. This was an arrangement of their joint affairs which Messer Griffo of the Claw was very willing to make.

I did not know all this as I stood there in the Place of the Holy Felicity, though I could guess at a good deal of it, for the tale of Griffo's love for Vittoria and of Vittoria's love for Griffo was written in the largest and plainest hand of write. But I could not guess the causes that had brought Messer Simone and Messer Griffo thus face to face before Messer Folco's house, in all this pomp and armament of battle. But I had plenty of friends in the crowd to question, and by the time that I had elbowed my way to the edge nearest to the antagonists--aiding my advance by loud proclamations that I was one of the Company of Death, a statement that insured me help and respect in my advance--I had learned all that it was necessary for me to know in order to understand the bellicose state of affairs. You shall understand them in your turn, but in the first place it is necessary for me to tell what had happened in those hours when I was snoring, and had led to the facing of those two armed forces in the Place of the Holy Felicity and in front of Messer Folco's home.

XXV
MEETING AND PARTING

Dante, when he left me, accompanied Messer Tommaso Severo to the house of Folco Portinari. He was very silent on the way, thinking troubled thoughts, but Messer Tommaso Severo talked, telling him many things to which he listened heedfully in spite of his cares. Messer Tommaso Severo told him that Messer Folco had greatly changed in his bearing toward his daughter, the which, indeed, he had already told me, and that he seemed to understand, as it were, for the first time, how precious a life hers was, and how lovely and how fragile. Severo believed that Messer Folco would now be willing, if only he could liberate his child from the weight of the Bardi name, to leave her all liberty of choice as to the man she would wed, even if that man had neither wealth nor fame to back him. Such changes of mood, the physician averred, were not uncommon in men of Messer Folco's temperament, who are led by pride and vanity and many selfish motives into some evil course without rightly appreciating the fulness of the evil. But when, by some strange chance, their eyes are cleansed to see the folly or the wickedness of their conduct, the native goodness in them asserts itself very violently, to the complete overthrow and banishment of the old disposition, and they are straightway as steadfast in the good extreme as of old they had been stubborn in the bad.

But what Messer Severo most spoke of was the strange delicacy of the physical nature and composition of Beatrice. Never, he declared, in all his long experience as a physician, had he met with any case like to hers. Although she seemed to the beholder to carry the colors of health in her cheeks and the form of health on her body, he asserted that she was of so ethereal a creation that the vital essence was barely housed by its tenement of flesh, and could, as he fancied, set itself free from its trammels with well-nigh unearthly ease. All of which he dwelt upon, because, being a man of science, it interested him mightily, and though he loved the girl dearly, it did not enter his wise head that what he said must cause a pang to the youth by his side, the youth who also loved her. But Dante made no sign that he heeded him to his hurt, but marched on doggedly, with a grim determination on a face that had aged much in a few days.

Florence was quiet enough as they trudged along through the streets that had been so crowded, so uproarious, yesterday. We soon settle down again after one of our little upheavals, and whether the event has been Guelph killing Ghibelline, or Yellow hounding Red, or Black baying at White, the next morning sees the sensible Florentines going about their affairs as composedly as if nothing ever had happened, or, indeed, ever could happen, out of the common. So when the pair came to the Portinari palace, the Piazza of the Santa Felicita was well-nigh as desolate as the desert. Dante glanced, you may be very sure, at that painted image of the God of Love that ruled above the fountain by the bridge, and it seemed to him as if the statue gave him a melancholy glance. Yet Dante was going to see his beloved, and he could not be downcast.

When the two were under the shadow of the Portinari palace, Messer Tommaso Severo ceased talking, and going to the little door, knocked thrice upon it, whereupon the warder within, after peeping for a moment through a grill, opened it and admitted the doctor and his companion. In silence Severo conducted Dante through the silent corridors of the great house, which seemed strangely quiet in its contrast to the gayety on the night when Dante last beheld it. The pair met no one in their progress through the palace. Severo informed Dante that Folco was within, but keeping his rooms in much gloom because of all that had occurred, and the physician made no offer to bring Dante to his presence. After a time Severo came to a halt before a certain door, on which he knocked again three times, as before. One of Beatrice's women answered his summons, and after a moment's whispered colloquy the girl withdrew. An instant later Severo pushed Dante into the room, and Dante found himself in the presence of Beatrice.

As Dante entered the room, Beatrice rose from the couch and advanced toward him with extended hands. "You are welcome, friend," she said.

Dante looked upon her paleness, and trembled and hardly knew what to say.

"My lady, my dear lady--" he began, and paused and looked at her wistfully.

Beatrice smiled sadly at him. "Our loves have fallen upon evil days, Messer Dante," she said. "It is but a few poor hours ago since we changed vows, and here am I wedded to your enemy, wedded to my enemy. Dear God, it is hard to bear!" For a moment she hid her face in her hands, as if her sorrow was too great for her.

Dante's heart seemed to burn with a fierce flame. "It shall not be borne, Madonna!" he cried. "I have hands and a heart and a brain as good as Simone's. I would rather play the knave and stab him in the back than have him live to be your lord. But there is no need of stabbing or idle talk of stabbing. This false wedlock shall be broken like a false ring."

Beatrice chilled the hope of his mind with a look of despair. "I do not know," she sighed, "I do not know. My father will do all he can. My father is a changed man in these hours. He weeps when he sees me, poor soul. But it is not sure we can break the marriage, after all."

"The Pope can break the marriage," Dante said.

Beatrice shook her head. "The Pope can do what he will, but he may not choose to tamper with a sacrament for the sake of two young lovers. It is all the world and its sober governance against two young lovers. It is all my fault, Dante."

Dante interrupted her with a groan. "Oh, my love--" he said, and said no more, for her look stayed him.

The girl went on, sadly: "If I had not yielded when I thought you dead, yielded in obedience, yielded in despair, we should be free now, you and I, to change many sweet thoughts into sweet words. But we are not so free, and it may be that we never shall be so free."

Dante compelled himself to speak bravely, combating her alarms. "Dearest, have no fear, have no doubt. Why, I will fight this Simone. Never smile at my slightness. All these weeks I have labored to make myself master of my sword, and I have mastered it. I tested my courage and my skill yesterday. Of my courage it is not fitting for me to speak, but my skill is a thing outside myself that I may speak of, and I found it sufficient. I will fight Simone, I will kill Simone, you will be free."

Beatrice sighed. "Are we right to talk so lightly of life and death, you and I? Are we not wasting time? I sent for you to tell you that if I can never be yours, I will never be another's. I have no right to kill my body, that I know, but neither have I the right to kill my soul; and of the two sins I will choose the lesser, and sooner kill myself than lie in loveless arms. I gave myself to you, my lover, that night, when we changed vows in the moonlight. I will kiss no other man's lips, I will share no other man's bed. I am your wife by the laws of God, and I will die before I dishonor my bridal."

Dante took her hand and held it in his. "Oh, if Heaven could grant me a thousand hearts to house my love in and a thousand tongues to give my love utterance, I should still seem like a child stammering over its alphabet when I tried to tell how I love you. All about me I seem to hear the swell of mighty voices that thunder what my lips are too weak to whisper, yet what they say is only as if a chorus of angels cried aloud what I say beneath my breath, the three words that mean everything--I love you!"

Before the warmth and passion of his words a faint color kindled in the girl's cheeks as she gave him back assurance for assurance.

"I love you, Dante, as you love me, and if, on this earth, we should never meet again, my love would remain unchangeable with the changing days. If I that am now young live to be old, I shall think, with death before me and Heaven behind the wings of death, that my withered body in the Holy Field shall quicken into the fragrance of spring flowers because of the cleanness and the sweetness of my faith. My love shall keep the spirit of the girl that was Beatrice fresh and blithe for the boy that was Dante when they meet again in Heaven beyond the frontier of the stars."

Her voice seemed to fail a little as she spoke, but she held herself erect, as if her unconquerable purpose lent her the strength she lacked. Dante stood before her, silent, in a kind of awe. His passion for the girl had always been so chastened by reverence, his desires so girdled about by mystical emotions, that it seemed to him in that memorable hour as if he and she were rather the priest and priestess of some fair and ancient faith than man and woman that were lover and lover. His great love seemed to burn about him like a fierce white flame consuming all that was evil, all that was animal, in his corporeal being, and leaving nothing after its fiery caress but a body so purified as to be scarcely distinguishable from pure spirit. So Dante felt, enchanted, gazing in adoration upon Beatrice, and reading in the rapture of her answering eyes the same splendid, terrible exaltation.

The spell lasted for an age-long while, and then Beatrice broke it, turning away from her lover's gaze, and as she did so Dante, lowering his eyes, saw how upon a table near the girl there stood a little silver casket, richly wrought with images of saints, and the lid of the casket was lifted, and in the casket Dante saw that there lay a single red rose, or, rather, that which had once been a red rose, but now lay withered and faded, the mummy of its loveliness. Dante looked at it in some wonder, and Beatrice followed his gaze and saw what he saw, and turned to him, smiling.

"Forgive me, friend," she said, "if in the joy of seeing you I forgot to thank you for your gift."

And Dante looked from the rose to her and from her to the rose, and his wonder grew, and he said, quickly, "I sent you no gift."

Then Beatrice gazed at him in surprise and told him. "One left this casket here for me this morning, a little while ago, shortly after I had sent for you, saying that it came from him whose name would be revealed by the treasure it contained. When I opened it I saw this rose, and I made sure it came from you, for I thought, 'This is the rose that I gave him, and he sends it to me in sign of greeting and of faith.'"

Dante shook his head, and he put his hand to his bosom and drew forth a small piece of crimson, colored silk and unfolded it, and within the silk there lay a withered red rose, and he showed it to Madonna Beatrice, holding it on his extended hand.

"This is the rose you gave me, Madonna," he said. "Ever since that day it has lived next to my heart." And as he spoke his wonder seemed growing into fear, and he looked again at the casket and the rose that it held.

"What, then, is this rose?" Beatrice asked. "And who sent it?"

Dante folded his own rose away in its coverlet of silk, and put it back into his bosom. He shook his head. He was still full of wonder, the wonder that was growing into fear. Before he could put his troubled thoughts into words there came a hurried knocking at the door, and Messer Tommaso Severo entered, looking anxious and alarmed.

"I fear there is some new trouble moving," he said; "there is one come to your father with grave tidings, for Messer Folco's face was troubled; but I know not what the tidings are."

Dante paid no heed to the old man's words. He took the mysterious rose from the casket, and held it toward Severo. "Here," he said, "is a token that was sent to

Madonna Beatrice this morning; do you know anything of it?"

Severo shook his head. "I know nothing of it," he said. "Who should send Madonna Beatrice a withered rose?" He lifted it for a moment to his nostrils. "For all it is withered," he said, "it has a strange scent, a strong scent." He looked at the girl anxiously. "Have you smelled it?" he asked.

"Yes," said Beatrice, "I have smelled it, and I have kissed it, for I thought it came from Dante."

The old man muttered to himself, examining the flower and peering curiously into its petals. He seemed as if he would have spoken again, but was interrupted ere he could do so by the entrance of Messer Folco looking very wrathful and stern. Folco showed no surprise at Dante's presence, and saluted him with grave courtesy. Before Messer Folco could speak, Severo slipped from the room.

Folco spoke. "Beatrice," he said, "here is bad news. Messer Simone of the Bardi is coming hither at the head of an armed following to claim you and take you."

Beatrice said nothing in reply to these words. She only clasped her hands against her heart and looked wistfully at her lover.

Dante spoke. "Surely this cannot be, Messer Folco, seeing that the Peace of the City was put upon him, as upon me, yesterday, before all Florence."

"Messer Simone is no stickler for principles," Folco said, sourly; "he cares for no laws that he can break. But in this case he claims to be acting according to his right, since the breaking of the peace comes from you."

"From me!" Dante stared at Folco in amazement.

But Messer Folco nodded his head emphatically in support of what he had just affirmed. "I have it all," he said, "from a friend of mine that has just come hotfoot from his neighborhood to give me warning, so that we may be ready to yield without making difficulties. Messer Simone affirms that you have broken the peace by visiting his wedded wife without his knowledge or consent, and that he is in his rights as a citizen, a husband, and a man in coming here to claim his bride and to defend her from your advances."

"I do no wrong in coming here," Dante said, sternly. "I came here without secrecy, as I had a right to come if you were not unwilling."

"Yes, yes," Folco said, "you came here without secrecy; but Simone's man, Maleotti, sees you and runs to tell his master, and presently his master will be here to claim his wife."

"What will you do, then?" asked Dante, studying the elder's face.

Messer Folco spoke proudly. "Folco Portinari will defend his daughter. Folco Portinari will defend his house so long as the stones of its walls hold together. My servants are arming now. I have sent to the Signory for aid from the Priors. If the Bardi beards me, let him look to himself." He turned to Dante, and addressed him. "Young man, I know you better than I did, and rate you higher. I overheard your talk with my daughter just now, as I had a right to do, and I esteem you a brave and honorable man. You have already shown that you can serve the state. If there comes a happy way out of this tangle, I shall be glad to welcome you again. But now it were well you should leave us."

Dante respectfully saluted Folco. "I thank you with all my heart," he said, simply, "for to-day's favor. I take my leave quickly, for I have a word to say to Simone." He turned to Beatrice, took her hand, and, bending, kissed it reverentially. "Most dear lady, farewell." He looked once, longingly, into the wide, tearless eyes of Beatrice, then turned and left the room rapidly.

With a loving glance at his daughter, Messer Folco turned and followed him. A minute later Tommaso Severo, entering the room with a look of grave anxiety on his face, was but just in time to catch Beatrice in his arms as she fell in a swoon.

As Dante made his way through the corridors of the palace, Messer Folco came after him hot upon his heels. "You will lose your way, Messer Dante," he panted, "if you have not me to guide you." He led Dante quickly by the way along which he had come, the two going in silence.

Suddenly Dante caught his companion by the arm, and addressed him eagerly: "Do me a good turn before I go," he said. "You see me with the Peace of the City upon me; I carry no weapon. Lend me a sword."

Messer Folco would have dissuaded Dante, urging him to put himself in some place of safety as speedily as might be.

But Dante shook his head. "I must have a sword," he insisted. "I wish to speak with my enemy at the gate."

Then Messer Folco, seeing that he was obdurate, and in his heart applauding his obstinacy, took him aside to a kind of armory, and there, from an abundance of weapons, Dante chose him a long sword, which he thrust into his belt. Thus weaponed, he followed Messer Folco to the gate of the palace and passed out into the fierce daylight, and as he heard the bolts shot behind him, he looked about him to see if there was any one hard by whom he knew. He saw a youth with whom he had some acquaintance, and called him to him, and begged him to go with all speed to Messer Guido Cavalcanti and tell him that his friend Dante waited for him and such friends as he could muster at the Portinari palace. And when the youth had gone Dante stood patiently, waiting for the things to be.

XXVI
THE ENEMY AT THE GATE

Dante had not long to wait. From all directions folk came hurrying into the Place of the Holy Felicity, presaging by their presence untoward events. Among these were certain friends of Dante's, youths that, like him, had enrolled themselves on the fellowship of the Company of Death and had ridden to Arezzo together. These he called toward him, and put them quickly in possession of what was toward, and those that carried weapons stood by him, and those that were weaponless hastened to find weapons and came back swiftly. As the square was filling with people there came along at a trot the few guards that the Priors, in their wisdom, had deemed it sufficient to send for the defence of Messer Folco's house, and these gathered together hard by the door and stood there, seeming to find little comfort in their business. Scarcely had they taken their places when a great roar from the farther end of the square announced some event of moment, and immediately thereafter Messer Simone rode forward on his great war-horse with a small army of soldiers, friends, and adherents after him. At the selfsame moment Messer Guido Cavalcanti and a number of his friends came racing into the square from the other corner and rushed in a body toward the door of the Portinari palace, where Dante was standing very quietly, seemingly all unconscious of the myriads of eyes that were fixed upon him. Thus, by the time that Messer Simone and his followers had advanced half-way across the square, there was a goodly number of well-armed and resolute gentlemen gathered about the doors of Folco's palace, and their strength was increased almost every instant by new additions to their count.

When Messer Simone saw the opposition that was intended to him, and who those were that offered it, he was hugely delighted, for he perceived now an excellent opportunity of getting rid of the majority of his enemies at a single stroke, as it were. The men he had with him that filled a goodly part of the square were far more numerous than those that had been thus hastily rallied against him, and he chuckled at his luck. But when he saw Dante where he stood he reviled him, calling him the thief that would steal a man's wife from his side, and summoning him to yield himself a prisoner instantly. He did this to put himself in the right with the people before he made an attack, and to disgrace Dante in their eyes. But Dante answered him very quietly, saying that he was a liar and a traitor that had cheated a woman with fables like a coward, and sent his fellow-citizens to death by treachery like a rogue. "But," so Dante went on, "liar though you be, and traitor and coward and rogue, as this is our quarrel, yours and mine and no other man's, I call upon you to dismount and meet me here sword in hand, that it shall be seen which of us two is the friend of God in this matter."

At these brave words many of the people cheered, and Simone was in a red rage at their cries, but he laughed at Dante and mocked him; yet I think he cannot have been so sure of himself as before, or he would have taken Dante's challenge for the pleasure of slaying him with his own hands. I am not sure that he would have slain Dante, and very possibly Dante might have slain him, for Dante's skill with the weapon was now marvellous for his age. But, however, that was not to be. Then Messer Simone bade Messer Guido and his friends stand away from Messer Folco's gates, for he had a mind to go in and get his wife. When Messer Guido denied him steadfastly, and called upon him to keep the peace, Messer Simone grinned, and, turning to his men, was for giving them the word to fall on. But even then another great roar from the crowd told of some new thing, and the trampling of many horses was heard, and over the bridge came a company of lances, and over their heads fluttered the Dragon-flag of Griffo of the Claw, and the great Free Companion and his fellows forced their way through the yielding throng and took up their station opposite Messer Simone and his friends, and it was very plain that it was their intention to oppose him. This was just the time that I got to the square, as I have already told.

Messer Simone's plans had been grievously marred by the, for him, untimely appearance of Messer Griffo and his lances. Up to that moment he seemed to have the city pretty well at his mercy. His party counted the more numerous adherents and the better prepared. The Reds were taken by surprise, and were largely scattered about among the crowd, instead of being drawn together into a solid body like the Yellows. In the seats of authority counsels were much divided, and, in view of such division, it was difficult, if not impossible, to take any decided action against Simone and his friends. Moreover, there was, or so at least it seemed to many who were not necessarily on Messer Simone's side, on the face of it, not a little to be said for Bull-face of the Bardi. The daughter of Folco Portinari was indeed his wife, and it seemed to those that were sticklers for the solemnity of the married state, however brought about, that he had every right to claim her, and, if put to it by unwise opposition, to take her from her father's house.

That the girl's consent to the wedding had been either extorted from her by menace or won from her by means of a sorry trick mattered little in the eyes of these disciplinarians. A daughter, according to their philosophy, had no right to have an opinion of her own as to her spouse. She was bound by the old rules and customs of the country to accept with submission, and not merely with submission but with meekness, and not merely with meekness but with gratitude, the husband that might be selected for her by the wisdom of her elders. All this volume of feeling--and it ran with a pretty strong current--was in favor of Messer Simone, and Messer Simone knew that it would be so in his favor, and counted on it, and made the most of it, displaying himself very obstreperously before the city as the defrauded husband.

Nor, as I have said, was the fact that Messer Simone had been a party--if, indeed, this could be proved against him, and were no more than mere malicious rumor--to a planned ambuscade, with its consequent slaughter of Florentine chivalry, found to weigh very heavily against him in the minds of many that belonged to the Yellow fellowship. A man must get rid of his enemies as best he can, after all, and the misfortune in this matter for Messer Simone was that he had flagrantly failed in his enterprise, and had rather strengthened than weakened his adversaries by his misadventure. Anyway, he may have had nothing whatever to do with the matter, and must for the present be accorded the benefit of the doubt.

All these things combined to make Messer Simone's rising a mighty serious matter, and his appearance at the head of his little army of followers before the house of Messer Folco of the Portinari a thing of sufficiently grave concern for

Messer Folco. Simone clamored for his wife, Simone insisted on his wife being de-livered over to him, Simone loudly announced his intention, if the girl were not promptly and peaceably surrendered to him, of laying siege to the Portinari palace and taking her thence by force.

Now, of the populace of Florence, that was soon set astir and buzzing by all this war-like circumstance, I think that the most part were against Messer Simone in this business, because of the general pity felt for the girl, and the general admira-tion for young Dante that was now proved poet and proved soldier, and the general sympathy for two young lovers troubled by adverse stars. But such sympathy could do little against the grim arguments of Simone, against those steady ranks of his adherents, heavily armed, and resolute to follow their leader wherever he might choose to lead them. Yet the people had found a leader in Dante, whose words had set their minds on fire, and the gradually increasing number of the Reds that had made their way to the place and were clustered about Guido Cavalcanti stiffened their fluent units into something like a solidity of opposition. But the odds were amazingly on the side of the Yellows in everything that was necessary for success, in readiness, in discipline, in weapons, in stubbornness of determination to do the thing they wished to do--as indifferent to the laws of the city as heedless of the laws of Heaven. The points of the game were all in favor of Messer Simone.

But when Messer Griffo of the Claw rode into the city at the head of his levy of lances, with Monna Vittoria in her male attire riding by his side, and the Dragon banner flapping over all, things began to wear a very different face. Messer Griffo and his merry men forced their way easily enough across the bridge, pushing steadi-ly through the crowds that gave way before them and cheered them as they passed, for Griffo of the Claw was popular in Florence. The company of mercenaries, as I have said, came to a halt by Messer Folco's house, and drew up in face of Simone and his forces.

Now, when I came upon the scene, I was still a little dizzy with wine and sleep, whose fumes my race through the streets of the city had not wholly dissipated, but I was beginning to collect my senses and to understand what was going forward. My Dante, standing with his drawn sword in front of Folco's door, the few and fright-ened civic guards about the Portinari palace, the group of Guido Cavalcanti and his brethren of the Red, the Bull-face Bardi with a multitude behind him, and in front of these the new-come Free Companions, calm as statues behind their master and the man-woman by his side--all these made up such a sight as I never saw before and have never seen since, though I saw much in my time when I was a worldling, but naught to equal that day's doings.

I have told you already how I forced and coaxed a passage through the throng on the piazza as quickly as I could, with the aid of my cry, "Make way for the Company of Death!" shouted with great assurance, as if I had at my heels all who had enrolled themselves in that strange brotherhood. As a fact, many of the company were ranked behind Messer Simone, serving his cause, and of those that rode with me to Arezzo, the most part were gathered together about Messer Guido Cavalcanti and backed Dante's quarrel, and, indeed, the company never served together as a company after that day. But the name was just then very pleasing to Florentine ears, because of the little triumph over the Aretines, and so the name of the company served me as a talisman to squeeze me through the press to the front, and so to place myself by Guido's side.

Messer Simone glared very ferociously at the new-comers, at Griffo of the Claw, that had lost him one toss already, and at the woman who rode beside him so gay and debonair in her mannish habit--the woman he had slighted, the woman who had, as he guessed, baffled his plans once, and had now come, as he might be very sure, to baffle them again. It was plain to him that he had lost the day. It needed no great tactician, no strategist, to perceive that the coming of the *condottieri* had turned the scale against him. They were better weaponed than his men, and when their strength was added to that of the adversaries already arrayed against him, he was gravely outnumbered. The arrival of the mercenaries had served to define the mood of many a waverer and to stiffen the courage of many that had been against Simone all along, but feared to make themselves marked men by publicly opposing him. The most prudent thing for Messer Simone to do--and I am sure he knew it--was to give up his game, withdraw his forces, and trust to the chance of some opportunity of revenge hereafter. This was assuredly the wisest course open to Simone to pursue. But Simone did not pursue that wisest course. His temper was worse than his intelligence.

When Dante, from where he stood, saw the coming of Griffo, he saluted him with his sword, for he rightly believed that he came as a friend to himself, or at least as a foe to Simone; and Messer Guido, that had a right to take a foremost place in the affairs of the City, especially in such a time and place where none of those in authority were present, went up to the *condottiere* and stood by his bridle, and spoke him fair, and asked him very courteously why he came thus among them. And Griffo answered, speaking also very courteously and quietly, that he had heard from a sure source that there were dissensions in Florence whereby some of his friends were in danger whom he would be sorry to have come to hurt--and as he spoke he saluted Messer Guido very civilly and also Dante--and that in consequence he had ridden over, he and his men, from the neighborhood of Arezzo, in the hope that perhaps he and they might be of some service to the authorities in aiding them to keep the public peace.

Now, Messer Griffo said what he said in a very loud voice, so that as many as might be should hear him. As the people were keeping very still since the coming of the mercenaries, out of eagerness and curiosity, very many did hear him, and naturally Messer Simone, that was only a few feet away, heard him. It seemed as if his rage and hatred boiled over within him, so that he could not abide in silence, but must needs give speech to his spleen. So he urged his horse a little forward and looked straight at Messer Griffo, and very fiercely. Then he called out, in a huge voice, "Florence has come to a poor pass if her peace depends upon a scoundrel and his strumpet!" And as he said this he pointed a great finger direct at Vittoria, and burst out into a horrible laugh. And Griffo showed no sign that he had as much as heard Simone, but the woman went pale under the insult, and tried to speak, but at first she could not.

At length, in a little, she found her breath, and she cried back at the giant: "You have won your wager, Messer Simone, and I wish you joy of your winning and the wife that loves another lord! But I would not have you now or ever, for I have found a better man!"

At this I guessed, and was right in my guesswork, that she meant Messer Griffo, of whom, it seems, that she had suddenly become overweeningly fond, as indeed he of her. Then Madonna Vittoria pulled with her right hand at a finger of her left, and drew thence a heavy gold ring that carried a great emerald set in its socket, and I remembered, as I saw that this was the ring she had staked in her wager against Simone's promise to wed. She rose a little in her stirrups, holding up the ring. "Take your gain, beast!" she screamed, and she flung the ring with all her force in Simone's face, and struck him on the left cheek and cut it open, and the ring fell clattering to the ground among the horses' hooves, and the red blood ran over Simone's face, very ugly to behold.

What happened then happened more quickly than I can write it down, happened more quickly than I could tell it across a table to a friend. With a cry that was more like the bellow of some beast of the field than any sound of a man's voice, Simone drove his horse against Vittoria, and, bending over his charger's neck, gripped the woman about the neck with both hands, and, lifting her out of her saddle, flung her across his crupper and held her there, squeezing at her throat. For what seemed to me an age, I and those near me stared at Vittoria's face, all red and swollen with the choked blood, made horrid with the starting eyes, its beauty ruined by the grasp of those two strangling hands. Simone was a madman at the moment, with a madman's single thought, to kill his victim, his fingers tightening and his blood-stained face twisted into a hideous grin. Before the ghastly sight men stood still, and knew not what to do--all but one man.

Griffo's sword rose in the air, shining like fire in the sunlight; Griffo's sword fell like a falling star for swiftness, and struck Simone between the head and the shoulder, slicing into the flesh as a knife slices into an apple. It was a well-nigh headless trunk that rolled from the saddle fountaining its blood. As the dead giant fell, Griffo let his sword drop clanging on the stones and caught hold of Vittoria, and, wrenching her from the relaxing fingers, clasped her senseless body in his arms.

In the fury of confusion that followed--the screaming and plunging of startled horses, the shouts and oaths and cries of men that seemed to themselves to have kept silence for a great while, and, finding voice as last, must needs use it inarticulately, like savages--I remember best how I saw Dante standing erect on the palace steps, with his sword held high above him, and his face was set and stern as the face of some herald of the wrath of Heaven.

"The judgment of God!" he shouted, in a voice so loud that I heard it above all the din, and many others heard it too, "the judgment of God! the judgment of God!"

XXVII
THE SOLITARY CITY

With the death of Simone the immediate brawl came to an end. In the first fury after his fall certain of his followers began to cry for vengeance, but the cry was not caught up with any fulness of assurance, and soon faded into silence. The men of the Yellows, so suddenly made leaderless and faced by enemies so many and determined, could not fuse into concerted action. They hesitated, looked foolishly at one another, and lost whatever chance they had of success. Messer Simone's body, almost decapitated from the stroke of Griffo, was fished up from underneath the hooves of his rearing charger, laid upon a dismounted door, covered with a cloak, and hurriedly conveyed away to his house. Madonna Vittoria, snatched just in time from the clutch of those cruel fingers, drew her breath in and out again; the blood that had suffused her swollen face flowed back into its proper channels; she quickened to existence clinging to her Griffo's breast. Messer Guido, taking to himself authority as the chief man of his party there present, called upon the party of the dead Bardi to disperse, and disperse they did, cowed by the presence of the lances of the Dragon-flag, even before the belated arrival of authority, backed by all the forces it could command, had made dispersal a necessity.

Authority, now that Simone dei Bardi was indubitably dead, held a united mind against Simone dei Bardi, and entertained no thoughts of punishing his slayer, who, indeed, would scarcely have been minded to tolerate their jurisdiction. Messer Griffo was left to ride unchecked to Monna Vittoria's villa with his lances at his back. In that villa Monna Vittoria recovered briskly, thanks to her youth and her health, and in that villa a little later the adventurer wedded the adventuress, and proved to the end of their days patterns of wedded content and pleasure. Messer

Simone's body was buried stealthily at night, and authority vindicated its dignity by confiscating his houses and his goods, though it restored to Madonna Vittoria her emerald ring, which was picked up on the field of fight, as some salve for her rough handling. So ended, as far as the feud of Reds and Yellows was concerned, that wild day which is remembered, whimsically enough, in the annals of Florence as the Day of the Felicity, from the name of the place where the contest began and ceased. From that day the words Red and Yellow as party terms ceased to be used, because the parties had ceased to exist. The Yellows fell to pieces with the death of Simone, and the Reds, having no appreciable antagonists, ceased in their turn to be.

As for my Dante, his joy in that day's work lived a short life. Let the story of his woe be told quickly. When the door of the house of Folco was opened to him, he faced its master on the threshold, clad in his ancient armor for the defence of his dwelling, and his face was strained with sadness, and he seemed gray with the double of his years.

"My child lies in a swoon," he said. "The physician cannot awaken her as yet. Go to your lodging. I will send for you when she comes to herself."

With that Dante had to be content, and he went back to the place where he abode, and he sat in his lonely room to await the coming of Folco's messenger. His heart was heavy within him, and his thoughts were troubled, and he feared the great fear. Then, to while away the weary time, and to stay his care from feeding on his spirit, he sought some work for his hands. He could write no verses, but because he was not without skill as a draughtsman he took up, wherewith to draw, his tables and a pencil, and he began to trace the face of an angel, and under his working fingers the face of the angel had the face of a girl, and the face of the girl was the face of Beatrice. But while he drew he became of a sudden aware that there was another in the room with him, although he knew that he had fastened the door behind him when he came in, and that none could have entered without his knowledge. Turning his head, he beheld that the God of Love was standing in the room, even as he seemed in the form of the image that stood over the fountain by the bridge. But now the bright feathers of his wings were faded, and his face was wan, and the garment that he wore was no longer red but black, and he looked very sadly upon Dante, and Dante felt his spirit grow cold and old within him before that melancholy gaze. Then the God of Love made a sign to Dante to rise and Dante rose, and

Love beckoned to him to follow and Dante followed. The God of Love went out at
the door and down the stair with Dante ever after him, and so into the air. No one
in the street saw that gloomy figure of Love, no one save Dante, and Dante followed
his guide through the bright evening, heeding no one, thinking no other thought
than to go where his mournful herald led him. The God of Love conducted him to
the house of Folco Portinari. Even as Dante came to the door the door opened and a
man came forth, and the man was Messer Tommaso Severo, that was setting out to
seek for Dante. Severo saw Dante, but he did not see the God of Love, and he told
Dante that he was on the point of seeking him.

And Dante cried out one word--"Beatrice!"

And Messer Severo answered the question in his cry, very slowly and sadly,
"Madonna Beatrice is dead."

Then Dante cried, "Take me to her!" And after that he spoke no other word,
but walked in silence and tearless by Severo's side till they came to the room where
Beatrice lay in her last sleep. The women that were about the bier drew away, and
the God of Love took Dante by the hand and drew him a little nearer to where the
girl lay, and Love stooped down and kissed the white face of Beatrice--kissed her on
the forehead and on the lidded eyes and on the pale lips. Dante heard the voice of
the God, that said, "It is your love that kisses her thus." But Dante spoke no word,
and there were no tears in his eyes; only he stood there a little while looking at
Beatrice, and then he turned and went his ways, unquestioned and unstayed, back
to his own place. When Messer Guido and I came to him later we found him sitting all alone in his chamber looking at a little unfinished drawing of an angel, and
murmuring to himself, over and over again, "How doth the city sit solitary that was
full of people? How is she become a widow?"

*   *   *   *   *

Here my tale comes to an end. The rascal Maleotti confessed later, on being
put to the question, that it was his master, Simone dei Bardi, who sent to Madonna
Beatrice the casket containing the rose, and that the petals of the rose had been poi-
soned by a cunning leech that was in Messer Simone's service, for Messer Simone

was sure that Beatrice would think it came from Dante, and Messer Simone was of a mind that if he could not have Beatrice no one else should have her. But when Simone heard from Maleotti of Dante's visit to the Portinari palace so soon after the sending of the casket, he felt sure that Dante would deny, as Dante did deny, the sending of the rose, and that the evil thing would scarcely have had time to effect its purpose. Then the flames of his jealousy blazed hotter within him, and he thought that Dante's presence in the palace would be an excuse for him to break the peace that had been put upon him, and that he might, after all, win Beatrice for himself. In this, as you know, he failed, and it is my belief that he failed in the first part of his plotting, for Messer Tommaso Severo, that had examined the rose, gave it as his opinion that though the petals had been impregnated with some kind of venom, their odor had not been inhaled by Beatrice sufficiently long to cause any malignant effect, and he affirmed that the fair lady's death was due solely to the woful agitations of the last hours of her life acting upon a body ever too frail to house so fine a spirit. However that may be, and I hope it was so, we found great satisfaction in the hanging of Maleotti. We would have hanged the leech, too, whom Maleotti accused, but he forestalled our vengeance by poisoning himself--partly, I think, out of hurt pride at the alleged failure of his cunning device.

I have little more to say--no more, indeed, than this: It has been said by many, and believed by more, that, after the death of his lady, my dear friend fell into a kind of moral torpor, in which all sense of things righteous and things evil was confused. Thus he went his ways, like the godless man of whom it is spoken in the Wisdom of Solomon, feeding on mean and secret pleasures, and consorting with the strange women that are called Daughters of Joy. I do not know that he ever did so; I should never credit it, though it is such folly as weaker men might fall into readily enough in the freshness of their despair. But I will set down this story which I have heard told of him. It relates that one night Dante drifted toward that quarter of the city where such light loves find shelter. There many women plucked at his sleeve as he passed, and, at last, surrendering to temptation, he followed through the darkness one that was closely cloaked and hooded. It seemed to him that they went a long way together, he and the hooded woman by his side, and though at times he spoke to her, she answered him no word. After a while they came to an open place that was moon-lit, and then the woman paused and pulled back her hood, and there for a moment Dante looked upon the face of the dead Beatrice. In that instant Dante found himself alone, and he fled from the place in a great horror.

NOTE

Those that in their travels in France have had the good-fortune to visit the Abbey of Bonne Aventure in Poitou can hardly fail to be familiar with the many and varied treasures of the abbey library. Most of these treasures were brought together by the erudite Dom Gregory, who had, among the other honorable passions of a scholar, an enthusiastic desire for the amassing of rare manuscripts. Perhaps one of the rarest of all the manuscripts in his great collection is that one which claims to be written by the Italian poet Lappo Lappi, and to set forth in something like narrative form an account of the loves of Dante and Beatrice. Students and scholars who have studied this manuscript have differed greatly in their conclusions as to its authenticity and its value. The German Guggenheim is emphatic in his assertion that the work is a late eighteenth-century forgery, and he bases his conclusions on many small inaccuracies of time and place and fact which his zeal and pertinacity have discovered. On the other hand, Prof. Hiram B. Pawling, whose contributions to the history of Italian literature form some of the brightest jewels in the crown of Harvard University, is inclined, after careful consideration, to believe that the manuscript is, on the whole, a genuine work.

Undoubtedly the sheets of parchment upon which the remarkable document is written are older than the fourteenth century, some time in whose first half Lappo, if he be the author, must have written the book. The keen scrutiny of powerful magnifying-glasses has revealed the fact that much of it is inscribed on skins which had formerly been used for the recording of a series of Lives of the Saints, whose almost effaced letters belong, without question, to the latter part of the twelfth century. Whoever wrote this story of Dante must have been at the economical pains to erase carefully the ecclesiastical script, thus curiously avenging so many palimpsests of Greek poets and Latin poets, whose lyrics have been scrubbed away with pumice-stone to make room for homilies and liturgies and hagiologies. If the writer of the story be indeed Lappo Lappi, it would be quite in keeping with his character, as we know it, to imagine him enjoying very greatly this process of obliterating some saintly relation in order to set down upon the restored surfaces his testimony to the greatest love-story of Italy. It is, however, unfortunately impossible to maintain with certainty that the writing is actually from the hand of Lappo. Though it appears to be a clerkly calligraphy of the fourteenth century, such things have been imitated too often to enable any but the rashest and most headstrong of scholars to give a definite and unquestionable opinion. One may cherish with reason a private belief that the thing is indeed Lappo's work in Lappo's writing, but with the memory of some famous literary impositions fresh upon us, very notably the additions to Petronius, we must pause and pronounce warily. It may be, indeed, that although the book be genuine enough in its creation, it was never intended to be regarded as a serious statement of facts, but rather to be taken as an essay in romance by one who wished the facts were as he pictured them. If this be so, the narrative is even less historically reliable than the **Fiametta** of Boccaccio.

In any case, the manuscript, whenever written, wherever written, and by whom written, is in a far from perfect condition. Though the care of Dom Gregory had encased it in a wrapping of purple-colored vellum, it still seems to have suffered from time and careless treatment. Probably its greatest injuries date from that period when, during the stress of the French Revolution, the treasures of the abbey library were hurriedly concealed in underground cellars, and suffered no little from damp and dirt during the period of their incarceration. Many portions of the narrative are either wholly absent or exist in such a fragmentary condition that, like a corrupt Greek text, they have to be restored by the desperate process of guesswork. Those, therefore, who thirst for the exact text of the tale, must either wait in patience for Professor Pawling's long promised edition, or satisfy their curiosity by a visit to the Abbey of Bonne Aventure in Poitou.

The Codes Of Hammurabi And Moses
W. W. Davies

QTY

The discovery of the Hammurabi Code is one of the greatest achievements of archaeology, and is of paramount interest, not only to the student of the Bible, but also to all those interested in ancient history...

Religion   **ISBN:** *1-59462-338-4*   **Pages:132**

MSRP $12.95

The Theory of Moral Sentiments
Adam Smith

QTY

This work from 1749. contains original theories of conscience amd moral judgment and it is the foundation for systemof morals.

Philosophy **ISBN:** *1-59462-777-0*   **Pages:536**

MSRP $19.95

Jessica's First Prayer
Hesba Stretton

QTY

In a screened and secluded corner of one of the many railway-bridges which span the streets of London there could be seen a few years ago, from five o'clock every morning until half past eight, a tidily set-out coffee-stall, consisting of a trestle and board, upon which stood two large tin cans, with a small fire of charcoal burning under each so as to keep the coffee boiling during the early hours of the morning when the work-people were thronging into the city on their way to their daily toil...

Pages:84

Childrens   **ISBN:** *1-59462-373-2*   *MSRP $9.95*

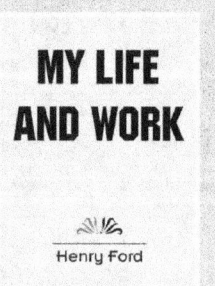

My Life and Work
Henry Ford

QTY

Henry Ford revolutionized the world with his implementation of mass production for the Model T automobile. Gain valuable business insight into his life and work with his own auto-biography... "We have only started on our development of our country we have not as yet, with all our talk of wonderful progress, done more than scratch the surface. The progress has been wonderful enough but..."

Pages:300

Biographies/   **ISBN:** *1-59462-198-5*   *MSRP $21.95*

www.bookjungle.com *email: sales@bookjungle.com fax: 630-214-0564 mail: Book Jungle PO Box 2226 Champaign, IL 61825*

The Art of Cross-Examination
Francis Wellman

QTY

I presume it is the experience of every author, after his first book is published upon an important subject, to be almost overwhelmed with a wealth of ideas and illustrations which could readily have been included in his book, and which to his own mind, at least, seem to make a second edition inevitable. Such certainly was the case with me; and when the first edition had reached its sixth impression in five months, I rejoiced to learn that it seemed to my publishers that the book had met with a sufficiently favorable reception to justify a second and considerably enlarged edition. ..

Pages:412

Reference   ISBN: *1-59462-647-2*   *MSRP $19.95*

On the Duty of Civil Disobedience
Henry David Thoreau

QTY

Thoreau wrote his famous essay, On the Duty of Civil Disobedience, as a protest against an unjust but popular war and the immoral but popular institution of slave-owning. He did more than write—he declined to pay his taxes, and was hauled off to gaol in consequence. Who can say how much this refusal of his hastened the end of the war and of slavery ?

Law   ISBN: *1-59462-747-9*   **Pages:48**

MSRP $7.45

Dream Psychology Psychoanalysis for Beginners
Sigmund Freud

QTY

Sigmund Freud, born Sigismund Schlomo Freud (May 6, 1856 - September 23, 1939), was a Jewish-Austrian neurologist and psychiatrist who co-founded the psychoanalytic school of psychology. Freud is best known for his theories of the unconscious mind, especially involving the mechanism of repression; his redefinition of sexual desire as mobile and directed towards a wide variety of objects; and his therapeutic techniques, especially his understanding of transference in the therapeutic relationship and the presumed value of dreams as sources of insight into unconscious desires.

Pages:196

Psychology   ISBN: *1-59462-905-6*   *MSRP $15.45*

The Miracle of Right Thought
Orison Swett Marden

QTY

Believe with all of your heart that you will do what you were made to do. When the mind has once formed the habit of holding cheerful, happy, prosperous pictures, it will not be easy to form the opposite habit. It does not matter how improbable or how far away this realization may see, or how dark the prospects may be, if we visualize them as best we can, as vividly as possible, hold tenaciously to them and vigorously struggle to attain them, they will gradually become actualized, realized in the life. But a desire, a longing without endeavor, a yearning abandoned or held indifferently will vanish without realization.

Pages:360

Self Help   ISBN: *1-59462-644-8*   *MSRP $25.45*

www.bookjungle.com *email: sales@bookjungle.com fax: 630-214-0564 mail: Book Jungle PO Box 2226 Champaign, IL 61825*

QTY

The Rosicrucian Cosmo-Conception Mystic Christianity *by Max Heindel*   ISBN: *1-59462-188-8* **$38.95**
The Rosicrucian Cosmo-conception is not dogmatic, neither does it appeal to any other authority than the reason of the student. It is: not controversial, but is: sent forth in the, hope that it may help to clear...   New Age/Religion Pages 646

Abandonment To Divine Providence *by Jean-Pierre de Caussade*   ISBN: *1-59462-228-0* **$25.95**
"The Rev. Jean Pierre de Caussade was one of the most remarkable spiritual writers of the Society of Jesus in France in the 18th Century. His death took place at Toulouse in 1751. His works have gone through many editions and have been republished...   Inspirational/Religion Pages 400

Mental Chemistry *by Charles Haanel*   ISBN: *1-59462-192-3* **$23.95**
Mental Chemistry allows the change of material conditions by combining and appropriately utilizing the power of the mind. Much like applied chemistry creates something new and unique out of careful combinations of chemicals the mastery of mental chemistry...   New Age Pages 354

The Letters of Robert Browning and Elizabeth Barret Barrett 1845-1846 vol II   ISBN: *1-59462-193-4* **$35.95**
by Robert Browning and Elizabeth Barrett   Biographies Pages 596

Gleanings In Genesis (volume I) *by Arthur W. Pink*   ISBN: *1-59462-130-6* **$27.45**
Appropriately has Genesis been termed "the seed plot of the Bible" for in it we have, in germ form, almost all of the great doctrines which are afterwards fully developed in the books of Scripture which follow...   Religion/Inspirational Pages 420

The Master Key *by L. W. de Laurence*   ISBN: *1-59462-001-6* **$30.95**
In no branch of human knowledge has there been a more lively increase of the spirit of research during the past few years than in the study of Psychology, Concentration and Mental Discipline. The requests for authentic lessons in Thought Control, Mental Discipline and...   New Age/Business Pages 422

The Lesser Key Of Solomon Goetia *by L. W. de Laurence*   ISBN: *1-59462-092-X* **$9.95**
This translation of the first book of the "Lemegton" which is now for the first time made accessible to students of Talismanic Magic was done, after careful collation and edition, from numerous Ancient Manuscripts in Hebrew, Latin, and French...   New Age/Occult Pages 92

Rubaiyat Of Omar Khayyam *by Edward Fitzgerald*   ISBN:*1-59462-332-5* **$13.95**
Edward Fitzgerald, whom the world has already learned, in spite of his own efforts to remain within the shadow of anonymity, to look upon as one of the rarest poets of the century, was born at Bredfield, in Suffolk, on the 31st of March, 1809. He was the third son of John Purcell...   Music Pages 172

Ancient Law *by Henry Maine*   ISBN: *1-59462-128-4* **$29.95**
The chief object of the following pages is to indicate some of the earliest ideas of mankind, as they are reflected in Ancient Law, and to point out the relation of those ideas to modern thought.   Religion/History Pages 452

Far-Away Stories *by William J. Locke*   ISBN: *1-59462-129-2* **$19.45**
"Good wine needs no bush, but a collection of mixed vintages does. And this book is just such a collection. Some of the stories I do not want to remain buried for ever in the museum files of dead magazine-numbers an author's not unpardonable vanity..."   Fiction Pages 272

Life of David Crockett *by David Crockett*   ISBN: *1-59462-250-7* **$27.45**
"Colonel David Crockett was one of the most remarkable men of the times in which he lived. Born in humble life, but gifted with a strong will, an indomitable courage, and unremitting perseverance...   Biographies/New Age Pages 424

Lip-Reading *by Edward Nitchie*   ISBN: *1-59462-206-X* **$25.95**
Edward B. Nitchie, founder of the New York School for the Hard of Hearing, now the Nitchie School of Lip-Reading, Inc, wrote "LIP-READING Principles and Practice". The development and perfecting of this meritorious work on lip-reading was an undertaking...   How-to Pages 400

A Handbook of Suggestive Therapeutics, Applied Hypnotism, Psychic Science   ISBN: *1-59462-214-0* **$24.95**
by Henry Munro   Health/New Age/Health/Self-help Pages 376

A Doll's House: and Two Other Plays *by Henrik Ibsen*   ISBN: *1-59462-112-8* **$19.95**
Henrik Ibsen created this classic when in revolutionary 1848 Rome. Introducing some striking concepts in playwriting for the realist genre, this play has been studied the world over.   Fiction/Classics/Plays 308

The Light of Asia *by sir Edwin Arnold*   ISBN: *1-59462-204-3* **$13.95**
In this poetic masterpiece, Edwin Arnold describes the life and teachings of Buddha. The man who was to become known as Buddha to the world was born as Prince Gautama of India but he rejected the worldly riches and abandoned the reigns of power when...   Religion/History/Biographies Pages 170

The Complete Works of Guy de Maupassant *by Guy de Maupassant*   ISBN: *1-59462-157-8* **$16.95**
"For days and days, nights and nights, I had dreamed of that first kiss which was to consecrate our engagement, and I knew not on what spot I should put my lips..."   Fiction/Classics Pages 240

The Art of Cross-Examination *by Francis L. Wellman*   ISBN: *1-59462-309-4* **$26.95**
Written by a renowned trial lawyer, Wellman imparts his experience and uses case studies to explain how to use psychology to extract desired information through questioning.   How-to/Science/Reference Pages 408

Answered or Unanswered? *by Louisa Vaughan*   ISBN: *1-59462-248-5* **$10.95**
Miracles of Faith in China   Religion Pages 112

The Edinburgh Lectures on Mental Science (1909) *by Thomas*   ISBN: *1-59462-008-3* **$11.95**
This book contains the substance of a course of lectures recently given by the writer in the Queen Street Hall, Edinburgh. Its purpose is to indicate the Natural Principles governing the relation between Mental Action and Material Conditions...   New Age/Psychology Pages 148

Ayesha *by H. Rider Haggard*   ISBN: *1-59462-301-5* **$24.95**
Verily and indeed it is the unexpected that happens! Probably if there was one person upon the earth from whom the Editor of this, and of a certain previous history, did not expect to hear again...   Classics Pages 380

Ayala's Angel *by Anthony Trollope*   ISBN: *1-59462-352-X* **$29.95**
The two girls were both pretty, but Lucy who was twenty-one who supposed to be simple and comparatively unattractive, whereas Ayala was credited, as her Bombwhat romantic name might show, with poetic charm and a taste for romance. Ayala when her father died was nineteen...   Fiction Pages 484

The American Commonwealth *by James Bryce*   ISBN: *1-59462-286-8* **$34.45**
An interpretation of American democratic political theory. It examines political mechanics and society from the perspective of Scotsman James Bryce   Politics Pages 572

Stories of the Pilgrims *by Margaret P. Pumphrey*   ISBN: *1-59462-116-0* **$17.95**
This book explores pilgrims religious oppression in England as well as their escape to Holland and eventual crossing to America on the Mayflower, and their early days in New England...   History Pages 268

QTY

The Fasting Cure *by **Sinclair Upton*** ISBN: *1-59462-222-1* **$13.95**
In the Cosmopolitan Magazine for May, 1910, and in the Contemporary Review (London) for April, 1910, I published an article dealing with my experiences in fasting. I have written a great many magazine articles, but never one which attracted so much attention... New Age/Self Help/Health Pages 164

Hebrew Astrology *by **Sepharial*** ISBN: *1-59462-308-2* **$13.45**
In these days of advanced thinking it is a matter of common observation that we have left many of the old landmarks behind and that we are now pressing forward to greater heights and to a wider horizon than that which represented the mind-content of our progenitors... Astrology Pages 144

Thought Vibration or The Law of Attraction in the Thought World ISBN: *1-59462-127-6* **$12.95**
*by **William Walker Atkinson*** Psychology/Religion Pages 144

Optimism *by **Helen Keller*** ISBN: *1-59462-108-X* **$15.95**
Helen Keller was blind, deaf, and mute since 19 months old, yet famously learned how to overcome these handicaps, communicate with the world, and spread her lectures promoting optimism. An inspiring read for everyone... Biographies/Inspirational Pages 84

Sara Crewe *by **Frances Burnett*** ISBN: *1-59462-360-0* **$9.45**
In the first place, Miss Minchin lived in London. Her home was a large, dull, tall one, in a large, dull square, where all the houses were alike, and all the sparrows were alike, and where all the door-knockers made the same heavy sound... Childrens/Classic Pages 88

The Autobiography of Benjamin Franklin *by **Benjamin Franklin*** ISBN: *1-59462-135-7* **$24.95**
The Autobiography of Benjamin Franklin has probably been more extensively read than any other American historical work, and no other book of its kind has had such ups and downs of fortune. Franklin lived for many years in England, where he was agent... Biographies/History Pages 332

Name	
Email	
Telephone	
Address	
City, State ZIP	

☐ **Credit Card**   ☐ **Check / Money Order**

Credit Card Number	
Expiration Date	
Signature	

Please Mail to: Book Jungle
PO Box 2226
Champaign, IL 61825
or Fax to: 630-214-0564

ORDERING INFORMATION

web*: www.bookjungle.com*
email*: sales@bookjungle.com*
fax*: 630-214-0564*
mail*: Book Jungle PO Box 2226 Champaign, IL 61825*
or PayPal *to sales@bookjungle.com*

Please contact us for bulk discounts

DIRECT-ORDER TERMS

**20% Discount if You Order
Two or More Books**
Free Domestic Shipping!
Accepted: Master Card, Visa,
Discover, American Express

www.ingramcontent.com/pod-product-compliance
Lightning Source LLC
Chambersburg PA
CBHW080904020726
47502CB00008B/2349